ARE YOU SIGNED UP FOR]

You'll get the latest news and info

exclusive excerpts, coming releases, sales, free books,

and more.

Check out our complete list of authors, too!

No spam, no junk. That's a promise!

Sign Up Here

www.dragonbladepublishing.com

Dearest Reader;

Thank you for your support of a small press. At Dragonblade Publishing, we strive to bring you the highest quality Historical Romance from some of the best authors in the business. Without your support, there is no 'us', so we sincerely hope you adore these stories and find some new favorite authors along the way.

Happy Reading!

CEO, Dragonblade Publishing

Happy Reading

Lily Harlem

LOVED BY THE LAST KNIGHT

Hawk Castle, Book 1
A Habsburg Historical Romance

by Lily Harlem

"What Mars gives to others,
Venus delivers to Vienna."

Dragonblade Publishing, Inc. is an imprint of Kathryn Le Veque Novels, Inc.
P.O. Box 23
Moreno Valley, CA 92556
ceo@dragonbladepublishing.com

Produced in the United States of America

First Edition April 2024
Print Edition

Additional Dragonblade books by Author Lily Harlem

Hawk Castle Series
Loved by the Last Knight (Book 1)
Adored by the Archduke (Book 2)
Embraced by the Emperor (Book 3)

The Lyon's Den Series
Lyon at the Altar

Loved by the Last Knight

Your world is crumbling around you—war, dissent, fear—then a knight in shining armor rides into town and sweeps you off your feet. Hell yeah, sometimes, it really does happen.

For Mary of Burgundy, conflict is approaching and the pressure to wed is mounting. Dukes, lords, earls, and even a king want her hand. All she must do is choose and her stars will align once more.

But who should it be? Who can fulfill her every need?

Tales of a handsome and brave knight in a land far away have filled the castle. She has never met him. He'll have to travel from Vienna and then fight for her lands when he arrives.

Is Maximilian of Austria up for the job? Not only as an intelligent leader and skilled warrior, but also as her husband and, just as importantly, her one and only lover for all of time?

Notes from the Author

While writing HAWK CASTLE, I have truly let my imagination run wild and free to create a fun, romantic romp through history in the company of an eclectic bunch of vibrant, powerful, and passionate men and women.

In other words, while this story is inspired by long-ago people and events, please don't quote HAWK CASTLE in your history thesis, as I can't be responsible for your grade!

By the way...

*Hawk Castle was the home of the very first Habsburg. There is some debate about how well it translates into 'Habsburg,' but it's nice to think it does.

**Maximilian really did write a book as mentioned in this one—complete with illustrations—about his journey from Vienna to Ghent to marry Mary of Burgundy. It's titled Theuerdank.

***Mary insisted upon having her beloved falcons and dogs sleeping in her bedchamber just three nights after her marriage to Maximilian. This says something of her love for animals and a lot of his love for her.

****When Mary and Maximilian first met, they spoke Latin to each other. Over the course of time, he taught her German and she taught him French. I haven't written LOVED BY THE LAST KNIGHT in three different languages, though. That would have been as tiresome for you, dear reader, as it would have been for me.

CHAPTER ONE

1476
Wiener Neustadt
Near Vienna, Austria

"I N THE NAME of the dear Lord, it's impossibly grand, Father."

"Ha. I fear not grand enough." Frederick III, Holy Roman Emperor, stabbed his finger at the ink-filled parchment sprawled across the dark table. "Perhaps it should be twice as big."

"I believe this will suffice. Already, it will practically fill the Apostles Choir." Archduke Maximilian of Austria studied the plans for his father's sepulcher that was to reside in St. Stephen's Cathedral. "It will take many years to craft. It is just as well you are not knocking at heaven's door."

"Indeed, it is fortunate that my heart beats strong." Frederick poured a goblet of wine and sat back in his throne-like chair with the base of the wine cup resting on his rotund belly. "Gerhaert is confident he is up to the task of creating it in a timely manner. Which is just as well; he is the only sculptor I would trust with creating my final resting place." Frederick burped and then took a sip of his drink. "I want it to be the most magnificent sepulcher ever made."

"I'm sure it will be, and yes, I have heard Gerhaert is extraordinarily skilled." Maximilian paused. "What is it to be made from?"

"Prized red marble from the Adnet quarry."

"Excellent choice." Maximilian ran his fingertip over the plans.

Golden autumn sunlight from a stained glass window created shadows as he moved.

The massive sarcophagus and platform were to be decorated with intricate images—coats of arms from all the ruled-over domains, and at least two hundred figures peering, standing, and climbing around arches. Atop, lying in pride of place, a crowned man, eyes closed, clutching a sword and orb.

"*Expensive* choice, though," Maximilian said. "Red marble."

"Let us not talk of finances."

Maximilian frowned. His father never wanted to talk of finances. He studied the supine figure in the plans. "This is your image?"

Frederick threw a grape into the air and caught it in his mouth. "Who else's would it be?"

Straightening, Maximilian walked around the table, coming to halt where a tray had been set, the surface of which was loaded with tafelspitz, apfelstrudel, and bread rolls. "Do you think"—Maximilian gestured to the food—"that the image is a good likeness of you?"

Frederick's eyes narrowed. "I don't know what you mean."

"Father, you are a large man. Riding, jousting, walking, and hunting are not things you enjoy and, quite frankly, your lack of outdoor pursuits shows."

"Ah, you mean I am a man who shows his health in a physical way." He rubbed his belly.

"Yes, and in all honesty, which I know you consider a virtue, you are fat, Father. Very fat." Maximilian was eternally grateful he hadn't inherited, thus far, his father's apple-round physique. They couldn't be more different to look at and he hoped it stayed that way.

"Perhaps that is the case." Frederick made a snorting sound. "Though likely, I will shrink and wither with age."

"And if you don't?"

"Then my lasting image will be one of sleek masculinity."

"But for years to come, mourners will see this statue and believe you, Holy Roman Emperor, to have been that way."

"What do I care?" Impatience laced Frederick's tone as it so often did. "It is how God sees me that matters, not mourners in one hundred, two hundred, five hundred years' time."

"But don't you think—?"

"Quiet, boy." Frederick threw back a gulp of wine. "I did not summon you to my chamber to confer about my waistline. I have more important matters to discuss with you."

Maximilian sighed, poured himself a goblet of wine, and then walked to the roaring fire. He stared into it, watching the orange and red flames dance. Why was it was that wood burned, but marble did not?

"I have made a decision about your marriage."

Thoughts of logs and marble flew from Maximilian's mind. He turned. "And here was me thinking you might have given consideration to political matters and *that* was what you wanted to discuss."

"What? No. They will work themselves out. As you know, what is important is that you marry advantageously. It is the only thing that matters right now." He paused. "And come to think of it, your marriage *is* a political matter."

Maximilian said nothing. He spent his days with his horses, dogs, and falcons, dancing, jousting, and by night enjoying the pretty girls at court. Marriage—that wasn't something he gave space or thought to. There was too much else to think about. Too much else to get pleasure from.

"We need an army we cannot afford, Maximilian. Austria is not rich, and France grows richer. All the time, the Ottomans are closing in and on top of that, I have grave concerns"—his father spoke through a mouthful of grapes—"that the Duke of Burgundy is getting rather above his station. Ha, why am I surprised? Hasn't he always been sickeningly pushy?"

"Charles the Bold, they call him. It is a clue to his nature." Maximilian shrugged.

"Indeed." Frederick pointed a finger at Maximilian. "And bold combined with ambition makes Charles an ongoing threat, despite my best attempts to thwart him over the years. He has an insatiable lust for territorial expansion. As if he doesn't have enough already."

"I am not marrying Charles just because you are worried about him gaining territory." Maximilian rolled his eyes.

"Don't be stupid, boy." Frederick sat forward but didn't stand—he didn't stand unless absolutely necessary. "It is not him you will marry, but his daughter, Mary of Burgundy."

Maximilian said nothing.

"For a long time, Charles has been making eyes at not only a royal title, but an imperial one," Frederick went on. "In the name of God above, he is meddling in matters with the Low Countries. And although the Battle of Grandson didn't go in his favor, he has inherited Guelders. I would wager he considers himself the new Alexander the Great, All-Conquering Prince."

"And you think *I* can stop him?"

"Not you, *us*, the House of Habsburg." Frederick sat back, as though exhausted. "Sigismund set the wheel in motion some time ago and—"

"Sigismund!" Maximilian's eyes widened at the mention of their troubled relative. "Why? What does he get out of this?"

"Why should he get anything?"

Maximilian thought for a moment. "He's still low on funds, isn't he?"

"I dare say his coins are limited."

"And the Eidgenossen are troubling him over his land in Alsace?"

"Most likely." Frederick held out his goblet. "Pour me more wine."

Maximilian scowled and did as bid. His father was the only person in the world he would deign to serve.

"Do not be too harsh on Sigismund, my son, for this marriage is very much my wish too. And, as it happens, the Duke of Burgundy's also."

"This has already been spoken of with him?" Maximilian's mind was set spinning and a prickle went over his scalp. His future wife had been chosen. The woman who would bear his children already had a face and a name. It was hard to get his head around.

"Oh, yes." Frederick took another mouthful of wine, then wiped the back of his hand over his lips. "We met, quite some time ago, Charles and I. Awkward, given his greed and what I was prepared to give to sate that hunger, but nevertheless worthwhile."

"How long ago did you meet?" It was hard not to feel betrayed that such a major event in his life had been planned but not discussed with him.

"Five years ago."

Maximilian drained his wine and slammed the goblet down. "And no one spoke of it to me. In all that time."

"You chose not to speak yourself until you were nine."

"I had nothing to say." Maximilian hated being reminded of his early muteness. In fact, he hated thinking of the siege his family had been subjected to in any shape or form.

"You were still a child when I met with Charles," his father said. "Your head filled with playing with your dogs, riding, and honing your fighting skills. Sadly, not your science studies and Latin. Poor Engelbrecht gave up on you."

"Poor Engelbrecht, I don't think so." His ears rang just at the memory of the Bible swiping him around the head whenever he made a mistake with his spellings or calculations. "The man is evil, an evil tutor and an evil man. He'll burn in hell, I can assure you."

"Do not speak of your teacher that way."

Maximilian sighed. This was an old argument. "And this betrothed of mine…" Maximilian swirled his finger in the air. "Margaret."

"Mary. Her name is Mary."

"Yes, Mary. She is willing?"

"A good daughter will do her father's bidding, just like a good son will. So yes, she is willing to marry."

"Marry *me*?"

Frederick was silent as he opened a wooden box at his side, the lid decorated with mother-of-pearl. He withdrew a letter. The red wax seal had been broken.

"What is that?" Maximilian asked.

"A letter arrived for you by envoy."

"For me. But…it's been opened."

"Yes."

"You read it?"

"I am at liberty to read the letter of any person in all of my lands and that includes you." Frederick gave Maximilian a look that said he wouldn't apologize and didn't, in fact, care about his son's objections.

"Whom is it from?"

"Find out for yourself."

Maximilian snatched up the letter.

Most dear Archduke Maximilian of Austria.

From my heart, I greet you.

I have been informed that it is both my father's and your father's wishes that we marry. Please accept this letter as a sign of my commitment to this endeavor and as my promise to be a true wife to you.

As a sign of your commitment, please deliver to me a gold ring set with a diamond.

Mary of Burgundy
Daughter of Charles of Burgundy.

Maximilian pulled in a deep breath. "It's a letter of betrothal."

"Indeed it is."

"And she wants a ring. A diamond ring, no less."

"So it seems."

Maximilian walked to the window and stared down at the misty courtyard. A black cat slunk past an urn with a limp mouse caught in its jaws. For a moment, Maximilian could identify with the mouse. Marriage was a predator, and he its prey.

And he, like the mouse, had been caught.

"And when will Mary come to Hofburg for the wedding?" Maximilian asked with an irritated edge to his voice. He hoped it wouldn't be for many months.

"She won't be coming to the palace."

"A proxy marriage?" Maximilian turned and laughed. "That will hardly produce heirs any time soon."

"You're right, it won't. So you, my son, will leave for Burgundy."

He was swamped by a sense of unjustness. "Me, go to Burgundy? No. She should come here. I am the man in this marriage. It is here, in Vienna, she will live. Schönbrunn in the summer months." He stabbed his thumb against his red-and-gold embroidered tunic. "That is how it will be. I insist upon it."

"Maximilian, perhaps if you had been a less frustrating student, you would have learned that your future wife is known as Mary the Rich for good reason."

Maximilian opened his mouth to speak, then closed it again. He hadn't known that. He should have.

"So you must go there, to her future lands," Frederick said.

"If she is so wealthy, what treaties must be signed?"

"None that I am aware of." Frederick's lips formed a tight line and he looked away.

"Are you sure?"

"Of course."

Maximilian was quiet, weighing up his options. He had a grand tournament planned for the spring. He had no intention of canceling it or letting it go ahead without him. But if he wanted to delay his trip to Burgundy, he'd have to play his cards right with his father, move his chess pieces with skill.

"Are you setting me a challenge, Father?"

Frederick studied him through narrowed eyes. A long moment passed, the sun going behind a cloud and shrouding them in cool, dim light. When weak, amber warmth spread over the chamber once again, Frederick nodded. "Yes. I believe I have set you a challenge. I challenge you to wed the heiress to many wealthy and powerful territories so that we can sleep easy in our beds and our sepulchers."

"And is there a timescale on this challenge?"

"There is necessity but not urgency for you to wed. Though if death takes Charles, that will change everything, and as you know, the man has a penchant for going to battle."

That was just what Maximilian wanted to hear. He would string this engagement out for as long as possible and stay in Austria, where life was entertaining.

He set back his shoulders and stood to his full height, a height that dwarfed most men. "I cannot say *no* to a challenge in a tournament, Father, and I will not say *no* to a challenge in life."

Frederick nodded slowly, as if wondering what demands Maximilian was about to make.

"We will send a letter of reply," Maximilian said. "Suggest a future wedding… in Cologne, perhaps."

"That would be agreeable."

"And I will travel to Burgundy prior to the marriage and escort her to Cologne to ensure she walks the aisle with me. Do not fear, Father. I will not let you down."

"I have no doubts of your success." Frederick nodded, his eyes still narrowed suspiciously. "You are of noble blood."

Maximilian puffed up his chest. He knew what his father needed to hear. "As a Habsburg, I do not understand the words 'defeat' or 'failure' or 'rejection.' It is our given right to rule and to guide. It is God's will that we lead and He will be with us every step and during every sacrifice."

"I am pleased you think in such a way, son." Frederick stood, wincing as though his feet pained him. "Though maybe you will find the company of one regal woman rather more fulfilling than that of a string of whimsical courtiers."

Maximilian frowned. "I never intend to be tied to just one woman. Marriage will not stop me from bedding whom I want when I want."

"Ah…" Frederick rolled his eyes to the ceiling and reached for the gold, jewel-embellished cross that sat around his neck. "God will be watching you, ensuring that you forsake all others in the bedchamber."

"God can look the other way." Maximilian huffed. He enjoyed chasing and copulating and then languishing in bed with pretty, soft, sweet-smelling female bodies. It was what he, what his cock, had been made for.

"God is all-seeing, as you well know." Frederick tapped Maximilian on his prominent, clean-shaven chin. "Do not anger Him. Do not anger your bride." His eyes flashed and his lips twisted. "You have to put everything else aside and be triumphant. Treat producing legitimate heirs as a battle that must be won."

"I will be triumphant, in time. That is my promise to you, Father." Maximilian spoke with conviction, with certainty, and he held on to that as he left the room, his boot heels clicking on the hard flooring. Because he would, eventually, do his father's bidding. It was his duty to continue the family bloodline, a fact he'd been told from a young age.

When the door shut behind him, he made his way from his father's wing, then stopped and stared at the vast, marble staircase that rose centrally in the palace. Guards stood in silence, dressed in red velvet, and staring straight ahead as they clutched sharp pikes. To his right hung a huge painting of his grandfather Ernest. Chubby-faced, flat-nosed, and with wavy, light-brown hair flowing from a fluffy, scarlet hat that seemed to Maximilian more like a nightcap. Ernest's eyes looked up and to the right, perhaps a nod toward his piety, or perhaps the direction in which he hoped to conquer lands. Maximilian wasn't sure.

What Maximilian was sure of was his path had been chosen. And to seal the deal, a letter of marriage acceptance must be written and sent on its long journey. But he could delay writing it for a while.

There really was no urgency.

CHAPTER TWO

Ghent, Burgundy

MARY SAT ASTRIDE her favorite horse with Jupiter, her falcon, perched on her outstretched arm. Around her, the low hills puffed like rising bread and the valleys below were torn at their bases with rushing, frothing streams.

The wind held a cheek-pinching chill. Winter had taken hold, but the white sun shone brightly, draping the hard earth.

"What is that?" Philip pointed to the right, his dark eyes flashing with excitement and the wind catching his black hair. "Over there."

"You saw something?" Mary peered at the swaying grass. Her cousin had an impressive knack for spotting stirrings.

"It's nothing," John said, his horse backing up a few paces and snorting. Like his brother, his dark hair was being mussed by the western breeze and his cheeks held a rosy glow. "Everything is sleeping." He yawned. "I wish I were."

"There is warmth today," Mary said. "I believe there will be creatures taking advantage of that."

"Cousin Mary, I like your optimism." John shrugged. "But we have been riding since daybreak and nothing has been seen."

"Perhaps if you had drunk less wine and bedded fewer courtiers yesterday eve, you would feel more inclined to enjoy the hunt." Mary scowled at him.

"The wine was good and so were the women." John chuckled and winked.

Mary rolled her eyes at him. "You're incorrigible."

"I try."

"There is something there. A rabbit, I think." Philip twisted in his saddle to face Mary. "Take off Jupiter's hood. I'm sure he'll get lucky."

"He does need to stretch his wings, if nothing else." With deft skill born of practice, Mary slipped the tiny, leather hood from her falcon's head.

Jupiter roused his feathers and stretched his neck, his beady, black eyes a stark contrast to the slash of yellow on his beak.

"Hey, boy," Mary said, tucking the hood into her pocket. "Are you hungry?" She smoothed the back of her index finger down his feathered chin.

He moved his head, small, sharp movements, no doubt picking up noises she could not hope to hear.

"Yes, there!" Philip stood up in his saddle and pointed. "Two of them. Rabbits."

"Set him free," John said, perking up at the prospect of a kill.

With a flick of her wrist, Mary released the cuff on Jupiter's left leg that was attached to her leather glove. "Go!" She raised her arm. "Go, my beauty."

Immediately, he took to the air. Sleek and powerful. A born predator. His agility never failed to catch her breath.

"He's spotted them," Philip shouted, urging his horse forward, his cape flapping behind him.

"They're running, toward the river." John dug his heels into the side of his horse. "Come on."

Mary followed her cousins, racing over the rough terrain, then jumping a patch of bog. In the distance, Jupiter had climbed high, but it was clear he hadn't lost sight of the scampering rabbits.

"Hurry!" Mary shouted, overtaking Philip at a gallop.

The sound of horses' hooves on hard ground filled her ears, the wind buffeted her face, and her hair flew out behind her. For a precious moment, the palace, the council, the worry of her beloved father being away at war was forgotten. There was only the here and now. The thrill of the chase. The beat of her heart. The strength of her surefooted horse.

"He's going for the kill," John shouted.

"Rabbit pie for us," Philip added.

Mary watched in awe as her falcon locked in on the rabbit that was rushing to the right. Its white tail bobbed as it twisted and turned, clearly frantic that it had found itself out in the open. Could it sense what was above? Did it know the end was nigh?

Jupiter turned, beat his wings to accelerate, then stooping, arrow-like, he sliced downward through the crisp air.

At the last moment, as earth and the rabbit approached, he opened his wings, claws extended, and lunged.

The rabbit was plucked upward, dangling helplessly.

"He got it!" Philip shouted, galloping even faster and coming alongside Mary.

Pride filled Mary. Jupiter was her joy. She'd had him from the day he'd hatched. Cared for him. Nurtured him. Trained him. Her father said she was the best falconer in all the land. And she was.

When they reached the kill, Jupiter was on the ground tearing at the dead rabbit's flesh.

Philip jumped down and grabbed the small animal, shoving it into a leather bag at his waist. Jupiter let out a shriek of complaint.

Mary whistled one long note and Jupiter's attention was instantly harnessed. He flew the short distance to her arm. "You're such a good boy," she said, plucking a strip of dried meat from her pouch. "Here's your reward."

He gobbled it up, still looking around for more prey. She gave him another morsel.

"We should get back," Philip said. "The light will be going soon."

"At least we are not empty-handed," Mary said. "I'll confess I thought we might be returning with nothing."

"I have never known that when hunting with you and Jupiter." John nodded fondly at the bird. "You must breed from him soon. Perhaps you will gift me one of his offspring."

"Indeed. I have thought of that for the future." She beamed. "And you, my dear cousins and friends, will both receive chicks from the first clutch."

"And we will be grateful," John said, then he rubbed his stomach. "But right now, I will be grateful to get back to Ghent and eat."

When they reached the stone turrets of home, the shadows had lengthened and at the portcullis entrance, flames leaped from a fire pit. Aymer, Mary's faithful fawn and white greyhound, stood beside it waiting for her.

Mary dismounted and immediately handed her horse to a stable-boy. Philip and John did the same.

She stretched out her back and rolled her shoulders as Aymer fussed for attention. The return ride had been long and cold. They'd traveled farther into the countryside than planned.

"Would you like me to take Jupiter to your chamber?" Philip asked. "So you can warm by the fire."

"Thank you." She smiled gratefully. Philip was always considerate, always kind as well as being a fine horseman. She wondered why he had yet to go to war. Perhaps God had decided it wasn't yet his time.

She handed a hooded Jupiter to Philip, then made her way past several guards and through the courtyard. She ruffled Aymer's fur as she went.

The moment she reached the tall, central building, the donjon, the heavy door flew open. Margaret rushed out and her high-pitched squeal filled the cold air.

"Margaret!" Mary said, grasping her stepmother's slender shoulders. "Whatever is the matter?"

"Oh, my dear child. Oh, dear Lord above, give us Your strength." Margaret flung back her head to stare at the stars. Several gray strands of hair had escaped her headroll.

Aymer barked.

"Margaret!" Mary said a little sharper. Her heart was clattering and a sense of dread snaked up her spine. "You're scaring me."

"And truth be told, I am scared right to the very bottom of my heart."

"What has happened? Tell me."

"Oh, how I wish I had joined you on the ride today. I wouldn't be the bearer of such terrible news." Margaret was always pale, but right now, she was ghost-like.

"Please. Tell me." Mary's voice had gone up a pitch, a rarity, but fear surrounded her.

"It is Charles, your father..."

They were the words Mary didn't want to hear. "You've had news?"

"Bad news." A tear formed and slipped down Margaret's cheek. "The worst."

Mary gulped. Her throat was tight. "Who brought this information?" It seemed a better question to ask than what the actual information was.

"A cavalryman, he journeyed from Nancy at great haste."

Mary nodded. "Nancy, yes. Go on."

"There is a report your father was killed in fierce fighting. Supplies were running out. Charles knew time was of the essence and was preparing to siege, but..."

"But?"

"The Duke of Lorraine's army ambushed, surrounding them in the forest and oh..."

"God give us strength." Mary drew Margaret into a hug, holding her tightly. "He is with the Lord?"

"We don't know for sure." Margaret pulled back, her teary eyes flashing.

"What do you mean?"

"There is no body. He is gone, his horse riderless, but there is no body to be found. The cavalryman said the slopes on which the battle was fought are heavily wooded and a fast-flowing stream takes everything fallen down to the valley this time of year." She let out a wail, her eyes closing. "Oh, my poor husband. My poor beloved. He is a wrecked and wretched ruined body. God bless his soul for all eternity."

"Come on, let's get you inside." Mary wrapped an arm around Margaret's waist. "This way."

What Mary really wanted to do was scream and holler and stomp her feet. Hit something. But she'd been brought up to hold herself with dignity at all times. And she would today, this day, her worst day.

But her father couldn't be dead. He just couldn't be. Would God really be so cruel to take both her parents while she was still so young?

They stepped over the threshold and went indoors out of the cold and rising wind. Aymer instantly herded them toward the warmth of the great hall.

The room was tall, ceilinged with a central escape hole for smoke, which rose from the fire beneath. Tapestries hung on the walls and the beams were patterned with signs of the zodiac. A wooden table with benches stood beside the fire, embroidered cushions making seating more comfortable. Along the western wall, beneath oiled-cloth-covered windows, stood a row of ornate chests, closed and locked, to keep mice from nibbling the important parchments within.

"You have returned, Mary." Jeanne dropped her hands from prayer and stood from her kneeling position. Light from the flame of a flickering tallow candle danced on her pretty face and caressed her long, chestnut-streaked hair.

"Yes. And I have heard the news."

"We are all praying. God will hear us. I am sure." Jeanne held out her arms. "My dearest, Mary."

Mary went into her embrace, gaining strength from her governess and loyal friend. "I hope so."

Margaret sat heavily, a strangled sigh scratching from her throat. "Oh, my Charles. My poor Charles."

"We must be patient and wait for more news." Mary took a goblet of wine from a courtier who had appeared with a laden tray. "There is little else to do." Her heart beat fast, the way it had during the hunt. Her senses felt alive, but at the same time, a great hole had appeared in her core and it was getting bigger with each passing second.

She sipped her sweet drink. Aymer nuzzled his nose into her palm, as though offering her his sympathy.

"Patience is indeed a virtue," Margaret said shakily while also taking a goblet.

Mary nodded and stared at the dancing flames. But she barely felt their heat caressing her cold cheeks. Her mind was racing. The death of her father, if it was indeed true, altered her status from heir presumptive to ruler in one fell swoop.

She'd been raised knowing this, of course she had, but perhaps it was naivety or foolishness, she wasn't sure which, but she hadn't given thought to the day it would happen. And now that it had, all she was aware of was the painful loss of her father.

A sudden flurry of activity behind her caught her attention. She turned and was greeted with four councilors, long robes swishing over the stone floor and deep frown lines marring their brows.

"Your Grace, we must claim your attention."

"It is with great concern we come to you."

"I fear disastrous tidings are coming our way."

"You must marry at once, Your Grace. Without delay."

CHAPTER THREE

"STOP." MARY HELD up her hand to silence the councilors. "We do not even know if my father is dead. There is no body. Do not presume he is gone."

"He could be walking on God's Earth as we speak," Margaret said, though the tears slipping down her cheeks took away the conviction in her words.

The councilor closest to Mary kissed his cross. "That is true and I hope it is, but we must prepare for the worst."

Mary sat on the bench, a sudden, bone-aching weariness overtaking her. It was as though her emotions had pulled a plug on her physical energy.

"Are you unwell?" Jeanne sat close and weaved her fingers with Mary's. "Can I get you something?"

"Having you here is a balm in and of itself." Mary smiled, though she knew it didn't reach her eyes.

Jeanne kissed the back of Mary's knuckles, then continued to hold her hand as though hoping to impart strength or at least take away some pain.

"You really must lend us your ear, Your Grace," the councilor went on. "There are matters of much import to discuss."

"I know." She frowned at him. "You want me to marry. You already said that."

"Immediately." He nodded and so did his colleagues. "Straightaway."

"I will not marry immediately." She tipped her chin. "Potential marriages have been plotted since the day of my birth. A little extra time will make no difference."

"I beg to differ." He set his lips in a tight line.

"You have many suitors to choose from," the councilor to his right said, "all of whom would secure your place."

"Do you mean *your* place, councilor?" She raised her eyebrows.

"The people of Ghent are relying on you," another councilor, with fat, wobbly cheeks and a bulbous nose, said, helping himself to wine. She recalled his name to be Hugo.

Mary thought of the people of Burgundy. She and Margaret had traveled the land listening to petitions and assuring towns and villages that the duke would not ignore them—he was a strict ruler and pacification was necessary.

"I would urge you to consider your future husband very carefully," Hugo said.

"You think me so foolish that I wouldn't?" She studied him with narrowed eyes and her jaw tense.

"No, Your Grace, my humble apologies." He shuffled from one foot to the other and looked down at the floor.

She took another sip of wine, then reached for a chunk of bread. Perhaps that would fill the hole in her stomach.

Oh, how she wished her father were in the room to tell her what to do. He was a shrewd man and had told her that marriage would garner support from whichever corner of Europe to which she betrothed herself.

"I have taken the liberty of listing your options." Hugo unrolled a scroll covered in intricate writing. He set it on the table. "I did not add Louis XI of France or his son, Charles, as I've been informed you have already refused them." His mouth turned down disapprovingly.

"I did not wish for either of those unions." Neither an elderly or infant husband was acceptable. Besides, the French king's demands of cession of territories that went along with the proposed marriage were preposterous.

Clutching the stem of her goblet, she peered at the scroll through the flickering light.

Ferdinand of Aragon.

George, Duke of Clarence.

Duke Francis II of Brittany.

Charles, Duke of Berry.

Philibert of Savoy.

Philip of Cleves.

"You have missed Nicholas of Anjou, and Maximilian, the Habsburg Archduke." She closed her eyes and pulled in a long, slow breath.

Just the name Maximilian conjured all kinds of emotions. She'd been privy to tales of his prowess as a fighter, his skills as a horseman and falconer, and she'd heard of his statuesque height. In her dreams he'd come to her, broad-shouldered, smiling, his arms a safe haven.

"Your Grace," Jeanne said quietly. "Are you faint?"

"Er, yes..." Mary opened her eyes. "I mean no, I am perfectly fine."

"You must choose a suitor," Hugo said. "They each have merits; each would secure your position. I would suggest you reconsider the proposal from the King of France and—"

"You think you know everything." She pointed at Hugo then swept her finger across the other councilors. "But you don't. None of you do."

"In which case, Your Grace, please tell us what information we are missing."

She stood and strode to the chests, staring down at the middle one with its ornate, iron cross set into the dark wood.

Aymer came and stood next to her and also stared at the chest.

"Some time ago on the instruction of my father," she said, her heart squeezing, "I sent a letter of betrothal to the Habsburg Archduke, Maximilian of Austria." The words pained her to say, for as yet, she hadn't received a response from Vienna.

Aymer whimpered and sat as though feeling her humiliation and frustration.

"The archduke," one of the councilors said. "A most interesting choice."

"A good match, I believe." She turned.

"And his response?" Hugo pressed.

She looked at first Margaret and then Jeanne. Both ladies knew of the situation and her vexation with Maximilian. "None as yet."

The councilors looked at each other, unspoken words passing between them.

"I will send another letter." She pulled open the chest and snatched out a piece of parchment. "This very night."

"Perhaps, my dearest Mary," Margaret said, "we should see how things unfold over the next few days."

"And write when you are level of mind," Jeanne added.

Mary sighed, her senses returning. "You are both quite right and I thank you for your wisdom." She looked at her councilors. "You are dismissed. I wish to be alone with my female companions at this time."

THREE DAYS LATER, as Mary was letting Jupiter catch bait from a length of rope in the inner bailey, an envoy clattered over the drawbridge.

His horse came to a skidding halt on the cobblestones and he leaped from the saddle. "Your Grace. I have news."

"What? Tell me." She held out her arm and Jupiter landed on it, instantly ducking his head to tear at the strip of meat she held for him.

"Charles, Duke of Burgundy"—he set his hand over his heart and closed his eyes—"is with God."

Her knees weakened; she feared they would not hold her up.

"And this is known for sure?" Her voice shook.

"Yes, his body was found. It seems his head was near sliced from his neck and—"

"Enough." She swallowed a rise of bitter fluid that had come up from her stomach. "Guard. Take Jupiter." Quickly, she hoodwinked the bird.

A guard rushed forward and took Jupiter from her.

"Be careful with him. No loud noises. Put him in my chamber."

"Yes, Your Grace."

Mary let her arms hang at her sides and stared at the beautiful, gray horse that had carried the messenger. It was breathing hard and sweat clung to its neck and rump. "You should care for your animal." She swallowed again and gestured to the horse. "He has served us well, traveling many miles."

"Yes, Your Grace." The messenger seemed relieved to have been dismissed and quickly led his horse to the stable quarters.

"Mary. What is it? What news?" Margaret and Jeanne rushed across the yard holding their gowns so high, their ankles were visible. They'd clearly been alerted by the noise of hooves.

Mary stared at them when they came to a halt in front of her. Her vision was a little blurry and her chest tight.

"Oh, dear Lord." Jeanne clasped her hand. "What is it?"

"Tell us. Find the strength." Margaret knotted her fingers beneath her chin, her knuckles paling, so tight was the grip.

Mary had the strength to say the words, but she didn't want to. Because saying them would make them true, would make her worst fears a reality.

She licked her lips and cleared her throat. Still, the words wouldn't come. They'd stacked up on her tongue and refused to budge.

"Your Grace… please." A tear slipped down Margaret's cheek. "I beg of you."

Mary took a deep breath, closed her eyes, and raised her face heavenward. "He's dead. His body was discovered."

"Oh, God have mercy!" Margaret crumpled to the ground with a wail.

Jeanne squatted at her side with an arm over her back. "He will have mercy. God is good." Her face twisted in distress.

Margaret wailed again, the spine-chilling sound rattling around the stone walls.

The guards stood, unmoving, unaffected, and Mary took strength from their solid, quiet stance. She'd never been one for hysterics and she wouldn't start now.

Hugo appeared, waddling over the courtyard, red cloak billowing. "What is it? What is happening?" Two courtiers followed in his wake.

"My father is dead. His body has been found," Mary said, maintaining his eye contact.

"God bless his soul." He kissed his cross and looked at her steadily. "And God bless the Duchess of Burgundy."

She didn't reply.

"And so now, I must implore you," the councilor went on quickly, "to marry as soon as you can. Burgundy must be ruled by a man; otherwise, France will claim it. The Estates General will be summoned immediately."

"Is that all you have to say to me?" She scowled at him. "During my moment of grief? All you can say is I must marry."

"I am sorry." He had the good grace to dip his head.

She didn't dignify him with an answer. Instead, she helped Margaret to her feet and along with Jeanne, led her stepmother indoors.

LATER THAT DAY, as Mary sat with Aymer, her thoughts strayed back to Maximilian. She'd never met the man, but she was angry with him. In fact, if he were before her right now, she'd perhaps stoop so low as to slap his cheek.

How dare he not reply to her?

How dare he treat her as though she were a commoner sending him admiring mail?

Did he not know the extent of her lands?

Suddenly, she heard shouting, a bang, two bangs. A thump and a jeer. She stood. "What is that?"

Jeanne looked up from her embroidery, eyes wide.

Margaret continued to sit, stooped over her rosary.

"I do not know," Jeanne said.

Mary stood.

Aymer followed suit.

Mary stared up at the small window. "They're shouting. The people."

"What are they saying?"

"They have heard of the duke's death."

"He was not a popular ruler." Margaret shook her head. "My poor beloved. He tried his best, did what he thought was God's will every day of his too-short life."

The four councilors swept into the room, four guards following. In an instant, the guards were flanking Mary. Tall. Protective. Silent.

Her heart rate picked up and a jolt of energy flooded her system. "Should I fear for my life? Is the mob so angered, we have an uprising on our hands?"

"It is true the citizens of Ghent are restless at the news," Hugo said.

A particularly loud bang and pop made Mary jump.

Margaret's prayers increased in volume.

Aymer barked.

"Shh, boy." She stroked his head and tried to shake the sense of feeling like a prisoner within her own walls. "Why are they so restless?"

She didn't really need to ask. The decrees of her father and grandfather had been far-reaching and unpopular. Plus, if she surrendered now and gave over rule to France, there would be no wars or war taxes. Her people would be wealthier.

"They are facing a change in rule, Your Grace," Jeanne said. "It is a chance to air their grievances."

"Air them very loudly." Mary scowled at the window. "I must think." She set her hands on her hips. What was she to do? And should she do anything this night?

"Unlike your father, you are popular and loved by your people," Jeanne said. "Can I suggest you speak to them?"

The guards stiffened, as though the very thought of taking Mary out into the baying crowd alarmed them.

Mary nodded slowly. "It brings some comfort to my broken heart to think that I am loved by my people," she said slowly because the noises outside the castle walls didn't make her feel loved at all, "but with no husband, no troops, and no power, what can I offer them?"

Margaret looked up, her teary eyes showing a hint of strength. "My dearest girl, I have faith in you. God has faith in you. I know you will come up with something."

A courtier rushed in. "Your Grace, the prison and hall of justice has been set alight."

Hugo frowned. "It is only a matter of time before Louis seizes your land, Your Grace."

Mary knotted her fingers so tight beneath her chin, her knuckles hurt. It seemed like all around her, problems were springing to life, growing, becoming unmanageable. It was a rockfall of disaster. A storm of doom.

"I could ask my brother for help." Margaret nodded. "Yes, that is what I will do. I should send for assistance at one."

"We can try," Mary said, her face somber. "But the King of England may well be otherwise engaged."

⋙✕⋘

A SHORT TIME later, Mary stood on the ramparts of Ghent Castle, clutching a scroll. The easterly wind held a dusting of snowflakes that skittered and swirled instead of falling to the ground. The sky was pregnant with fat-bellied clouds as dark as a rook's chest and promising heavier snow to come.

To her right stood Margaret, and to her left Jeanne. Each woman wore a black cloak lined with wolf fur and held tightly in place with a brooch displaying the crest of Burgundy. A flag flapped above them, snapping and curling the image of a gold-and-red cross.

Upon her head, Mary wore a simple, silver crown encrusted with jewels. It had been placed there moments ago by her stepmother, the Duchess Dowager, during a small inauguration ceremony attended by a handful of clergy and councilors.

The sea of expectant faces that had come out into the bitter cold stared up at Mary. A few people held torches, others pitchforks, and all were wrapped against winter's cruel fingers.

She held up her hand.

Silence fell.

"The duke is dead!" Hugo shouted. "Long live the duchess!"

A series of boos and shouts.

"My fellow Ghent citizens," Mary called above the noise, "I come to you today with God's love and peace." She cleared her throat.

"Give us back our privileges."

"Yeah, return what is rightfully ours!"

A brackish cheer pierced the cold air.

"On this day…" Mary said as loud as she could while still maintaining what she hoped was dignity. "I come to you in joyous entry as my father's heir."

A hissing round of snarls and jeers.

"Was I not your beloved princess?" she said, holding out her hands. "Do you not trust me?"

The crowd quieted.

She made the most of the moment. "I thank you for being here. Many have fled, fearing France will take our country. But you, brave citizens of Ghent, stand here, by my side. Many also say I should marry, give you a duke, but what of our wealth? Does my chosen husband deserve to claim that?"

"No! What is Burgundy's stays Burgundy's," someone shouted, his deep voice spreading over the crowd.

"I agree, kind sir, and do not forget that I am my father's daughter," Mary went on. "My heart beats in time with his—his blood runs in my veins. I offer you my service as ruler and promise to govern with wisdom and charity. And when I do marry, you will have nothing to fear." She paused and pulled in a deep breath. "I have spoken at length with the Estates General regarding a draft known as *The Great Privilege*." She paused and swung her gaze over the crowd. "It will only be my heirs who have claim to your country, not him—not my future husband."

A few people looked at each other and nodded. She noticed Hugo puffing up his chest and tilting his chin in a satisfied way.

"And also within this charter," Mary went on, knowing it was her only chance at gaining the respect she needed, "I intend to restore local rights."

A cheer. Pitchforks stabbed the air.

"Let her speak. Let her speak," the man with the deep voice bellowed.

She nodded, feeling like she'd gained some ground. "I am renouncing the levy given by my father, relieving you of the debt."

Silence. Mouths agape. Eyes wide. People looked at each other to see if they'd heard right.

"Your ears do not deceive you." Mary had always found giving was more rewarding than taking. "And I promise you this: to always take council in matters of war and peace. For with my title comes responsibility and God's trust to care for you, the good citizens of Ghent, the Low Countries, Burgundy, and beyond, should our claims widen." She paused. "It is my promise to you, to always act with caution and council's advice."

"God bless Mary! God bless Mary! God bless Mary!" The crowd's chant started off quiet but quickly grew to a deafening below.

She turned to Margaret.

"Well done." Margaret smiled. It was the first time she had done so since her husband's death.

Mary stayed on the ramparts until her cheeks felt frozen and her fingers numb. But her heart was warm. She'd pleased her people, staved off a full-scale uprising, and she hoped, solidified her position.

When she arrived in her bedchamber, out of habit, the first thing she did was check on Jupiter and coo to him. He ruffled his feathers, sleepy; he'd eaten well that day.

It was then she noticed a scroll had been placed upon her pillow. Curiosity piqued, she snatched it up. The seal was intact—a seal that held the Habsburg crest of lions, feathers, armor, and a shield. "What? When did...?" She glanced at the door.

With shaking hands, she tore at the seal then gathered her skirt and hopped onto the bed. She spread the scroll out using the flats of her palms to keep it in place. A knot of nerves formed in her belly.

Mary, most illustrious Princess of Burgundy and Luxemburg,

I wish to thank you for your letter of betrothal. I agree—our union would be of great advantage to both of our houses.

I also humbly apologize for the length of time it has taken me to respond and hope you will still accept me as your husband.

If that is the case, I suggest a proxy marriage on the last day of April. And do not fear: Your gold diamond ring is forthcoming.

Archduke Maximilian of Austria.

CHAPTER FOUR

MAXIMILIAN TWISTED TO the right, heaving his colossal sword upward and grunting as he did so. His shiny, new field armor might have looked spectacular, but it was weighty, dragging on his shoulders and restricting his hip movements.

His opponent, Lars, backed up then stepped to the right, easily avoiding Maximilian's sword as it swung through the air at neck height.

The heft of the sword's momentum had Maximilian leaning to the left. He went with it, a well-rehearsed dance, and avoided a return stab.

But this was not a fight to the death. It was a display, a spectacle for the people of Vienna to truly appreciate both Maximilian's prowess as a warrior and the strength of the Habsburgs.

Not that that made it any less exhausting.

Through the narrow slit of his helmet, Maximilian spied the crowd's rapt faces as he lunged again for Lars.

Sweat dripped down his nape and his armpits were damp. He kept on going, swirling away from Lars's counter-strike then raising his sword high. For a moment, he kept it there, the weight of it seeming to press his body into the ground, then he brought it down with a sideways slice, grunting as he did so.

It caught Lars's leg, but no harm was done. His armor was also strong and fine. Even so, Lars fell to the ground, landing on his back, sword held between his two hands.

Maximilian brought his blade down on Lars's sword, not as hard as he could have, but still with enough strength to produce a pleasing clash of metal for the crowd.

He then tore off his helmet and threw it to one side, grasping Lars's sword and holding it aloft with his own.

The victor.

He beamed at the enthralled sea of faces.

Breathless and high on applause, Maximilian walked across the arena and stood before the podium.

"Father, you are here?"

Frederick sat on a large, dark, wooden chair, red upholstered and with the letters *AEIOU* carved in an arc over the top.

"Your eyes do not deceive you." Frederick sliced a hunk of cheese from a slab as large as his hand.

"I wasn't sure if you'd come out of your chamber today."

"I wouldn't have missed this for anything." He'd spoken with his mouth full.

"You please me. I hope the tournament pleased you."

"You're certainly imaginative."

"And cunning." Maximilian straightened as two servants began to remove his armor. "Very cunning."

"Enlighten me." Frederick put down the knife and studied Maximilian.

"You see..." Maximilian gestured to the sand-covered arena. "This might look like a show, simple entertainment, but what it's actually doing is cementing in people's minds the power of the Habsburgs. It is reminding them of our skills and our unwavering control over Vienna."

"A market as such...to show us off." Frederick nodded slowly and then swung his gaze around the departing crowd. "Yes. Yes. That is certainly one way to look at it."

Maximilian bent forward as his torso armor was removed. The breeze suddenly seeped through his black undergarments. He'd been overheating for two hours and the cool felt good.

"And talking of political matters…" Frederick waved for a goblet of red wine to be passed to Maximilian. "I have grave news."

"Pray tell." He took the wine.

"As you know, your proxy marriage to Mary of Burgundy is only days away."

Maximilian frowned and drank deep. This was a subject he preferred to avoid with his father. Unless of course… "Has it been called off?"

"No." Frederick shook his head. "In fact, the opposite. The union is of even more importance."

"And why is that?"

"News has arrived that Charles of Burgundy is dead. Killed in the fight against the Lower Leagues at Nancy. At first, it was merely a rumor, a whisper spreading like mist, but now it has been confirmed. His body laid to rest in God's house near to where he fell."

Maximilian crossed himself.

Two courtiers at his side did the same.

In that moment, Maximilian realized he must secure Mary of Burgundy as his wife. His father wasn't insistent about many things. But this seemed to be one subject that had hammered a nail into his determination.

"You set me a challenge, Father," he said, steeling himself. "To wed Mary of Burgundy and produce heirs."

"Indeed I did."

"And I will not let you down."

"I am glad to hear it. But go soon, my son, to Burgundy. Do not continue to dally."

"I would do no such thing."

His father ignored him. "You must quash her other suitors, for any

32

heir of a man like Charles is not likely to be without admirers of good standing. Respect for a proxy marriage is non-existent to some."

"Other suitors? Admirers? What do you know?"

"It is foresight." Frederick touched the spot between his eyebrows. "Any woman who has inherited such lands is quite the prize. The wolves will be sniffing around her as we speak. That is something my heart and mind are sure of."

"Wolves." Maximilian frowned and a sudden stab of possession hit him. He had never met Mary, knew nothing of her, other than her good breeding and great riches, but she was promised as his. He would not tolerate wolves sniffing around her.

He looked up as Lars approached, free of his upper armor and his brow red lined and perspiring.

"What has happened?" he asked, looking between Frederick and Maximilian. He slammed his hands onto his hips. He was still breathing heavily.

"Charles the Bold has been killed," Maximilian said. "Leaving Mary his sole heir."

"Your betrothed?" Lars raised his eyebrows at Maximilian.

"Indeed." Maximilian couldn't help the scowl. His day was taking a different turn to what he'd planned, but at least the tournament was nearly at its end. Seven days of spectacles—jousting, fighting, dancing, falconry, and music—had wowed the citizens of Vienna and been a resounding success.

"The proxy marriage," Frederick said, "will secure the deal as much as possible in this delicate situation, and then Maximilian will travel to Burgundy and become Mary's husband the moment he arrives. And arrive you must, for you are my only son. Who will rule Vienna if something happens to you? Who will keep the Ottomans in the east at bay?"

Maximilian drew in a deep breath. There was no way out of this. No longer could he pretend the sending of a letter and promise of a ring had brushed away the duty of marriage and producing heirs. No longer could he ignore the calendar and hope the date of the proxy would never arrive. He took another big gulp of wine. "You will accompany me, Lars." It was not a question.

"I would be honored." Lars pressed his hand to his chest. "And I will do my upmost to protect and serve."

"You see he gets there, Lars." Frederick bit into a rosy-red apple. "With God's speed and in one piece."

"Of course, Your Highness." Lars dipped his head. "I have been put on this Earth to serve the holy Habsburg family and I will do so with every breath I take."

"I will sleep better knowing you are with Maximilian." For a moment, Frederick's gaze softened on Maximilian, but then it hardened again. "A herald will announce your coming. So do not delay."

"I will not, but, Father, there is much to do before I leave. Gather the best men, horses, and falcons. Trunks to pack. Weapons to polish and stow for safe passage. Armor to order and—"

"You will not delay." Frederick's jaw tightened.

"But these things take time and I must be prepared. The realms through which I will pass have been ravaged by plague and war."

"So it is just as well Herrs Barr and Tolk have come to your assistance?"

"Herr Barr, he is just a merchant." Maximilian frowned. "And unless I am mistaken, so is Tolk."

"Wealthy merchants," Frederick said, "who have gifted you, Maximilian, with horsemen, horses, armor, and weapons."

Maximilian stared at his father. "You wish me to be beholden to *merchants?*"

"No, I wish you to get to Burgundy alive and soon." He waved his hand at Maximilian as though wafting away a fly. "And one day, when you have power and wealth, you can repay them."

Lars set his hand on Maximilian's shoulder, as though taking some of the weight of his anger and frustration.

Maximilian gritted his teeth. He hadn't even taken Mary as his bride and he was accruing debt that Burgundy must pay. It sliced at his pride and gnawed at his honor. But he had a duty to do, one that was bigger than him, bigger than the Habsburgs, even. It was to Vienna, Austria, the lands he would one day rule when he became Holy Emperor of Rome.

⟫⟫⟨⟨

MAXIMILIAN LEFT VIENNA with a heavy heart. Saying goodbye to his young sister had been hard. Frederick was plotting to marry her off, as though she were a commodity with which to strengthen the empire.

Much in the way he was being used.

"It is still better," Lars said as they rode side by side on black horses. They'd left the hills and were gaining steadily on the flat lands.

"What is better?"

"To be us, rather than paupers."

Maximilian huffed. "Yes, I suppose you are right."

Lars grinned. "So don't look so down of heart."

"My heart has nothing to do with it."

"Oh, no?"

"No, it is my head." He tapped his temple. "It is the thoughts that swirl, non-stop. I can't get peace from them."

"Sounds to me like you have worries to address."

"You know I have." He pointed at the sky. "But lately, I have been pondering other things. Like why is that blue? What makes storms? How can we use the weather rather than be slave to it? Is it best to battle in summer or winter? What advantages are there to each season?"

"Those are indeed big thoughts."

"I have been reading works from Italy, Florence in particular."

35

"Between tournaments, hunting, and seeking out pretty courtiers, I fail to see when you'd have had time for reading."

"I don't sleep well." Maximilian huffed.

"And what have you read from Florence?"

"That things are changing in that corner of Europe. The need to learn, to understand the world is a real thing. I'll confess I wish I were riding east so I could experience some of the new ideas that could revolutionize farming, war, and power. It is though they have seen a light we have yet to."

Lars was quiet for a moment, then, "Can anything be more important than power?"

Maximilian laughed, but it held little humor. "At one time, I might have said love was more important."

"But not now?"

"I am as good as wed to a woman I have never seen. Where is the love?"

"You are not the first and will not be the last to wed this way."

Maximilian turned to Lars. "Can I tell you one of my fears?"

"I will bear the weight of it with you, my friend."

Maximilian paused. He sighed. "I have prayed to God that she is not an ugly maiden with warts and smelly feet."

Lars laughed. "I have never heard any such rumor about Mary of Burgundy."

"Rumors can be quashed, especially if they are fact." Maximilian watched a murmuration of starlings dancing en masse on the horizon. Why did they do that?

"I understand that as your wedding night approaches, these fears claim more of your thoughts, my friend," Lars said. "But I am sure they will be unfounded."

"My purpose, as far as my father is concerned, is to create an heir. What if I…?" Maximilian pulled a face and glanced down at his groin. "What if I…?"

"Can't get it up?" Lars said. "Why? Have you had a problem before?"

"No. Of course not." Maximilian scowled. "But black, stumpy teeth, big ears, flappy breasts... Even if I close my eyes, I fear my cock will still not rise to the occasion."

"Then you have only one choice." Lars threw him a serious glance. "Which is?"

"To keep praying that she isn't an ugly wench and your cock not only approves, but *performs* when the occasion arises."

"If that is the case, I must have more time to pray. Tonight, when we set camp, we will plan on staying for several days. Give the horses and the men a rest after four weeks of traveling."

"Several days?"

"Yes." Maximilian gripped the reins a little tighter. Delaying was expensive and if he ran out of money, he'd have only one choice and that was to ask Mary for more.

⇒⟫⟩⟨⟪⇐

FOUR WEEKS LATER, Maximilian set up camp just outside Ghent. He'd drawn out the journey, it was true, and near Cologne, he *had* had to request additional funds from his betrothed. They'd come quickly, ensuring him of her keenness to still be wed to him. Melchior Pfintzing, Maximilian's personal clergyman, thought this to be an excellent sign of God's will for them to be joined in holy matrimony.

"Please do not cut off my head for saying this..." Lars poured his third goblet of wine and seated himself in Maximilian's tent, ankles crossed, a position that implied he was staying for a while.

"Should you risk saying it, then?" Maximilian washed his hands and face in a bowl of spring water, then pressed a cloth towel against his cheeks. "Or do you not care for your head? Perhaps breakfast wine has made you reckless." He continued to wash his torso, soaping up a

37

rag and scrubbing his chest and underarms.

"Yes, perhaps it is the liquid breakfast that has made me bold." Lars paused. "But I will say it anyway. The time has come to ride into Ghent." Lars drank, studying Maximilian as he did so, then, "King Louis is loitering in the wings, plotting, scheming. You must claim what is yours." He paused, leaning forward. "Claim your wife today. This day. Do it now, my friend. Before it is too late."

Maximilian sighed.

"Send word," Lars went on, "that you will arrive at noon. You could be wed by sunset."

"You are right, of course." Maximilian pulled fresh black under-garments on. "Let us armor up and go."

"Really?" Lars's eyes widened in surprise.

"Yes." Maximilian clapped. "You speak wisely. Now come on. Before I change my mind."

"Which we both know you can't. Not really." Lars knocked back his wine and stood. Closing his eyes, he swayed.

"And now you are drunk on my wedding day." Maximilian shoved Lars's shoulder.

Lars staggered to the left, his arm nudging the canvas wall. He burped. "No. I am perfectly sober and of sound mind." He pressed his fingers to his lips and grinned. "Let's summon the nobles, hoist our flags, and mount our steeds."

Ghent grew larger on the horizon, dominated by the castle's tur-rets, ramparts, and impressive donjon. The scatter of houses that led from the sturdy castle had orange-tiled roofs that were shaded by ancient trees. A brook edged with swaying reeds babbled toward the town and overhead swifts let out their high-pitched calls. The place had an air of tranquility, as though sleeping in the warm, midday sun.

But that wouldn't last for long.

The horses had rested well and so trotted energetically, silken tails held high, necks curved, and looking particularly smart as the men had taken the time to brush and clean their rump cloths and attach plumes of feathers between their ears.

Strangely, Maximilian had a sense of calmness come over him as he approached the outer walls. He still felt energetic and alert but also ready for the challenge, not just of marriage, but also of governing Ghent's good people, who could now be seen working in fields, sowing, plowing, tending. He had no intention of being a tyrant; he wanted citizens to prosper and live happy lives and have healthy children.

Hooves clattered on cobbles, alerting everyone of their arrival into the town. People came onto the street to greet him. Some cheered and waved, others stared wide-eyed. A few studied him with obvious suspicion.

Ghent smelled of bread and lavender. Many citizens wore clothes made of fine, embroidered fabrics. A few waved the Burgundy flag.

"Archduke Maximilian."

He drew to a swift halt.

A slender, young woman stood before him, blocking the passage of his horse. She wore a tall, peaked hat, atop it a length of lace that hung down past her nape to her shoulders. Her mouth was wide and her eyes dark.

Mary. I have met my wife. Finally.

He waited for a flip of his heart. Nothing. He waited for his breath to hitch. It did not. A surge of desire and longing? Not a drop.

Lars burped again.

The woman frowned up at Lars. "Archduke Maximilian of Austria?"

"No." Lars pointed at Maximilian. "That is he."

"It is a pleasure to meet you, Duchess." Maximilian hoped she didn't hear the disappointment in his voice. This woman was by no means ugly, but she wasn't appealing to Maximilian's taste. Still, he would have to bear it. At least he couldn't see any warts from where he sat up on his horse.

"Oh, good Lord, I am not she." The woman raised her eyebrows. "The Duchess of Burgundy has sent me in her place to greet you. I am Jeanne de Commynes, the Lady of Halewijn."

A great rush of relief swept through Maximilian. He glanced at Lars. Lars was gazing at the woman as though he'd never seen a female before, his mouth a little slack and his eyes unblinking.

Maximilian cleared his throat. "When will I see her? My bride."

"She is preparing herself. We heard you had left camp and so we are readying for the wedding ceremony."

He nodded.

She stepped closer, eyeing his horses' big, shining hooves. And then she breathed in noisily, her nostrils flaring. She closed her eyes.

"Whatever are you doing?" Maximilian asked.

"Smelling you." She eyed him suspiciously.

"*Smelling* me?"

"The duchess fears you do not bathe with enough frequency." She raised her eyebrows, as though daring him to say otherwise.

He frowned. "I most certainly do bathe. As frequently as the opportunity arises."

"So you don't smell?"

"Can you smell me?"

"Not from here."

"And you wouldn't from here." He pressed his hand to his chest. "I can assure you of that."

Lars chuckled.

"What is funny?" Maximilian snapped at him.

"Nothing." Lars tried to suppress his smile but with little success.

"And can you read and write?" Jeanne asked haughtily.

"Can *you?*"

"Indeed." Her lips pursed.

"And, I'll inform you, so can I." How dare she? Of all the nerve…

"Count?" Jeanne held up her hand, fingers spread. "The duchess needs a man who can count to more than five."

"I have a good brain for mathematics. Perhaps the duchess doesn't have an aptitude for numbers and that is why she needs a husband."

"There are many reasons why she needs a husband." Jeanne folded her arms and after a glance at Lars, she took a step backward. "You should dismount and follow me. The duchess is waiting, and it has been a very long wait."

"I will apologize to her for the delay." He swung his armor-heavy leg over his saddle and landed on the hard ground with a metallic thud.

She stepped back and looked up at him. "And you will also apologize for the expense?"

He cleared his throat and passed the reins to a courtier. "A necessary expense. Now, lead the way."

She turned, and then with chin tilted and gown held from the dusty cobbles, she walked through the crowd.

Maximilian followed, heavy cape embroidered with Habsburg crest flicking behind him. Lars and Melchior were close on his tail. He was aware of the curious gazes. And he invited that curiosity. He would govern with authority and thoughtfulness. Soon, these people would be *his* people.

They passed over a moat bridge, beneath a portcullis, and into the inner walls of the castle. A flight of pure-white doves took to the sky, abandoning a sprinkle of grain on the ground. To his right, a blacksmith worked at a glowing furnace, thick smoke billowing. A cart was midway through being unloaded of sacks and barrels and the workers paused to stare at him.

Jeanne continued to lead the way, through a doorway, along a dark corridor lit only by a handful of fat candles, then into a vast room with a fire burning brightly in the center. Tapestries hung on the walls and a great bench was heavily set with a banquet—urns of soup and stew, piles of bread, fig stuffed apples, veal chops, pork, honey, almonds. His stomach growled at the sight.

Four small high windows had their parchment coverings pinned back to expose the blue sky beyond. Bright, diamond-white light shone in through them like reaching fingers. Two shards hit a deep-red rug, one landed on a brown-and-white dog that was studying him with wary eyes, and the other landed on a woman.

She was petite, and her floor-length, cream-colored gown was made of fine material with exquisite golden details on the bodice and the long sleeves. Her headwear consisted of a tall, pointed hennin covered with a flowing, white veil that draped over her shoulders.

She was looking straight at him with soft, gray eyes. Her reddened lips were set in a straight line, neither smiling nor disapproving.

He stopped in his tracks beside the table, his clanking armor silencing as he stared at what appeared to be an angel before him. "Mary of Burgundy?"

"Yes." Pause. "Archduke Maximilian of Austria?"

"That is I." He swallowed, his throat suddenly tight. In the name of heaven, the way the sunlight fell created a halo above her head. This was his immaculate bride. God had truly blessed him.

The silence stretched, a void waiting to be filled.

Her skin was pale and delicate, like the finest china, and her slender shoulders set in a way that told him she was strong despite her fragile appearance. He was instantly drawn to know more, to know *everything* about her, and at the same time, a surge of protectiveness came over him, a desire to protect her over everything, at all costs, even his own life.

His heart did a strange beat, seeming to miss one, then banging against his ribcage twice to catch up. He sucked in a deep breath as a new, fiery heat burned in his core, warming him from within. It was like nothing he'd ever felt before.

Instantly, he knew what the gripping, intense new feeling was.

He'd just fallen in love.

CHAPTER FIVE

MARY STARED AT the silver giant towering before her. He seemed to fill more space than just his physical presence; it was as though his soul permeated the entire room. Seeping into every corner, knowing everything, touching everything at once.

She had an urge to fidget, something she never did, but forced herself still.

His jawline was strong and masculine. His dark-blond hair was ruffled and his brow a little damp, no doubt from wearing a sallet. His nose wasn't perfectly straight, indeed a little hooked, but it suited him. And his eyes, they were the blue of a deep lake, and clear and intelligent.

He removed his gloves and set them on the bench beside a plate of pickles.

Aymer stood, though he didn't take a step forward.

Mary glanced at Maximilian's hands. They were clean, nails short, the skin a little work-worn, perhaps. A sense of relief produced a sigh. Mary couldn't abide uncleanliness, and if his hands were clean, it bode well that he washed and bathed with frequency and the rest of him was clean. Indeed, she'd sent Jeanne out to greet him with instructions that if she'd found him to be a stinking, uneducated beast, she was to order him back to Austria immediately.

"You're very tall." Her voice seemed suddenly loud in the quiet room.

"And you're very small." He smiled, just a little.

His smile changed his face from warrior to nobleman and the sudden switch almost made her gasp. Perhaps he would prove to be tolerable.

"I humbly apologize for the delay," he said, his voice deep and accented. "It was quite the journey, one worthy of a book. Perhaps one day I will get the time to write it."

She waited for him to go on.

"Avalanches, lightning strikes, shipwrecks, murder plots, duels, and pitched battles. A tale, indeed." He tilted his head slightly, the smile still dancing on his lips.

Mary remained quiet. Shipwrecks? Really?

He pulled in a deep breath, seriousness seeming to come over him. "I wish to offer condolences for the loss of your father, the duke."

"That was some time ago, but I thank you." She inclined her head. "But we should marry soon. My Estates General wish to me marry the Dauphin of France. They do not agree with our marriage."

"Why must you do as they say?"

"I was pressed into a corner when my father died, my own people turning against me. I was forced to create a treaty which gives the council and estates power over matters of importance."

"Tear it up. Tear it into one hundred pieces, if you wish. You are the duchess." He frowned. "And, by the way, your council is clearly of low acumen. The very notion that you might marry Charles is ridiculous. He is a child. A spoilt and indulged one at that."

"Indeed. But that is not the only reason I do not wish for the marriage. My father and the King of France were mortal enemies. It is a union I cannot entertain. The duke would roll in his grave."

"Their hatred of each other over these last few years is a well-known fact." Maximilian stepped closer, so close, she could see the stubble growing on his strong chin and the darker ring of blue that lined his irises. "And now fate and God have it that I will be the one who gets the good fortune to wed you."

"It makes good political sense for your family." She raised her chin. "Does it not?"

"It will make the King of France an enemy of the Habsburgs. He is a dangerous enemy to make. Now I think of it, I am not sure how sensible that is!" He chuckled softly.

"You are refusing? After this long journey? After all of this time?" She frowned up at him and fought not to raise her voice. Aymer came to her side, as if sensing her frustration. "Now you are here you are too frightened to marry me?"

"I did not say that." He took her hand in his. "I definitely did not say that."

His skin was warm and his touch firm but gentle. Her heart rate picked up a little more. It was as if the room were fading around her. All she saw was Maximilian. His face, his wide shoulders, and the way his black undergarment sat slightly rucked around his thick neck and stretched over his chest.

"I am always ready for a challenge," he went on. "The challenge of taking a wife, I am up for. As I am for the challenge of a battle with King Louis to defend our lands and people."

"That pleases me to hear. But we must take action soon. The French are moving in; they are in Picardy. I have the citizens sheltering in my churches. They are fed and clothed but want to go home. I need a duke at my side. A duke on whom I can rely, who can think with me, act with me."

"You know what you want, Duchess, and what you need. I like that."

"Of course. Is there another way to be?"

He smiled, as though she'd pleased him greatly. "'In youth and beauty, wisdom is but rare.'"

A small thrill went through her. "You know the philosopher Homer?"

"As, it seems, do you." He stooped down onto one knee, stiffly, slowly, his armor clanging. A frown crossed his face, as though the position were uncomfortable.

"Maximilian?" Her heart rate picked up and for the first time in many months, she allowed hope to take shape.

"Duchess Mary of Burgundy." He held up an exquisite diamond ring. "Give me your hand, this day, and I will give you my sword, my wisdom, and my loyalty until the day I die. I *can* promise you that, and I *will* promise you that."

She swallowed, emotions pricking at her eyes. For so long, her only support had been her stepmother and closest friend, Jeanne. She hadn't been lonely, but she had felt alone in the face of the council and King Louis and that had made her feel weak.

And she hated feeling weak.

Yet now…now her long-awaited betrothed, Maximilian, was here and sliding a ring onto her finger.

"You have my hand," she said, her voice a little shaky. "And the church is ready, as is the bishop."

"Then lead the way." He stood, straightening once again to his full height and still holding her hand. "And we will become man and wife."

"And you intend to wed in your armor?"

"Ah." He looked down at himself. "I had not planned that, but seeing you stole all other thoughts." He smiled. "I will indeed change into something more befitting of a groom." He took her other hand. "Though I beg you, Duchess, do not change a thing about yourself. You are simply exquisite." He paused and let his gaze dip down, then up, her body. "More beautiful than I could ever have imagined."

Now she did fidget, shifting from one foot to the other and then looking left and right and down at Aymer, who was still studying Maximilian as though unable to decide if he was friend or foe.

"I am not saying you are beautiful because they are the words that should be said to a man's bride." Maximilian released her left hand and with the crook of his thumb, tipped her face to look up at his. "I am saying it because it is true. You are a vision of beauty that is almost blinding."

She stared at the man she'd feared might arrive at her home and show himself to be a big, stinking brute.

"Perhaps this marriage," he went on, "will gain us more than political power. Perhaps it will gain us each a friend in the other."

"A friend?"

"It would be a good place to start, don't you agree?"

She did agree, but he didn't wait for her to reply.

Instead, he turned and bellowed, "Lars! Where are you? I need to change for the ceremony."

One hour later, Mary stood with Margaret and Jeanne to her left and Bishop Arquette to her right.

On the bishop's other side, Maximilian held himself rod-straight, arms behind his back and chest puffed out. He still wore his cloak, which was embroidered with the Habsburg coat of arms and pinned with a large, golden brooch in the shape of an eagle with its wings spread. Now it was paired with a plain, dark tunic and pants, leather boots, and a sheathed, silver sword that nearly touched the red altar rug.

She didn't care for the material of his clothing. It appeared rough and well-worn. It was a Godsend that Ghent was the home of clothmaking. She would ensure, from this day forward, his outfits would be befitting of a duke.

Lars, who appeared to be a close acquaintance of Maximilian's, stood beside her groom, as well as his personal clergyman.

The bishop held up a Bible, his face somber.

The crowd hushed.

As the service began, Maximilian kept his attention on her, his mouth set in a serious line and a small crease marring his otherwise smooth brow.

She swallowed. The intensity of his gaze had a little coil of nerves winding up in her belly.

Tonight would be their wedding night. Their marriage would be consummated. What would Maximilian be like in the bedchamber?

A beast who would throw her to the bed and take her over and over again? A man who would want to claim her morning, noon, and evening? Or a husband who would care for her comfort as well as his own pleasure? Mary had nothing to go on, other than talk from her married lady friends. She was a virgin, as was befitting, but with that came many concerns.

"I now pronounce you man and wife," the bishop said, crossing himself. "As is witnessed by our Lord above and the lords and ladies of this House of God. May you be blessed with sons and good health in the years to come."

For the first time since entering the church, Maximilian smiled, his cheeks balling and his eyes sparkling. "Amen." There was something a little wicked, slightly devilish in the timbre of his voice.

Mary glanced away, a rise of heat growing on her chest. Once more, she had to resist the urge to fidget. It seemed her new husband had a knack for making her restless—making her want for something she wasn't sure how to describe.

"Congratulations," Margaret said. "To you both. This is an excellent union for Burgundy and Austria. And now we will feast."

"Many thanks to you, Dowager." Maximilian nodded at Margaret and offered Mary the crook of his arm. "Let us celebrate our good fortune in coming together."

Mary said nothing and slipped her arm through his.

He grasped her hand, took a deep, almost-satisfied breath, and led her past the congregation. His paces were slow and his sword shifted with each step. A flute played, and a pair of doves was released. A small girl scattered petals before them, a delicate path of powdery pink.

Mary got the sense that Maximilian, like Margaret, was particularly pleased with their union. It was the tilt of his chin. His stride. The sparkle in his eyes.

Once in the Great Hall, a hum of conversation accompanied guests taking their seats. Huge urns dripped with flowers, fat candles flickered, and the tables creaked under the weight of the gargantuan feast.

Mary glanced at Philip, who was studying Maximilian. She hoped her marriage wouldn't change her friendship with her cousin. For so many years, they'd adventured, laughed, and learned together. She couldn't imagine not having him in her life. He'd been a constant during times when everything around her had changed.

"Dear wife." Maximilian held her chair while she sat, then pushed it in. "Please relax and enjoy yourself."

Aymer slunk beneath the table, settling by her feet with his tail between his legs.

"Thank you."

Maximilian sat at her side and reached for his wine. He took several noisy, big gulps.

Jeanne raised her eyebrows.

"You are thirsty?" Mary asked him.

"I am."

"And hungry?"

"Very." He took a piece of bread and a hunk of pork then added pickles, fig-stuffed apples, and butter to his plate.

Her eyes grew wide. "You are *very* hungry."

"I will need my strength for later."

"Later?" Oh, dear Lord. He was going to be a wild man in the bedchamber, energetic, rampant, and with stamina. That must have been why he was filling himself up with food. He'd need the energy. She squirmed in her seat and reached for her own wine. What had she done?

"Yes, later," he said, smearing butter on the bread. "I am to govern at your side, am I not? We have much to discuss. Likely, our conversation on political matters will take a long time. See us late into the night."

"Ah, I see." Surely, governing wasn't the only thing on his agenda for their first night together? "Political matters, yes, yes of course."

Next to her, Jeanne blew out a long breath, as though she'd been anxious on Mary's behalf about Maximilian needing his physical strength.

"And," he went on when he'd finished a slice of pork, "I do not wish to be like my father."

"What do you mean?" Mary popped an almond into her mouth.

"He might be Holy Roman Emperor, my father, but he is lazy."

"*Lazy!*" She was surprised that Maximilian would accuse his father of such a sin.

"Yes, he enjoys feasts, he rarely leaves the grounds of his home, and he can be insular at times. I'm pretty sure he couldn't summon the physical strength to hold a lance or attend a day's hunting." He leaned closer, his wide shoulder brushing hers. "Indeed, I've heard a rumor that Pope Pius II once exclaimed that my father rules while sitting down." He drank more wine. "An accomplishment he shouldn't be proud of."

"I agree that is not something of which to be proud." She nodded at his sword. "And I've heard rumors that you are quite the swordsman."

"It is true I enjoy sparring. It is better than going to battle."

"In sparring, you get to keep your head. Always a bonus."

"True." He chuckled. "Tell me, what do you enjoy?"

She raised her eyebrows. "You really want to know?"

"Of course."

"I'll admit I have a love for falconry. I have hunted with Jupiter—"

"Jupiter?"

"My falcon." She smiled. "He is the best falcon I've ever had. He's calm and very intelligent. We rarely come home empty-handed."

"'We'? You and Jupiter?"

"Yes, but also my cousins, John and Philip." She nodded at Philip, who was now talking to his father. "That is their father, Lord Ravenstein, talking to Philip. Lord Ravenstein is master of my horses."

"And where is John?"

"He was called away."

Maximilian nodded slowly. "We should hunt together. You and I."

"I would like that very much." She smiled. "If it would please you."

"It would. But you must eat more." He nodded at the few crystalized spices and three cherries on her plate.

"It is not becoming for a duchess to gorge." She placed her hands on her lap.

"But this is your wedding feast. The food is sumptuous." He reached for a boiled and peeled egg and a slice of bread and put them on her plate. To that, he added a spoonful of white fish and several figs. "I insist you enjoy this food as well as gain nourishment from it."

Mary glanced at Jeanne, who had only a few nuts and spices on her plate.

Jeanne shrugged and turned to Margaret.

Margaret appeared to be watching Maximilian closely. "Mary, my dear daughter, if your husband wishes you to eat, I think you should do as he advises."

"It is not a hardship." Maximilian chuckled and bit into an apple. "And we should send God our thanks for this plentiful feast."

Mary nodded and picked up her fork. Pushing some fish onto it, she ate daintily.

"Very good," Maximilian said. "Everyone, eat, I insist." He nodded at Jeanne and Margaret and then sent his attention around the room, seeming to settle his gaze on the few women at the benches. "My wife and I do not wish for anyone to leave our wedding celebrations hungry," he boomed. "Eat, drink, and be merry."

Mary salted her egg, her mind rushing with thoughts. Her new husband was making changes already. He was young, it was true, younger than she, but his years did not detract from the air of authority he held.

When the feasting had finished, servants cleared away the plates, bowls, and urns and the benches were pushed to the side of the room. Beside the fire, which had been refueled and now flickered merrily, a band consisting of a harp, vielle, and flute set up. The musicians, all dressed in red with flat berets, began to play.

"Ah, this is good." Maximilian tapped his fingers on the table.

"You enjoy music?"

"Very much." He turned to her. "Don't you?"

"I do indeed." She smiled, pleasantly surprised that he had an ear for rhythm.

"Ah, my bride. I have something for you." He tapped the pockets of his jacket, frowned, then stood. He dug into his tunic pocket. "Here." Sitting back down, he set a silver medal on the table in front of her.

"What is it?" she asked, picking it up.

"A medal. I've had it struck to commemorate the joining of our two families. I wish you to have it as a reminder of this day."

"Thank you." She had not been expecting such a thoughtful gift. "It's very detailed."

"I hope you like it. See? Our family crests."

"I do like it, very much." She turned it over and studied the delicate image of The Virgin and Child set between two saints. An inscription read, in Latin: *Tota pulcra es amica mea et macula non est in te.* "It is a nice sentiment."

"It is more than a sentiment, it is a truth."

"But you could not have known that you'd find me pure and beautiful before today."

"It was something I prayed for." He took her hand, brought it to his mouth, and swept his soft lips over her knuckles. "And God has not only heard me, He has been very generous." He leaned closer, so close, she could feel his breath on her ear as he spoke. "And now, sitting here, I find not only beauty, but also intelligence."

"And intelligence is attractive to you?" She turned to face him, their noses almost bumping.

He smiled. "More than you could ever imagine."

She swallowed and stared into his eyes. They shone with desire. A sensation like stroking fingers tickled up her back and over her scalp. A small tremble went through her, clenching her belly, then settling lower down, between her legs.

"Tell me," he whispered, "Do you like what you see when you look at me?"

"You are clearly a fine warrior and an accomplished horseman."

"I did not ask you to list my skills." He swiped his tongue over his bottom lip, leaving a soft sheen there. "I asked if you like what you see when you look at me."

"You are big."

"I know." He raised his eyebrows.

"And strong."

"Go on."

"And you have…"

"What?"

"A nice face, a noble face, and your eyes are so very blue."

"You think I have a nice face." He nodded, as though that pleased him. "Good, that is good." Suddenly, he stood, the legs of his chair scraping on the hard floor. "And now we will dance, our first dance, my beautiful wife."

"Dance?"

"Yes, for this is a celebration, we will dance the carole, sing, and enjoy music together." He gestured to Margaret and Jeanne. "Come, I insist we have fun. Everyone looks so serious here." He took Mary's hand and tugged her to standing, laughing as he did so.

His laughter was infectious and she giggled as he pulled her to the center of the hall.

Music filled the room, and other guests joined them, standing in a circle holding not hands, but fingertips.

"And we begin, good people of Burgundy," Maximilian shouted. "Begin!"

He set the dance in motion, tugging Mary three steps to the right. Everyone followed, kicking their left feet across the right, then stepping back three steps again.

The light of the flames caressed everyone's faces while the flute twittered like an excitable bird. Guests began to smile, laugh, and relax into the dance.

After a minute, the rhythm changed and the circle drew in, clapped three times, then stepped backward.

Mary found herself getting breathless as she moved and swayed to the beat. She kept glancing at Maximilian and found each time she did, he was watching her.

The group returned to stepping clockwise, then anticlockwise, kicking out their legs. The flutist picked up the pace; he went so fast, Mary wondered if he was trying to trip people up. But no one seemed to mind. There was much laughter.

When the music finally stopped and the dance ended, Mary bent forward, giggling, her cheeks hot.

"It seems I have a wife who can dance," Maximilian said, pushing his hand through his hair and sending several strands shooting upward.

"And I a husband with a talent for fancy step work."

He smiled, almost wickedly, and cupped her elbow. "You'll be relieved to know"—he leaned closer and lowered his voice—"dancing is not *all* I'm talented at."

CHAPTER SIX

THE UNDERCURRENT IN Maximilian's words had nerves tumbling through Mary. She glanced up at the windows. The sky was dark and peppered with stars. Her wedding night was almost upon her.

"Here." Maximilian poured her more wine. "Drink this."

She did as he'd instructed. Perhaps it would help with the ordeal that was to come.

"Your Grace," Jeanne said, appearing at her side, her cheeks also a little flushed from dancing. "Would you like me to help you prepare for your wedding night?"

"Yes." Mary nodded. "Thank you."

Maximilian inclined his head, a half-smile playing on his lips. "I will come to your bedchamber in due course."

"Do not rush," she said.

"Oh?" He raised his eyebrows. "Why not?"

"Her Grace takes a while to prepare for bed," Jeanne said, looping her arm around Mary's waist. "All must be perfect, naturally."

"Naturally," Maximilian said with a grin as he threw a grape into the air and then caught it in his mouth. "And I would expect nothing less."

"Oh, God help me." Mary gasped as Jeanne steered her through the crowd. "Lord have mercy on me. Oh…"

"All will be well. Have faith." Jeanne squeezed her closer.

"Have faith? *Have faith*…?" Mary's stomach roiled as they left the room. The quiet of the corridor made her ears ring.

Aymer rushed along at her side.

"Have you *seen* the size of my husband, Jeanne?" she said. "And a great warrior at that, muscles and strength. Oh, what will be left of me by morning? I will be wrecked, ruined, and sore."

"It is true what you say. He is big, and his friend Lars is also quite the brute."

"Brute, exactly… Oh, I should have married Philip. I am sure a night with him would not be as terrifying as this one. Philip is gentle and caring."

"If you are so scared, why did you marry Maximilian? It was you who chose him."

"It was my father who chose him, remember. And it is also because Burgundy needs him. We cannot let our land and people fall to France."

"And you need an heir."

"I know…but…" Mary watched Aymer dash ahead as if checking the way was clear.

"But what?" Jeanne asked.

"I don't believe Maximilian's father, the Holy Roman Emperor, told him about a treaty he made many years ago with my father, during what I gather was a rather tense meeting. Maximilian would have mentioned it before the ceremony, I am sure of it."

"Your fathers had a treaty?" Jeanne opened the door to Mary's bedchamber. "Tell me more."

"It is a contract that stipulates Maximilian cannot inherit Burgundian lands. It is further sealed in the Great Privilege Act, as you know. So upon my death, everything—lands, titles, and possessions—will go directly to our children, God willing we have them, and he will lose all of his power here."

Jeanne nodded slowly. "It is not something I can imagine a man like Maximilian accepting with ease. Not now that I have met him."

"But maybe he does know." Mary sat and waited for Jeanne to unpin her hennin. Aymer lay over her feet, keeping them warm. "Maybe his father explained it and he still wanted to go ahead with the union."

"That is something you can pray for." Jeanne lifted off the head-wear and Mary's pale-brown hair tumbled free. "But do you want my advice, Your Grace?"

"I do. I really do." Mary unclipped a brooch and set it on the dresser.

"If I were you, I wouldn't say anything. It was a deal made between your father and his. And an act you constructed in a dire moment. And if you both live long, happy lives, as I will pray each night that you do, it will never be a subject that needs addressing, or at least not for many years."

Mary couldn't imagine she'd be that lucky. Sweeping such a thing under the carpet…could she?

With a sigh, she stood and waited while Jeanne undid the buttons on her gown.

Then she raised her arms and Jeanne lifted her dress over her head, the many layers rustling as it was drawn past her ears.

Standing in a plain, white woolen undergarment, the shoulder straps thin and the soft material skimming to her ankles, she nodded. "You are right. I have more pressing worries tonight than a small clause in the odd treaty here and there."

"You have, but remember what Margaret told you. Relax as much as you can, close your eyes, and pray that it won't last long. Pray that he will be quick to plant his seed."

"Why must we women endure such a thing?" Mary took the warm, wet cloth Jeanne handed her. "On top of menses, and child-birth."

"Men, they have nothing to worry about." Jeanne paused. "Except going to battle and being speared by a sword, pike, or arrow, I suppose."

Mary pushed away an image of what her father's last moments must have been like. "Yes, there is that awful unpleasantness." She downturned her mouth.

"Unpleasant, indeed."

Soon Mary became lost in her thoughts of the night ahead as she washed, cleaned her teeth, and brushed her hair.

Jeanne was quiet, and Mary was grateful. It felt like she were going to battle, with Maximilian. And she'd be no match for him. He would be able to do as he chose with her.

Knock. Knock.

Jeanne stopped folding linen. "He is here."

"Yes." Mary's heart clattered. "It is time."

Quickly, Jeanne disposed of the wash water and pushed a clean chamber pot under the bed. "I will pray for you." She kissed Mary's cheek. "And I will also pray that he is kind and gentle and quick."

"Thank you." Her mouth was dry. She wished it were already morning and the ordeal were over with.

"Mary. It is I, Maximilian. Let me in."

"Go, Jeanne." Mary nodded at the door and clasped her hands together. "I will be strong. Do not fear."

"I know you will be, my dearest, beloved friend."

Jeanne rushed to the door and pulled it open. "Your Grace. She is ready."

Maximilian didn't speak.

"Aymer," Jeanne said, turning. "Come with me."

Aymer whimpered and looked up at Mary.

"Go," Mary said, pointing at the door. "You can't stay in here, not tonight."

Aymer stood and sloped out, thin tail slotted between his legs. He paused beside Maximilian and sent him an accusing, withering look before slipping from view.

Maximilian entered the room then closed the large, oak door. He flicked the lock.

The clunking sound of the key added to Mary's nerves. She hoped she wouldn't be sick.

He strode into the room, his sword banging against his leg. Then he stopped and unpinned his cloak. Without saying a word, he draped it over a chair, the heavy material falling almost to the floor.

A fire smoldered in a grate beside the four-poster bed. Having been on all day, the room was warm, but right now, Mary felt hot, as though her blood were on fire.

She wished the fire had gone out.

She wished Jeanne hadn't filled the room with so many flickering candles.

He undid his belt and with it removed also came his sword, which he laid atop his cloak. Next came his boots and socks.

With each passing second, her anxiety grew. Seeing him here, in her space, made him bigger somehow and made it all the more real. This was no dream, this man before her. He was her husband and she his to claim.

He tugged his shirt from his breeches, then pulled it over his head, exposing his torso. He was solid but lean with a smattering of chest hair, and his skin kissed by the sun. A scar ran over his left pec and a silver cross sat on a chain and rested just below the hollow of his throat.

He straightened and stared at her.

For a moment, it was like there was some kind of other force between them. Something strong, instinctual, as though they were the only people who existed.

But it only lasted a moment; her nerves were fraying and the anticipation was too much. "Just do what you need to." She forced herself to uncross her arms and let them hang at her sides. She took in a deep breath, then blew it out through pursed lips.

He stepped onto the bedside rug beside her. His eyes narrowed as he studied her intensely.

"We are wed," she said, her voice tight, "and now we must produce an heir."

"I hope our children"—he reached for her left hand and pressed it between both of his—"will have your beauty and grace."

She looked straight ahead, at the cross sitting against his smooth flesh. Three dark-green gems sat within it. "And I that our sons have your strength and skills," she managed.

He didn't reply. Instead, he came closer still.

His scent wrapped around her, spice and leather, and something male she hadn't encountered before. It wasn't unpleasant.

"My bride." He pressed her palm onto his warm chest. "You have already stolen my heart. And now, it is my intention to win yours." He rested his hand over her left breast.

She trembled and locked her knees. Her nipples were hard and she knew he'd be able to feel the one beneath his palm.

"Do I have a chance?" he whispered. "To win your heart?"

"I…I don't know."

His eyebrows twitched. "You don't know?"

"We have only just met."

"But you like what you see. You've already admitted that."

She studied his torso. Shadows danced over his toned muscles; his nipples were small and dark. A fan of hair went from his navel to the waist of his pants. "I like what I see well enough."

"Good." He slipped his hand from her breast upward, over her throat, up the column of her neck, then cupped her face in both of his palms. "That is a good place to start."

She kept her hand on his chest and was sure she could feel the beat of his heart, or was it her own pulse pounding through her body?

"You have never lain with a man?"

"Of course not."

He stared into her eyes. "Have you kissed a man?"

"No, of course not. I have never kissed a man, nor a woman, for that matter."

He smiled, creases darting from the corners of his eyes. "I should have been clearer."

She didn't reply. His closeness had set her senses alight. What was he going to do next?

Still holding her face, he drew closer. "You will only ever be kissed by me," he said. "There is only me, for you are mine."

And then his lips touched hers, gently, softly.

She closed her eyes and was guided by his delicate movements. When his tongue found hers, she gasped, though the sound mixed with his throaty moan. He tasted of wine and apples, fruity yet dark, and she felt so small and delicate at his side, but not vulnerable. His touch was tender and mild.

After a minute, he pulled back but kept her face cupped in his hands. "You are so sweet. The most delicious thing I have ever tasted."

She bit on her bottom lip. She could still taste him. "We should... You should...release your seed now." She paused, trembled. "But I'll confess you will have to lead the way. I have no idea how and—"

"Shh, my love." He pressed a finger over her lips. "That will not be happening tonight."

"It won't?" Surprise caught in her words.

"You've gone twenty years untouched. We can wait until you don't tremble with fear at my touch." He tucked a lock of hair behind her ear. "It may surprise you to learn that I am a man who cares as much about a woman's pleasure as I do my own."

"I do not expect it to be a pleasurable experience. Tolerable at best."

"Then you have a lot to learn, and I am a lucky man, as you are a blank canvas just waiting for me to fill you with experience." He swept his lips over hers again. "Delicious experiences that will have you gasping my name and begging for more." He took her hand and led her to the bed. "Come, let us sleep. It has been a long day."

"You mean...?"

"I mean what I just said." He peeled back the covers of the bed and settled beneath them.

She stared at him.

"Come. Join me." He patted the white sheet next to him and settled his head on the feathered pillow.

"But...you are sleeping in your breeches?"

"I am doing my best to be chivalrous, but I am a mortal. To be naked beside you, that may test my willpower a little too much."

She didn't understand what he meant, but his smile was genuine and kind, so she slipped under the heavy covers next to him.

He pulled her to him, aligning their bodies. "Good night, my sweet wife. Sleep well and dream of our future together."

For the first time in a long time, Mary let out a contented sigh as she closed her eyes. Her new husband was handsome and wise and it seemed he was kind too.

But would she really be gasping his name and begging for more? How could that possibly be? She didn't believe it.

>>>><<<<

DAWN BROUGHT WITH it the sound of birdsong and Aymer whining on the other side of the bedchamber door.

"Nuisance dog," Maximilian muttered, squeezing Mary close but not opening his eyes.

"Oh, please don't be harsh with him. He likes to sleep in here with me. He'll wonder why he's been kicked out." Mary set her hand on Maximilian's chest, her fingertips resting on the silver cross.

"Sleep in here?" He opened his eyes. "Not on the bed, I hope?"

"Yes. And why not? He's warm."

"You have *me* now. I am much bigger and warmer than him."

"That is true, but he will not understand." She felt a little irked on Aymer's behalf.

"He will have to. I will not have a dog looking at me as though I have stolen something from it. Which is exactly the look he gave me last night."

She sat and decided to change the subject…for now. "Jeanne will be here soon with a breakfast tray for us to take in the solar."

"Good, because I am famished." He raised his arms above his head, flashing dark underarm hair as he stretched.

"After all you ate yesterday? How can you be famished, Maximilian?"

"Today is a new day. My stomach is empty." He grinned.

There was a sudden loud banging on the door. Aymer went quiet.

"Who is it?" Maximilian called.

"It is I, Bishop Arquette."

"The bishop?" Maximilian downturned his mouth. "What is he doing here? I thought you said Jeanne was bringing breakfast."

"I don't know why he is here." Mary shrugged. "He doesn't usually visit in the morning."

"What do you want?" Maximilian called.

"Let us in! Let us in now. We demand it." The bishop's tone was impatient. "This very minute."

Maximilian stood, the morning good humor leaving his eyes. "Who is '*we*'?" He strode toward the door.

"I am accompanied by councilors," the bishop said, "and we demand you open this door to us."

"You *demand*, huh?" Maximilian swiped up his sword. He discarded the scabbard and held the weapon at his side, the point directed at the floor. His back was taut with muscle and his shoulders tense. "I am not used to demands being made of me by bishops and certainly not when I have barely roused from my bed."

Mary snatched the covers up to her throat. What was going on?

Maximilian flicked the key in the lock and pulled open the door.

Aymer galloped across the room, flying onto the bed to land next to Mary. Quickly, she gathered him close.

Behind Aymer, the bishop rushed in. Hugo and two other councilors hovered on the threshold with their arms folded.

"Show us the sheets," the bishop said, pointing at the bed. "Show us the virginal blood as proof this marriage has been consummated." He tipped his chin, as if daring to be disobeyed.

"You wish to see blood?" Maximilian asked. His eyes narrowed as he stared at the small man who was almost hopping on the spot before him. "You wish to see *my wife's* blood."

"Yes. I do. And the councilors are insisting upon it also." The bishop gestured to the doorway. "Are you not?"

"It is true," Hugo said, stepping in. "And it is quite the proper thing to do." His jowls wobbled. Today, his cheeks were extra red. He didn't look at Mary.

"The proper thing to do," Maximilian repeated through gritted teeth.

Mary didn't know her husband well, but she knew enough to know he wasn't impressed with the demand. In fact, he looked furious.

"Yes," the bishop said, "show us the evidence."

"You think…" Maximilian raised his sword, his biceps bunching. "That you can burst into my wife's bedchamber and demand to see our bedsheets?" He directed the tip of the glinting sword at the bishop.

"It is God's will that I do my duty." He eyed the sword warily.

"Your duty…" Maximilian took a step forward, the sword now no more than an inch from the bishop's throat. "Was to marry us. The rest we can do ourselves."

"I must see proof that your bodies have joined." He tilted his chin and his eyes flashed.

"I will tell you now that our bodies have joined and you will believe me without proof, Bishop. Some things are private between a man and his wife."

"But, no, that will never do. I—"

"My cock works very well," Maximilian suddenly shouted as he cupped his groin. "And my wife's cunny is wet and willing. My word is all the proof you need."

Hugo's eyes widened. "Really, that is quite...and I..."

"I must insist upon—" The bishop's words were cut off as Maximilian jabbed the sharp end of the sword into his upper chest, denting his flesh.

"You will insist upon nothing from me, your duke, or my wife, the duchess." Maximilian's voice was low and dangerous as if he were speaking over sharp sand. "And what is more, you will never enter this room again. I am the only man permitted in my wife's bedchamber. Any other man stepping through the door uninvited will have a choice of two things..."

The bishop's mouth pressed into a tight line. His brow was shining with sweat.

"What two things?" Hugo asked with a shake in his voice.

"He can either choose to be gutted from here to here." Maximilian gently drew the sword from the bishop's chest to the base of his round belly, almost, but not quite, touching him. "Or..." He swung the sword in Hugo's direction. "He can choose to have his throat slit." He slashed from left to right heart-stoppingly close to Hugo's neck. "It may take a few attempts if I am sleepy like now, so expect pain and misery."

Hugo whimpered and stepped back. He bumped into the other councilor, who quickly tugged him from the room.

Maximilian turned the sword back on the bishop. "We can put this uninvited entry into the duchess's bedchamber as a lesson learned or you can choose gutting or beheading right now. I will leave the choice entirely up to you, Bishop." He raised his eyebrows. "Which is it to be?"

Bishop Arquette clasped the rosary around his neck and looked at Mary. "Your Grace, I beg you to see sense and appease the council and—"

"You should obey the duke," Mary said, stroking Aymer's head. "For it is clear my husband is a fine warrior and a man of steely determination. It would be wise not to anger him, don't you agree?" A flush of pride went through her as she described her new husband's skills.

The bishop swallowed, sent his eyes heavenward as though consulting directly with God, then took a step backward. His face was pinched, his lips tight like a rosebud, and his eyes glowered with anger and frustration.

"Goodbye." Maximilian flicked his hand in a dismissive wave. "And do have a glorious day."

The moment the bishop had stepped out of the doorway, Maximilian kicked the door shut with a loud bang.

He turned, still holding his sword, and laughed. "What a bunch of bumbling fools. Do they really think they can order *me* around?"

CHAPTER SEVEN

"SO WHAT WILL we do today?" Mary asked as they feasted on a breakfast of porridge, bread, apples, and honeyed figs in the solar—the private room adjoining her bedchamber. "I have some scrolls here in Ghent you could look at, some monetary details too. Unless there is something else you need? Much of my father's reporting is at Coudenberg and we should travel there soon."

"Mmm..." Maximilian was studying a red-and-gold tapestry on the wall. It was a picture of a unicorn, a lion, and a pomegranate tree. A peaceful scene and of the finest quality. He liked it a lot.

"Maximilian?"

He turned and poured juice from an ornate, black jug into a pottery mug. "I should like to meet your falcon, Jupiter."

"You would?" She smiled, though a flash of surprise went over her pretty eyes. "I can have him brought to this room."

"I thought you'd want to show off his hunting skills. Why don't we ride out?"

"Have you not spent enough time in the saddle of late?"

"That is true, but you weren't with me. And the day is bright, perfect for riding." It was important they had a bond if she was to trust him and they were going to be a united couple. What was more, he wanted to spend time with her, his wife, not poring over parchments. It was their honeymoon, after all.

She cleared her throat. "I will have the horses saddled and get

Philip to prepare Jupiter and a bird for you. I must be sure they have not been fed or they will not hunt."

"Philip?" A slight crease marred the gap between his eyebrows. This man kept getting mentioned. "He must be involved?"

"My cousin has always helped me with my falcons." She shrugged. "He is very skilled with them."

Maximilian said nothing as he cut a chunk off his bread and smothered it in butter.

"I will see to it now." She lifted a small, brass bell and rang it.

Jeanne appeared at the doorway. "Yes, Your Grace."

"We are going hunting. Can you see that the horses and falcons are prepared? A fresh steed for my husband; his horse deserves a rest."

"Of course." Jeanne smiled. "Very good."

Maximilian imagined his bride's lady friend would be desperate to ask Mary questions about the wedding night. But Mary would have to lie. They couldn't risk having a sham marriage. Maximilian was in no rush to consummate. Much as he desired Mary, and his cock had grown hard when he'd kissed her, he wanted her to want him in return. Where was the satisfaction if she didn't?

⇶⇷

OUT ON THE grasslands, the summer sun beat down. The horses sweated and flicked their tails at flies. But Maximilian barely noticed the heat or the view.

Mary was obviously an accomplished horsewoman and on a gray mare with a hoodwinked falcon perched on her left hand, she looked even more regal, even more beautiful. A tapestry should be made of her image this way. He would gaze at it endlessly.

The warm day had given dots of color to her pale cheeks, and a few strands of her hair had escaped her short hat and now caught on the breeze. She sat with her back straight and a deep-purple cape draped from her shoulders over her horse's rump.

Her keen eyes surveyed the surroundings. "Over there. I saw something." She gestured to a patch of long grass. "Do you want to send your bird, Maximilian? I think it was a hare."

"No, send Jupiter so I can see him in action."

Maximilian's horse pawed at the ground. He was a big, black stallion with a thick mane and feathered fetlocks. He had spirit too, not liking to stand still. Maximilian wondered who had chosen a restless horse for him.

"Are you sure?" she asked.

"Yes. Go."

Quickly, she undid the hood and sent her bird into the air.

But Maximilian didn't watch Jupiter. Once again, he watched his new bride. It was clear she adored her falcon. The way her eyes softened when she looked at him, spoke of him, it made Maximilian long for her to look at him that way. And now, as Jupiter soared with wings spread, she appeared captivated. In love, almost.

"Philip," she called. "He has something. Go get it."

Maximilian hadn't even seen the bird stoop and dive for the kill. But now he turned to Philip, who kicked his horse into a gallop and raced down the slope.

"The lands around here are plentiful," she said, beaming at Maximilian. "I am sure you will also catch something, then we can feast on our bounty this eve."

His horse pulled, wanting to follow the other horse. Maximilian turned it in a circle, using just one hand on the reins because of the bird perched on his other. "Yes, I would like that very much. This is proving to be a fruitful first day of marriage."

Any irritation at the fractious horse left him when she kept her smile and her focus on him. It was as though she were seeing deeper into him, further into his soul, and enjoying what she saw. His idea to do something she loved was paying off.

"This day is pleasing you?" she asked.

"Naturally, I have finally wed Mary of Burgundy, and I am outdoors on a fine horse in a land of plenty. I am very content."

"Good." She paused and bit on her bottom lip, studying him. "I wish you to be happy, even though my lands have problems to be addressed."

"You wish me to be happy?" He raised his eyebrows.

"Of course. A happy ruler will be without spite toward the people and will make good decisions."

"I do not believe myself to be a spiteful man." He chuckled. "I prefer to laugh."

She didn't answer, and after a moment, turned to watch Philip, who was returning with a large hare attached to his saddle. She looked up, spotted Jupiter soaring, and whistled.

The bird returned to her, landing with grace, and took the morsel of meat she offered it.

"We should head to the bluff," Mary said. "I would like you to see the view from there—it is exceptional, and there is always good hunting."

"Lead the way."

The coppery, evening sun had dipped low in the sky by the time they'd returned from the grasslands and the air was finally cooling.

Mary had slipped from her horse and told Maximilian she would see him at dinner.

Philip, with his hands full of catch, nodded curtly at Maximilian. He then turned toward the castle kitchens, disappearing into the shadows of the ramparts.

"Finally tired this one out," Maximilian said, patting his horse's neck as a stableboy took the reins. "He's a feisty one."

"He is, Your Grace, but he is fast. A favorite of the duchess's cousin."

"Philip?"

"Yes." The horse was led away.

Maximilian wandered over the courtyard wondering why Philip had given him his favorite horse for the day and not ridden it himself. Was it as a test of Maximilian's riding ability or a gesture of welcome? It was impossible to know.

But Maximilian couldn't get rid of the itch in his spine the man gave him. It was an unpleasant feeling stemming from the fact that Philip knew his wife much better than he. Had known her longer, had grown up with her—had no doubt considered himself a suitor.

Did he still?

Maximilian's boots thudded on the cobbles as he made his way to the rooms he'd been given use of. But just before he stepped through an archway, he stopped. On the ground lay a falcon's perfect tail feather. It was silver with gray-brown stripes that led upward from the delicate point.

He picked it up and ran his fingers over the silken, flattened side then brushed over the elegant tip.

Lars appeared beside him. "How was the hunt?"

"You should have joined us." He kept hold of the feather but dropped his arm to his side.

"I happily would have, had it not been for the pain in my head this morn."

"Too much local wine, my friend."

"Possibly." Lars strolled with him. "Did it go well? The hunt?"

Maximilian forced thoughts of Philip aside. "Yes, it did. Mary is a fine horsewoman and an excellent falconer, as good as a man—better than many, perhaps."

"It is a fact Jeanne told me."

"You have spent time with Jeanne?"

"Yes, she showed me where to unpack your things. A hot bath has been drawn."

The thought of bathing was very appealing.

"I heard you had a mishap with the bishop and a few of the councilors this morning." Lars raised his eyebrows.

"A *'mishap.'*" Maximilian huffed. "If you are referring to me promising to gut them and slit their throats should they step into my wife's bedchamber again, then yes, we had a mishap."

Lars threw him a grin. "What a way to make friends."

"I do not wish them to be my friends. I wish my wife to be treated with respect."

"And can I ask how your wedding night was?"

"No." Maximilian shoved Lars's shoulder. "You may not."

Lars staggered to the side, chuckling. "Fair enough. But you can't blame me for being curious."

"I would not ask you about your sexual conquests."

"But I am unmarried; they are of much less import."

"Exactly, a marriage is important and so is the trust and discretion that goes with it." He stopped outside the door to his rooms. "But I will tell you I find her very beautiful, very witty, and she has an intelligent head on her shoulders. My fears were unfounded."

"It is true she has neither warts nor smelly feet. Or at least not that I have noticed."

Maximilian laughed. "Yes, that is true, thank God." He pointed the feather at Lars. "I will see you in the Great Hall. We are eating the hunt."

He looked at the feather. "What is that for?"

Maximilian grinned. "Wouldn't you like to know?"

THE MEAL WAS plentiful and the game meat perfectly prepared.

Maximilian sat at the bench with Mary, Jeanne, Margaret, and Lars. Compared to the wedding feast, it was a small group and he felt relaxed after bathing in his bedchamber.

Not that he had any intention of sleeping in there. His place at night was beside his wife.

As soon as the meal was over, he took her hand and leaned close. "I wish us to retire. It has been a long day with much exertion and there are still things we must give our attention to."

She looked at him, her eyes full of questions. "You do? There are?"

"Yes. Unless you are still hungry and wish to stay here a while longer."

"No, I have eaten plenty."

"Yes, I am pleased to see that." He touched her soft cheek with the back of his index finger. "But now I want you to myself. I do not wish to share you with people, horses, or falcons for another moment on this, our first full day of marriage."

She swallowed and nodded, then quickly looked away.

He hated that he still saw apprehension in her expression. But at least it wasn't the red-hot fear that had seared there yesterday.

"Good ladies and gentlemen," he said, standing. "My wife and I bid you a goodnight." He set his hand on her slim shoulder and squeezed.

She stood and glanced around the table with her chin tilted. "Goodnight, all."

Aymer jumped up and circled her legs.

Mary rubbed him between his ears, then stopped. She frowned slightly. "Stay," she said, pointing at him. "You stay with Jeanne."

Aymer hung his head, his eyes sad.

Maximilian was pleased she'd taken account of his words. The marital bed was no place for her dog.

After a round of biddings for a good night, Maximilian led her from the room with his hand placed on the small of her back. She was a whole head shorter than him and he'd reckon barely half his weight. But that just made her more appealing and the instinct to protect her and please her burned hotly inside of him.

She didn't speak as they made their way to her bedchamber.

He wondered what was going through her mind but didn't break the silence.

At a guess, he'd say she was expecting him to consummate the marriage, take her, claim her, plant his seed. But he had other plans— plans he hoped would switch the apprehensiveness in her eyes to raw desire.

CHAPTER EIGHT

MARY STEPPED INTO her bedchamber. Her stomach felt like it was swarming with butterflies and her heart was thumping. She missed Aymer's close and comforting presence but had decided not to go against her husband's wishes, for tonight at least.

Candlelight flickered around the room, stretching up the stone walls and casting shadows on the floor. The fire was lit, though not roaring, and the scent of lavender hung in the air. Her bedchamber didn't feel like a safe haven anymore—it felt like the unknown was lurking in every corner.

Once again Maximilian locked the door with a decisive turn of the key.

She clasped her hands and fought down a tremble of nerves. She was sure any moment now, he would throw her to the bed, strip her naked, and ravish her like a wild beast. She'd be helpless against him. Totally at his mercy.

"I am supposing, as you bathed before dinner, you do not need Jeanne to help you prepare for bed?"

"No." She removed her padded roll headdress, slipped off her shoes, and stood on the rug beside the bed curling her toes into the stiff fibers. "I do not."

He nodded and shrugged out of his jacket. He then peeled off his tunic, revealing his naked chest. After setting a sheathed dagger on the table, he stooped and discarded his boots.

Mary watched him closely, studying the way his muscles and tendons bunched and flexed beneath the surface of his skin. It fascinated her. Everything about him seemed not just big but tight and strong and his movements were careful and definite.

He didn't remove his pants. Instead, he stepped up close, his body heat radiating onto her. "My love," he whispered. "Can I kiss you again?"

She stared into his face and nodded, surprised that he was even asking.

Gently, he pinched her chin and lowered his face to hers. Their lips connected and she fluttered her eyes closed, remembering how she'd enjoyed the sensation of him kissing her the evening before. This time, she was a little braver and sought his tongue, finding it as he deepened the kiss.

He moaned softly.

The low sound made her heart skip and her belly tightened. A strange new need seemed to grip her core and heat settled in her breasts and between her thighs.

He pulled back, very slightly. "Do you like me kissing you?"

She set her hand on the ball of his shoulder. "Am I doing it right?"

He smiled. "I don't think there is a wrong way."

"Oh. That is good, then."

"So you like it?"

"Yes."

Once again, his lips came down on hers and their tongues danced and stroked. The dark, wine-laced taste of him heated her further and her nipples tightened against her undergarments.

His breaths became quicker, heavier and he cupped her face, drawing her closer still. Then suddenly, he released her, stepped back, and closed his eyes. His chest expanded as he inhaled deeply and his fists clenched.

"Maximilian?"

He opened his eyes and smiled, the tension seeming to fall away from him. "Stay exactly where you are."

He walked to his jacket and pulled out a falcon's tail feather and what appeared to be a ribbon made of black silk. He laid the feather on the bedside table next to an ornate bowl she kept for jewelry.

"Now," he said. "Close your eyes."

"But why? Shouldn't we—?"

"Do you trust me?" He stood before her with the length of silk stretched between his fingers. "Have I done anything to make you doubt my affection and commitment to you?"

"No...I don't think so."

"So trust me. I will not hurt you, but I will show you how it should be between a man and a woman. Prove that it's not what you think it is."

"How do you know what I think?"

"I can see it in your eyes." He pressed the cool silk over her face, blocking her vision. "And I want to change what I see. The best way to do that is for you to only feel, nothing else."

"I don't know, I..."

"Shh." He stepped behind her and tied the ribbon just beneath the crown of her head. "Let the darkness take you and instead only feel and remember I prize you, I adore you, I will make you feel only good things."

His words filled her with apprehension but also curiosity, an emotion she'd suddenly discovered could rival fear.

"Imagine the rest of Burgundy does not exist," he murmured beside her ear. "There is only you and me. Nothing else matters."

She didn't answer, but she did try to do as he'd said. It was quite easy because at this moment, he'd become her world.

"I will show you pleasure," he went on, working free the back buttons on her gown. "I will show you what your body was made for."

Her breaths were coming fast, her breasts hitching against her gown. And then her gown was slackening around her ribs. This was a looser gown than she'd worn the night before and it soon sat around her hips. With a little tug from Maximilian, it was down to her ankles and off.

She shivered, despite the room being warm and still wearing her silk undergarment.

"You will soon be hot," he said, his lips touching the curve between her neck and shoulder. "Do not fear." He spread the kisses further, to her shoulder, then brushed her hair to one side and kissed up her neck.

Each trace of his mouth had her heart rate quickening.

"You taste of petals and spice," he whispered. "And I am going to kiss you all over."

Oh, dear Lord. He couldn't mean that, could he?

After a rustle of blankets, he slid his hand around her waist and urged her to the bed. "Lie down. Make yourself comfortable."

She couldn't see anything, not even a crack of light, so she gingerly climbed onto the soft bed and lay down on her back, arms at her sides, legs tight together, head resting on the pillow.

The mattress dipped at her side and his body aligned with hers.

"Tell me," he said, tracing the shape of her nose, her lips, and her chin. "Have you ever touched yourself?"

"What kind of question is that?" Why did her voice sound so breathy?

"I told you to trust me, and this is important."

For a moment she was quiet. "Once... when bathing."

"And did it feel good?"

"I was told it wasn't supposed to, that is was a sin."

"Ah, I see." His finger traveled down her neck to her right shoulder. He pushed at the thin strap until it hung down her arm. He repeated the action on the left side.

She let out a trembling sigh.

"From now on," he said, "pleasure is not a sin. It is something you deserve in mountain loads."

"I don't understand."

"You will." He tugged the undergarment downward, past her waist, exposing her breasts fully.

She gasped and pulled in a deep breath, jutting her chest upward. Her nipples tingled and her skin goosebumped. She had to fight the instinct to cover herself.

"You're so beautiful," he murmured.

"I… Please, we should just…"

"Do not concern yourself with anything we should do. I am in control." He kissed her mouth.

She found the taste of him, the kiss, reassuring and relaxed a little.

"Now tell me," he said onto her lips. "Can you feel this?"

The lightest touch tickled into the hollow of her navel.

"Yes." Her eyelashes flickered against the ribbon.

"Shh, it is only a feather. That is all I am touching you with."

"A feather?"

"It is fitting, is it not, considering your love of falcons?" The touch moved higher, to her sternum, leaving a trail of sensation.

"I suppose." She swallowed and pressed her legs together.

"And a feather could not be more gentle, am I right?" He stroked it over her right nipple, once, twice, three times, then circled it.

"Oh!" She reached for him and found his solid upper arm. "Maximilian, what are you doing?"

"Showing you how wonderfully responsive your body is, my love."

Her nipple felt like it had hardened to a pebble. That was quite the response to a feather.

He switched to the left nipple, his breaths warm on her shoulder.

She bit on her bottom lip as a delicious weight seemed to grow in her breasts.

"It will only feel better," he said, caressing the outer edge of her breast with the feather tip. "The more you feel, the better it will be."

"I will take your word for it."

"I can do better than that. I can prove it."

Suddenly, her left nipple was immersed in wet warmth. He'd taken it into his mouth.

She sucked in a breath and speared her fingers into his hair. Oh, it did feel good. She'd never imagined it, never could have predicted it. But his tongue, his lips, the gentle suction had her arching her spine for more.

For several minutes, he worked her. She forgot about the blindfold, about her undergarment being shoved to her hips. All she concentrated on was what he was doing to her. The way he was making her feel.

Then he switched to the other breast and treated it to the same attention.

She ran her palms over his shoulders and back, learning the shape of him and exploring the expanse of smooth flesh. He was like a great, marble statue she'd once seen in a cathedral.

Soon his kisses went lower. He shuffled down the bed, tracing her flat belly, and to the curve of her waist.

Her undergarment was once again tugged, over her hips and down her legs. Fully removed. She was utterly naked.

"Oh, God help me," she murmured.

"You do not need His help," Maximilian said softly. "I will care for you."

"I thank you." A tremble ran through her voice.

"You do not need to thank me for treating my wife with gentle respect." He paused. "Can you feel the feather again?"

"Yes."

He was running the tip up her left leg, knee to hip. The stroke of it going from hip point to hip point had her quivering. He drew it down to her right knee.

"Close your eyes again. Forget the rest of the world and everything in it."

How he'd known her eyes were wide behind the ribbon, she didn't know. But she did as he'd asked and closed them once more.

"And now like this." He pushed her right leg, bending her knee, revealing the lips between her legs.

She pressed her head into the pillow—embarrassment a hot fist gripping her and making sweat pop on her brow.

"Just feel," he murmured.

The feather was there, shimmying up her inner thigh. When had that part of her body become so sensitive?

When he reached her cunny, she held her breath. He stroked over it so lightly, it could have been a butterfly wing touching her. But still, she tensed her internal muscles and her abdomen hollowed.

He continued the feather's journey, sliding down her right inner thigh. "Don't fight it. Just let your body react, Mary."

"I'm trying."

"You're doing so well." He caressed her again with the feather, stroking over her sensitive flesh—flesh she was sure was a little damp now. "Remember when I said I was going to kiss you all over?"

"Yes."

"You should know that is about to happen. Please, do not be shocked."

"Shocked? Why would I...? Oh..." Her mouth opened and stayed open.

Maximilian had slid between her legs and was kissing her there. On her cunny lips. Kissing her like he had her nipples. His tongue stroking and caressing and exploring.

"Oh, dear Lord, forgive me." She gripped his hair and pointed her toes. Surely, this wasn't a normal thing for a married couple to do. It must have been a dreadful sin, one she hadn't even thought of or heard of.

He moaned softly, as though finding his own pleasure from kissing her cunny.

She clamped her legs to his hard body. He was so big and rock-hard.

He flicked his tongue over her sensitive bud and her cunny clamped in response—but it was strange, as though she was empty and needed something to fasten on to.

Over and over, he worked her bud, circling it, sucking on it. Soon, the sensation was all she could think of and she was glad of the blackness—she didn't want distractions from the strange, new pressure growing in her pelvis.

A musky scent tickled her nose and the gentle sucking noises of his kisses filled her ears. And then she felt more than his tongue—his fingers were stroking her too, sliding up through her lower lips and finding her entrance.

"Oh, please, I don't know if... Maximilian... Oh..." She writhed on the bed, but he stayed with her.

Her gasped words and bowing spine seemed to spur him on. He increased the pressure on her bud, lapping at it with determination, the point of his tongue stiff.

She drew up her knees, arching for more.

He gave it, slipping one long finger into her entrance.

She cried out, not in pain, but in absolute relief at feeling him there. It was wild and erotic and the pressure in her bud couldn't be contained. He was flicking at it in a way that made her feel ready to burst, but it was good. It was a release she needed.

"Maximi... Oh... What is happening...I...?"

She remembered his words. *Trust me.* It was what she had to do.

She held her breath as the pressure reached a point she couldn't contain. Bright lights flashed through her darkness and she curled forward, yanking at his hair. And then it released, the sweet and sour, hot and cold feeling she'd never experienced before. It traveled from her cunny over her flesh, reaching every corner of her body.

She cried out again, bliss mixing with wonder as she spasmed around his finger and her pulse raged in her ears.

Whatever had just happened to her was nothing short of a miracle, and it was her husband who had made it happen. She ripped off the blindfold and stared down at him, just to be sure it really was Maximilian creating such honeyed magic between her thighs.

"Maximilian," Mary gasped. "Oh...please...please." She could hardly catch her breath and still, he toyed with her cunny. "I... What was...?"

He lifted his face from between her legs and grinned up at her. His chin was shiny and his pupils wide. "Did that feel good?"

"What did you do to me? I mean..." She paused to catch her breath. "I have never... You just..."

His grin stretched wider and a flash of male pride crossed his eyes.

"Please tell me if you know," she begged.

He slipped his finger from her cunny and moved up and over her so his chest was hovering against hers. "I do know."

He kissed her and she tasted herself, slightly salty and warm. The flavor was shocking but erotic.

"Please tell me. Am I abnormal?"

"No." He chuckled softly. "You are perfectly normal, perfectly perfect."

She stared into his eyes.

"That was the pleasure I was talking about," he said. "The pleasure I want you to feel every time we join as man and wife."

"*Every* time?"

"Yes, and I see it as my duty to ensure that happens."

"You mean...I can do that more than once?"

"Oh, yes, you really can." He swiped his lips over hers then dropped to his back at her side. "Likely more swiftly and frequently than I can."

"I just didn't...know." She stared at the canopy above the bed. She'd thought herself to be intelligent and worldly wise, yet she hadn't known her body could explode in pleasure.

What else did Maximilian know that she didn't?

CHAPTER NINE

WHEN MARY STIRRED, the sound of rain hitting the castle was the second thing she noticed. The first had been Maximilian's warm body against hers and his arm keeping her locked in place.

He was breathing slowly, still asleep, and the cover had slipped to below his chest.

She rested her hand over where his heart was and let her fingertips settle over the small smattering of hairs at his sternum. The light was dim, but still, the diamond set in her ring sparkled.

He was hers to touch, just as she was his.

He was *her* husband—a husband who was skilled not just on a horse and on the battlefield, but one who indeed had talents in the bedroom. It wasn't something she could have possibly known about Maximilian before she'd chosen to marry him, so now she felt lucky—lucky to have made the right choice. To have a man by her side and in her bed who, so far, hadn't shown himself to be a monster.

She hoped that continued.

He stirred and she looked up at his still-sleeping face, enjoying seeing him unguarded while he dreamed. Usually, he was smiling, but now his mouth was slack, his lips slightly parted. He had a sprinkling of stubble on his chin and over his top lip, and his dark eyelashes were longer than she'd noticed before. His hair, which was long to his nape then cut across his forehead, was messy, sticking up at all angles, likely from where she'd dragged at it, pulled it, weaved her fingers through it the night before when he'd put his face between her legs.

A tremble went through her at the memory. The bursting feeling he'd produced, like wine and spice fizzing inside her, had been incredible. And what was more, it seemed he was intent on creating that inside her frequently.

And when he'd entered her, with his finger, far from being an ordeal, she'd needed it—craved it, almost.

She set her lips softly on his warm flesh, just above her hand, and kissed him tenderly. Then she sat as gently as she could so as not to disturb him.

But the moment she stood from the bed, he spoke. "Mmm, where are you going?"

"To call for breakfast," she said. "I am hungry."

He chuckled softly and opened his eyes. "Bedchamber activities create an appetite, it is true."

She felt her cheeks flush as she pulled on a robe and lifted the brass bell.

"It's raining," he said. "No hunting today."

"No, not today." She glanced at the corner of the room where Jupiter usually rested on his perch. It was strange not seeing him there.

She rang the bell.

Woof. Woof.

"Oh, Aymer," she said, unlocking, then opening the door. "How long have you been sitting outside?"

He bounded in, long legs lolloping, then leaped onto the bed, the sheets rucking beneath him.

"In God's name!" Maximilian sat bolt upright as Aymer landed on him, tongue hanging out and long, whip-like tail wagging furiously.

Mary laughed. "He'll settle in a minute. He's just not used to being away from me."

"Well, he'll have to get used to it. I am your bed companion now."

Why couldn't she have both? She pouted, but her husband didn't notice.

"Your Grace, you called?" Jeanne appeared.

"I bid you good morning, Jeanne," Mary said. "Do you think you could organize breakfast for my husband and me? We will take it in the solar again."

"Of course." She looked over Mary's shoulder at Maximilian sitting in bed.

Her eyes widened slightly, no doubt surprised to see his naked upper torso and wildly messy hair.

"Jeanne?" Mary studied her friend's curious, almost-admiring, face.

"I, er, yes, of course. I will get it now for you, Your Grace." She bobbed her head and disappeared.

"I suppose he does have a cute face," Maximilian said, stroking Aymer's head, then tickling him behind his ears.

A little piece of Mary's heart melted at the sight. She loved Aymer; he was her faithful, constant companion. And to see Maximilian being so tender with him, despite him being so big, touched a very deep part of her soul.

She closed the door and walked to the bed, sitting on the edge. "I could have the chests opened for you to go through the scrolls," she said. "I am sure you will want to familiarize yourself with the finer details of the duchy."

"No, not today."

She raised her eyebrows. "I could have them brought to the solar; it is warmer in there."

"Yes, the solar is a pleasant room on an inclement day."

Aymer flopped over Maximilian's feet and let out a sigh.

"And we should stay in there today, nice and warm and dry," Maximilian said. "But I was thinking we should read together."

"Read?"

"Yes, I would like to know more about what you read." He nodded at a small, clasped book wrapped with golden cloth set on a table beside a vase of white roses.

"It is true I enjoy to read more than just my Book of Prayers."

"Homer?" He took her hand in his and turned it palm up.

"You know I do."

"Who else?" He traced his finger over the lines of her palm.

The tickling caress had a shiver of warm sensation traveling up her arm and over her scalp. She hitched in a breath.

"Poetry," she managed, all authors leaving her mind.

"We will sit by the fire, drink wine, and you can read poetry to me. And if you would like, I will read to you also."

"What do you like to read?"

"I'm interested in the big questions, the thoughts of the scholars in Florence and Milan. Though I read many things." He nodded. "Yes, we will read together today."

"If that is what you wish."

"I wish for it more than poring over numbers and deeds and treaties." He chuckled.

The mention of treaties had her stomach tightening. Luckily, there was a knock at the door then Jeanne and a courtier came in holding two trays laden with food and drink.

"Your Grace," Jeanne said. "We will stoke the fire in the solar."

"Thank you." She'd been saved from the treaty conversation for a while at least.

After breakfast, Maximilian took himself off to his bedchamber to prepare for the day, and, he said, to consult with Lars on a few matters.

Mary took her time over her morning ablutions. Her mind kept drifting back to the evening before. The delicious feel of the feather on her skin. Maximilian's mouth on her…down there, a place she'd never thought she'd be kissed. She quivered, inside and out, as she remembered the sweeping, crazy, wondrous feelings that had burst through her holding her hostage to pleasure.

She'd glanced at the clock, thinking about the hours before darkness. What would her third night of marriage bring?

As Jeanne was brushing her hair, there was a knock at the door.

Aymer jumped up and stared at it.

"Who is it?" Mary called.

"It is I, Margaret."

"Come in, please."

Her stepmother rushed in holding her gown to stop from tripping over it. A worried line sliced over her brow.

Aymer trotted over to greet her, tail wagging.

"Whatever is the matter?" Mary asked.

"Philip has asked me to tell you that Jupiter is all out of sorts today. He's not eaten and Philip is worried that he is missing you, missing being in your bedchamber. It is all he has ever known."

"Oh, dear." Mary's heartstrings pulled. She couldn't bear it if anything happened to Jupiter. What if he dropped down dead of heartbreak? She'd never forgive herself. "He should come back in here. Immediately."

"Are you sure?" Margaret set her hands on Mary's shoulders. "What will Maximilian think?"

"It will not concern him." Mary waved one arm in the air. "He does not spend much time in here. Only long enough to..." She cleared her throat. "He has his own bedchamber."

"I think you'll find he does spend a lot of time in here," Jeanne said, appearing. "He has been here each time I have knocked since you wed."

Mary nodded. "It is true. But Jupiter was here first. My husband will have to get used to him."

"But with Aymer as well," Margaret said. "It is quite the animal park in here and—"

"If he wants to be with me, he'll have to accept my animals." Mary folded her arms.

"Who will have to accept your animals?" Maximilian strode into the room, his deep voice seeming to rumble over the stone walls.

Mary turned and her heart stuttered in a way it never had before. It wasn't an unpleasant sensation—in fact, it filled her with a mix of anticipation and excitement. He was so big and handsome. Freshly shaven, his skin glowed with health, his eyes flashed with curiosity and intelligence, and his hair was now once again neat, no lasting evidence of her grasping fingers.

"Jupiter is pining," Margaret said. "The duchess has asked for him to be brought in here to her."

He turned to Mary. "You want the bird in here?"

"Yes, it is where he's always slept. He will be no bother in the corner, on his perch. And if something happened to him be-cause...because...it would break my heart and—"

Maximilian held up his hand. "In that case, and if it is what the Grand Dame wants. That is what she will have."

"'Grand Dame.'" Mary touched her face. "What a name! How you age me."

"You are wise beyond your years, my love."

Margaret clasped her hands and rocked back on her heels as a satisfied smile tilted her lips. "It is good to see this union off to a good start." She paused and the smile slipped. "But there is work to be done. Duchess, you have a country to govern and France presses ever closer. Strategies must be considered. Your new husband, the duke, must put his mind to this matter."

"Do not fear. My man Lars is working on it." Maximilian opened the door to the solar that had a fire roaring in the grate and a table set with cake and jugs of mead. "And governing can wait a few days. My wife and I have poetry to read."

"Poetry?" Margaret repeated, her eyes wide, as though not believ-ing her ears. "'Poetry to read'?"

"Yes. Indeed." Maximilian made a sweeping gesture with his arm.

"Wife, this way if you please. I intend to have you all to myself for the rest of the day." He paused. "Dog and falcon notwithstanding, of course."

SEVERAL HOURS LATER, Mary was relaxed and warm by the fire. Aymer was at her feet, and Jupiter on his usual stand in the bedchamber, sleeping now that he'd finally eaten.

She'd read some scripture and mythology to Maximilian and in turn he'd read an amusingly written chronicle about mountain goats.

"Would you like me to read you a poem by Deschamps? I think you would like him." She switched books and settled back in the cushions of her soft chair.

"I have read some of his work in the past." Maximilian stretched his arms high and yawned, then slotted his hands behind his head, elbows sticking to the sides. He looked as content as a man could be sitting beside the fire, full of cake and mead and being read to.

"You have?" she asked.

"Do not look so shocked when I have similar tastes to you."

"It is not that."

"Then what is it?"

The truth was he continued to surprise her with his knowledge of things other than battles and tournaments. "I had not realized Deschamps's work had reached Vienna."

"Indeed it has. As have many works." He paused. "Why do you think I'd like this one especially?"

"You like food, husband of mine!" She giggled.

He grinned. "Pray, go ahead. I am listening."

Mary read. When she got to the last few lines, she leaned forward, watching his face… "'It's clear a spice like clove. Can drop its guard. It won't be busted. There's just one thing these people serve. Always never asking…mustard.'"

Maximilian clapped and roared with laughter. "Yes. Yes. Mustard, always mustard, he is right. Those people of Burge, Ostend, Antwerp, and Ghent. Mustard!"

Mary loved the sound of his laughter. It was deep and unrestrained and echoed around the high-ceilinged room.

She closed the book. "I wish I could give this poem to all the citizens of Burgundy so that they could read it and laugh."

"Your wish may just come true." He reached for an almond, threw it into the air, and caught it in his mouth, crunching noisily.

"What do you mean?"

"My father has talked to me of a new printing press that is being experimented with in Salzburg."

"Printing press?"

"Yes, I am intrigued by the idea. It would mean mass printing. Pamphlets, books, documents of law. Can you imagine how much information you could spread on pieces of paper crammed with knowledge?"

"You have forgotten one thing."

"What is that?"

"It is only useful if citizens can read."

"True." He held up his finger. "And I have thought of that. If images can also be included, it would be a powerful tool for rulers to pass on information and laws to the illiterate. Don't you agree?"

"Yes." She nodded, imagining being able to put something into every house in the land that held her words exactly. "It really would be something."

"I intend to make use of it, the moment it is available." He stood and walked to a tapestry and appeared to study a lion closely. "And if a person printed out books about their life, the stories of their life, I mean detail their loves and losses, even when he or she died, the book would be a memory to the world not just that they had existed, birth and death, but *how* they existed." He turned with his hand on his chest. "Their story, not a myth or a fable or a list of facts, but the intimate details of their emotions. Whom and how they loved."

She also stood, her gown skimming the base of her ankles. "I like your ideas."

"You do?"

"Yes."

He stepped up to her and cupped her face. "I never imagined I would be this happy on this day here with you. It is like we have always known each other...or at least were meant for each other."

"I feel the same."

He bent his head and kissed her. It was the same gentle kiss as before. A meeting of mouths and tongues in a gentle dance.

Feeling bold, she slipped her arms around his neck and pressed up close, wanting to be reminded of the solidity and strength of his body.

He moaned softly and spread the kisses from her mouth over her cheek to her neck.

"Maximilian," she whispered and she tipped her head back, loving the delicate tickling trail he left. "Oh..."

He found her mouth again.

Cupping his cheeks, she followed the way his jaw moved as he kissed her. There was more passion there now, as though an urgency was growing. His breaths were coming faster and he moaned and slid his arms around her waist, hauling her to him.

Their bodies connected, their chests, their groins, and even through her gown, she could feel the hard wedge of flesh straining at his breeches.

She gasped and pulled back, freeing herself from his arms. She was panting and a hot flush had risen on her cheeks.

He frowned, his chest rising and falling.

Her attention was stuck on the bulge behind the material of his breeches. It was so long and thick. Her heart galloped. His manhood was huge. It would tear her in two. This union would never work. How could it? She'd only just taken his finger. The whole thing was a disaster. It was clear they were not meant for each other at all.

He turned back to the tapestry and straightened his tunic, snapping it into place.

She stared at his broad shoulders, thoughts colliding, fear growing. "I think…I should… We should… Oh, dear Lord…"

He held up his hand. "We will go for a stroll around the castle gallery before dinner."

She said nothing and clasped her hands beneath her chin, sending a quick prayer to God to have mercy on her poor husband, who must surely be deformed to have such a big appendage.

"Just give me a minute," he said, his voice tense. "And then we will stretch our legs. We have been sitting long enough."

"Of course. Yes. Of course." She rushed from the solar with Aymer at her feet. Tears formed. They would never have children. She would never produce an heir for Burgundy or for Maximilian. Quickly, she snatched up a kerchief and dabbed at her eyes. She didn't want him to see her distress. It would only compound his feelings of failure.

"My love." Suddenly, he was behind her, his hands on her shoulders.

"Oh!" She turned, not wanting him to see her upset. "I…"

"Why are you crying?"

CHAPTER TEN

SEEING MARY CRY squeezed Maximilian's heart. He felt ashamed, too. He'd meant to kiss her gently, reverently, but his cock had had other ideas and lust had shot into his system. She did something to him no other woman ever had. Delicate but strong, innocent but responsive, intelligent and forward-thinking. It was an intoxicating mix and had he known it, he wouldn't have gone so long without a woman before arriving. He'd have made sure his stamina had been at full barrel when he'd arrived in Ghent.

"I'm sorry, I didn't know," she managed, her voice cracking.

"Know what?" He took the kerchief from her and dabbed her damp cheeks.

She sucked in a breath as though holding back a sob.

"I'm the one who should be sorry. I was too forward," he said. "I didn't mean to frighten you. Please, forgive me. I beg you."

"Frighten me?"

He shifted from one foot to the other. His cock was still semi-erect and it wasn't particularly comfortable being contained in breeches. "Yes, when you felt my manhood, I am sorry to frighten you."

"Oh, you didn't frighten me, you just shocked me. I mean, I had no idea…"

"No idea about what?" His head was spinning. What was going on? What was she talking about?

"That you are so…so… I am so sorry… Really, I am."

"Mary." He tipped her chin to stop her staring at his groin. "What are you sorry about?"

"That." She paused and pulled in a deep breath. "That you are so deformed. So terribly deformed. I am so sorry that this happened to you."

"*Deformed?*" His eyes widened as the word bounced around his head. "You think I am deformed?"

"Yes, I don't know much about married life, but I know that…" She flicked her eyes downward. "*That* has to go inside me and… You know as well as I that it will never fit. You have a deformity of…of…of it!"

"I do not!" He'd spoken sharper than he'd intended.

"You do." She pulled away from him. "I felt it. I saw it through your…"

Aymer circled her legs, then stared accusingly up at Maximilian. He was clearly cross with Maximilian for upsetting his mistress.

In the corner, Jupiter let out a series of shrill calls and roused his feathers.

"There is nothing wrong with me." Maximilian caught Mary's arm and turned her to him again.

She spun, gasped, and stared up at him, her body stiff and tense.

Aymer barked loudly. Jupiter flapped his wings, rattling the perch to which he was attached.

"I am not deformed, Mary. I am perfectly normal—actually, no, I am *better* than normal. I am Archduke Maximilian of Austria and I have a very fine specimen of a penis."

"A very fine specimen?" Her mouth hung open.

"Yes." He looked down at Aymer. "Be quiet, dog."

Aymer let out another three yaps, then ran behind Mary. Jupiter still squawked. He needed hoodwinking.

"So you're not…?"

"Deformed? No, I most certainly am not and I'd thank you not to use that word again when talking about my...about me."

"Oh...I..." She wriggled free of him and wrapped her arms around her waist, as though hugging herself. "But...?"

"But nothing." He grabbed her white fox fur and threw it over her shoulders, and quickly, he fastened the clasp. He then pulled on his cape. "Come, we will walk. The exercise will do us good."

And he had to get out of the solar before he well and truly showed her just how well his cock worked. Maybe taking it slow was backfiring on him.

Thankfully, she allowed him to lead her from their private rooms and down the hallway. She sniffed twice, then tucked her kerchief away.

After a few minutes, they stopped to look out of an opening in the wall. Ghent lay before them. Smoke streamed from chimneys and rain had shined the cobbles. A farrier worked below, evident by the chiming of his hammer on metal.

"Tell me," he said. "How did your first name come about?"

"My first name?" She looked up at him, clearly surprised by the question.

"We all have a story, Mary."

"Yes, but mine... Well, it would be a twisted tale in a book about my life."

"Now I am intrigued."

She smiled and his heart seemed to relax and his nerves realign. "I was born at Coudenberg Palace, which you probably know."

He didn't but nodded anyway.

"At the time, a guest of our house was Dauphin Louis of France."

"King Louis now?"

"Yes."

"Pray, go on." This was not the story Maximilian had been expecting.

"My father was not there—he was out at war, or planning it, I suppose." She paused. "But apparently, Louis was a bag of anxiety when my mother was in labor. Pacing outside the door, demanding every five minutes to know how mother and child were doing. So when I was born and swaddled, my grandmother took me out to him so he could see all was well."

"Your first engagement with royalty, only minutes old."

She laughed softly. "I've never thought of it that way."

"It's a truth."

"It is. And it was Louis who requested that I be called Mary after his mother."

"That is quite the tale." Maximilian paused. "But now, we find, not only did he want you to marry his son, or even himself, he wages war on Burgundy, your homeland. The child he was so fearful for he now considers an enemy or at the very least someone to defeat."

"A man I used to know. But not any longer." She shook her head sadly. "And we must face up to him at some point."

"I know. And we will. *I* will. Soon, the plan will be formed."

"So what about you? Where does the name Maximilian come from?"

They started walking again.

"My father, he had a dream about a saint, a pretty obscure one, called Maximilian of Tebessa."

"A dream, that is all. To get your name?"

"It left a significant mark on him, this dream, because the saint had warned my father of imminent peril. My father was involved in many dealings, and some could have gone very wrong for him, but he believed this dream taught him caution. In the end, nothing was particularly perilous and he thanked Saint Maximilian of Tebessa for her foresight by naming me after him."

"I like that story too."

"I am glad." He paused. "And I would imagine you had a lavish christening, Mary."

"Apparently, it was a splendid affair, though I don't remember." She laughed. "Louis was named my godfather. Can you believe that?"

"A wolf in sheep's clothing."

"Indeed."

The scent of beef and broth suddenly filled the air. Maximilian wanted to brush thoughts of Louis away. He was a problem for another day. "Let's eat."

"You are hungry again?"

"Always." He nodded at the ramparts. "And the sun has nearly set."

"Yes, we have spent much of the day reading."

"A very pleasant way to be entertained. I'm sure we'll do it again many times." He stopped and touched her shoulder.

She also stopped and turned to him.

"Are you quite well now, my love?"

"Yes." She smiled, though it was a little shaky. "I am."

"Are you certain?"

"Yes. Thank you for asking."

"Because all will be well. Trust me."

"I do. I've trusted you before and all was well." A rise of color bloomed on her cheeks. "More than well."

He tucked a strand of hair behind her ear. "You will always be able to trust me and rely upon me. Never doubt that."

AFTER A HEARTY meal of stew and bread, Maximilian excused himself and his wife once more. Margaret hadn't joined them for dinner. Lars and Jeanne were talking about bolstering the Burgundy army and how to pay for horses, armor, pikes, and swords. Melchior was eating quietly, as though deep in theological thought.

Preparations for war weren't something Maximilian wanted to

think about yet. It was enough that Lars was going through the scrolls and accounts for him. Soon, he knew, his days would be filled with plans of battle and victory.

Right now, he had other issues to address.

Namely, the fact that his wife thought not only was he deformed, but that they'd never fit together.

Her bedchamber—or *their* bedchamber, as he thought of it, for he didn't like the cold bed in his—had a large fire glowing in the ingle-nook, candles perched on sconces, and was pleasingly warm. A refuge from the cold evening.

Aymer jumped up at their arrival and Jupiter eyed Maximilian warily when Mary removed his hoodwink.

A tray held strawberry tarts and mulled wine. He helped himself and as he chewed the tart, he discarded his cape.

After fussing with Aymer and patting the bed for him to jump onto it, Mary removed her fur and yawned.

"You are tired?" Maximilian asked.

"A little. A rainy day does that to me sometimes." She sat on the edge of the bed. "Lack of sunshine, perhaps."

He pinched up a sugar-soaked strawberry and walked over to her. "Here, this will remind you of the sun's sweet warmth." He smiled. "Open up."

Her dainty mouth opened and he popped the strawberry onto her tongue.

"Mmm." She closed her eyes and chewed. "Cook is so good with preserving strawberries. I'm sure this is one of my favorite flavors of the year."

He tilted her chin up and lowered his face. "*You* are my new favorite flavor."

She smiled and as her lips curled, he set his mouth over hers.

There was no hesitancy in her kiss. She stroked her syrupy tongue with his and rested her small hands on his chest.

It was time for her to learn a few things.

He broke the kiss and straightened. Then he placed his hands over her palms to keep her touch tight on his chest. "I want you to understand," he said, "so you are not fearful of me, or what does have to happen."

She didn't say anything but swallowed, the gulp audible.

"Here," he said. "Feel here."

He slowly drew her right hand down his tunic, over his belt, to his groin. He set it over his cock and kept it there. "Feel me," he whispered.

"Maximilian...I..." Her eyes widened.

"Do not be scandalized. We are man and wife. Feel me. Feel my manhood."

A furrow appeared on her brow as she gingerly cupped her palm over the material, squeezing his cock gently.

"But...before..." she said. "It was so big. I mean...I wondered how you could even ride a horse with that...thing."

"That *thing*..." He suppressed a chuckle and lifted his hand from over hers. "Is not hard all the time."

"Oh. I see." She squeezed it a little firmer. "I suppose that makes life bearable for you, then." She traced the outline, up to his cock tip and back down the other side with her index finger.

"But if you keep doing that, it will grow hard." He locked his knees as blood did indeed rush to his groin. Her first sweet touch was so erotic.

"It will? Because you like it?"

"How could I not like your hands on me, my beautiful Mary?" His cock was hardening; he was halfway to full erection now.

She watched her own movements as she traced its outline with the point of her finger. "It's getting big again."

"Yes. Do you want to see it?"

She drew in a shaky breath.

Aymer sat up, as though sensing his mistress's un-sureness.

"My love, we do have to become physically acquainted." A coil of desire was winding up in his belly, anticipation gripping him. "At some point."

She nodded and looked up into his eyes. "So show me it."

He clenched his jaw, unbuttoned the flap on his breeches, then reached into his undergarment.

He pulled out his cock.

"Oh, dear heavens above," she said, snapping her hand to her mouth in shock. "What a color it is."

He frowned at his erection. "It is a perfectly normal color for a cock. Do not say I am deformed again."

"That is not what I meant." She leaned closer, studying it intently. "I just thought it would be the same as your face."

He could feel her warm breath. Lord, give him strength. His balls tightened. He was fully hard now. A flashing image seared over his brain—him pushing her to the bed, rucking up her gown, sinking deep, pounding hard, spilling his seed in glorious, wild thrusts.

But no, that couldn't happen. He wanted his wife's heart before he took her body.

Not that he didn't want her body. Or at least his cock, really, really did.

He reached upward with his left hand and gripped the horizontal beam that ran from the two bedposts. He'd use that as an anchor. While he was holding that, he would have control.

He took his cock in his other hand and smoothed up it from root to tip.

"Maximilian." She said his name on an outward breath and it was the sexiest sound he'd ever heard.

"Mary…" His heart rate had picked up. His pulse was loud in his ears. "Touch me, like this."

Hesitantly, she raised her right hand. He took it and wrapped her dainty fingers around his engorged cock. He placed his hand over the top to keep hers there.

Aymer barked. Jupiter let out a high-pitched call.

For a moment, the animals distracted him, pulled him from the moment, but then Mary copied his actions of moments ago, working him root to tip.

"Yes." He stared down at her enrapt expression. "Just like that."

"But it's still so big. It will never fit inside me."

"It will. When you are wet and wanting, we will fit perfectly."

"The way I was last night?"

"Yes, just like that." Finally, thank the Lord, she was beginning to understand. That knowledge gave him hope. Her words also reminded him of the night before and he closed his eyes picturing her laid on the bed, legs spread, his face between them. The memory of her taste, her tight, hot cunny gripping his finger, rushed back to him.

He groaned and clasped the beam harder until his fingers ached. He wanted to come—he couldn't go another night without releasing. The last two had been very uncomfortable.

"Am I hurting you?" she asked.

"No...no...it's good." He blew out a breath through pursed lips and tightened his grip over hers. "Don't stop."

She didn't. She kept rubbing his cock, firm sure strokes that fueled his desire further.

He reached up and grasped the beam with his other hand, his torso stretching. She was a natural and his balls were retracting in preparation for release. He'd never had so little stamina. Mary would be his undoing. She was like no other woman who had ever touched him.

"Oh, God, yes, yes..." The beam creaked as he dragged at it.

Aymer jumped off the bed barking and that set off Jupiter into a series of high-pitched caws.

"Please, keep...keep doing that..." He gasped, fearful the animals would distract his wife.

"I'm worried I am hurting you. You appear in pain."

"I'm not in pain." He forced his teeth to un-grit. "It's pleasure... Oh, in the name of..."

He released his seed. He didn't even try to hold back. It had reached the pinnacle and the relief was instant.

"Oh!" Mary gasped.

"Oh, God, yes." He clenched his buttocks and rocked his hips into her touch. "Thank you, oh... That's it... That's so..."

He gripped her hand again, keeping it around his cock. Another blast of release spurted from him, a rope of bliss that coated both of their palms.

"Maximilian." Her voice was high and excited. "I had no idea..."

With his left hand, he cupped her chin and stooped to kiss her—an unrestrained kiss that was full of desire and passion.

She was breathing fast, and so was he. Their tongues tangled. Satisfaction swamped him and as it did, he stopped her hand moving on his cock.

"My love," he said against her lips. "I have never felt anything as wonderful as your touch."

"Did I do it right? Was that supposed to happen?"

"Do you really need to ask? Surely, you heard and felt that you did it right and..." He lifted her hand up. It was sticky with cum, fluid shining in her palm and between her fingers. "And yes, this exactly what was supposed to happen. This is my seed. This is what will give us heirs."

Her eyes widened. "So what should we do with it now?"

"Nothing." He kissed her warm brow. "There will be more."

Aymer jumped onto the bed and nuzzled Mary's neck.

"Lie down," Maximilian said firmly to him.

Aymer ignored him.

"Lie," Mary said. "Lie down, Aymer."

He obeyed.

LOVED BY THE LAST KNIGHT

Jupiter flapped.

"There are too many animals in this room," Maximilian said.

"But it was their bedchamber first. Before you." Mary licked her lips and smiled. He swore she fluttered her eyelashes too.

And in that moment, he knew he'd never be able to deny his wife anything. She could have anything she wanted. Her happiness had become his world.

Oh, and beating back King Louis XI of France. That was also pretty important.

CHAPTER ELEVEN

"THE SUN IS shining again today, so we will ride," Maximilian announced the next morning.

"With the falcons?" Mary smiled. She'd enjoyed their previous day out hunting very much.

"No." Maximilian shook his head as they strode into the sunny courtyard, a glinting sword bouncing against his leg. "We will simply enjoy the views and each other. Ah, there's Lars."

"Good morning, Duke and Duchess." Lars nodded at Mary. "Can I be of assistance?"

Aymer sniffed around Lars's leather boots.

"Yes. You will ride with us today, and Jeanne also. And tell the kitchen to pack us a sack of bread and cheese, wine and fruit."

"A sack of food." Mary studied her husband's handsome face. "Whatever for?"

"You will see." He took her hand and kissed her knuckles. "Ah, Philip." He lifted his head and clicked his fingers. "Come here."

Philip walked over. He nodded formally at Mary and then addressed Maximilian. "How can I be of service, Your Grace?"

"My wife and I are going riding. Jeanne and Lars also."

"I will prepare myself too."

"No, for I will take your horse, and you will stay here."

"Oh, but…" He looked at Mary. "I have always ridden out with the duchess, to ensure her safety and—"

"She has no need of you now," Maximilian said. "I will ensure her safety."

Mary opened her mouth to speak—Philip was right, he did always ride out with her—but she closed it again. Maximilian had a frown line between his brows and there was a note of determination in his voice—one that gave her the impression his mind was made up.

"And, Philip, you will keep Aymer with you," Maximilian said. "All day. And see to Jupiter too."

"But Aymer likes to run with the horses and..." Mary said.

"Not today." Maximilian cupped her cheek and his voice softened. "Trust me, not today. He will be happy with Philip. Isn't that true, Philip?" He kept his eye contact with Mary.

"Yes. Of course, Your Grace," Philip said.

Mary studied her husband's eyes. There was a flash of something she didn't recognize in them when he spoke to Philip. Almost as if he didn't like him. Yet Philip had done nothing wrong. Indeed, as a gesture of welcome, he'd given Maximilian his horse, a fine steed, to ride out on.

"Good," Maximilian said, turning and rubbing his hands together. "We will leave before noon."

⇻⟫⟨⇺

A FEW HOURS later, the Ghent valley stretched out before them. Skylarks twittered above, and butterflies flitted around a patch of daisies.

Half an hour previously, they'd seen a herd of red deer. Maximilian had bemoaned not having his bow and arrow on hand.

"Over there, down by the river, that is where we will go." Maximilian pointed ahead.

"For what?"

"Alfresco dining. Have you never enjoyed a meal in God's great

107

outdoors?"

She laughed. "I am sure I have eaten outdoors before."

"Ah, but not like this." He kicked his horse on. "Lars, Jeanne, you stay here. Keep watch. We do not wish to be disturbed." He threw a smile at Mary. "Come, wife, let us indulge ourselves as newlyweds."

"We will wait here," Lars said. "I will give the call of an eagle should you need to be alerted."

"Very good."

"Your Grace," Jeanne said. "But what if… Can I…?"

"I will be quite safe and well with my husband. Do not fret." She knew she'd neglected her friend since her wedding day. Usually, they were together constantly, told each other everything. But Maximilian had spun her life on its head. He was her constant companion.

For now, at least.

They made their way down the gentle hill toward the bustling river. Once there, a startled heron took to the sky and Maximilian spotted boar prints in a patch of mud at a watering spot.

"Burgundy is a fruitful place," he commented.

"Which is why it cannot fall to France. Louis can have no claim on our cloth or our game."

"I will see that he does not." He pointed ahead. "Ah, there will do nicely."

She trotted alongside him, coming to a stop with him at a section of long, swaying grass that blocked this section of bank off from the hill they'd just ridden down. A copse of oak trees to the left gave a screen to where she knew a small, long-abandoned shepherd hut sat, the elements having reclaimed the roof and two walls.

Maximilian jumped gracefully to the ground, tethered his horse, then reached for her waist.

She let him lift her to her feet. Not that she couldn't dismount—of course she could—but she enjoyed him caring for her and enjoyed the display of his strength. It was as if she weighed no more than a dormouse to him.

"You are even more beautiful today," he said, kissing the tip of her nose. "I am sure God has arranged it so your beauty grows with each passing night, while you sleep."

"You flatter me so."

"It is the way I see you." He grinned suddenly, then, with a flourish, removed his black cape. He wafted it high into the air, then let it float to the soft, green grass. "My Grand Dame, a dry spot to place your regal behind."

She laughed. "Why, thank you, kind sir."

Carefully, she sat, her gown gathering around her. "Ah, this is a nice place."

The river babbled at her side, and all around her, the grass danced on the breeze, creating a gentle whisper.

Maximilian secured her horse, removed his sword, then untied the sack of food and wine. He sat beside her and began plucking cheese and apples and goblets from the sack.

"You did not wish for us to have company during our alfresco dining?"

"No." He poured a goblet of wine and passed it to her. "No people, no dogs, no falcons. Just us."

"And the horses?" She removed her light hat and placed it on the cape. Her hair fell around her shoulders.

"A practical necessity." He took a drink of wine, then sliced cheese. "We have a busy bedchamber."

"Do you hate it so much? Aymer and Jupiter?"

"I don't hate them in the slightest, quite the opposite, but a man does occasionally allow himself the selfishness to desire his wife to himself. *All* to himself."

A dark flash seared over his eyes and again, for the hundredth time already that day, she thought of him finding and taking his pleasure the previous night. His big cock had been so hot and hard in her hand, his body like a bow primed for firing an arrow. At one point, she'd thought the entire bed might collapse around them, he was hauling on it with so much gusto.

And then his seed, warm and sticky, had burst from the slit in his cock. She hadn't been expecting it to be like that, but of course, how else could it be?

"Drink," he said, touching her goblet. "It is good wine."

"It is. The best." She took several sips.

"And Cook has packed pork pies." He chuckled. "I suppose she has heard of my fondness for them." He bit into one, crumbs sprinkling.

If there was one thing she might change about her husband, it was his habit of eating fast and somewhat messily. Other than that, she wouldn't change a thing.

"Tell me," she said. "What is your parents' marriage like?"

He shoved the last of his pie into his mouth. When he'd swallowed, he spoke, his attention on a patch of swaying grass. "My mother died when I was eight."

"I am sorry." She touched his arm, over his linen shirt.

"I missed her greatly. She gave me a warmth my father never did."

"Did he show your mother warmth?"

Maximilian huffed. "No, they showed no warmth to each other. I believe my mother tried to be affectionate to start with, at the beginning of their marriage. But ultimately, she gave up. I recall her saying he was taciturn and miserly. Not a nice way to think of your spouse."

"And was it true?"

"To a point. Yes, I suppose it was. Tell me about your parents' marriage. Margaret is your stepmother, isn't she?"

"Yes, though more like a friend to me. We have a lot in common and she always has my best interests at heart. Indeed, it was she who suggested that it was you I should marry."

"And you took her advice."

"Of course. After I lost my mother, at a young age like you, I could not have been blessed with a better woman to stand in her place." She glanced away. It still hurt that her mother had been taken to heaven so young.

"I am sorry for your loss," he said, taking her hand. "But can I ask how Charles and Margaret's marriage was?"

She shook her head sadly. "There was no malice, but also no interest after she failed to produce a male heir. I feel like my father gave up on her, and me sometimes. He was always away, waging war, fighting battles, hunting. That's not to say I didn't love him dearly, I did. And I miss him desperately."

"It is still a fresh wound."

"Indeed, but I have not had the luxury of grief." She finished her wine. "I have lands to rule, a greedy king on my doorstep, and an heir to produce."

"Ah, yes, about that heir." He took her goblet and set it aside.

"I beg your pardon?"

He'd drawn his face close and was studying her intently.

"It is time," he said. "For us to consummate this marriage and perhaps, if God sees the time is right, we will be blessed with a son in nine months."

"Outside! Surely, that is a sin." She clasped her hand over her mouth and looked around.

"Where did you think Adam and Eve performed the act?"

"The Garden of Eden was a place of innocence." She frowned at him.

"Ah, true. Well, we must make do with the Garden of Ghent." He chuckled softly and pulled her hand from her mouth. "And we must do this, and here we are alone—we will not be disturbed and there is no rush. And you, my sweet bride, look utterly relaxed and sun kissed and beyond beautiful." He leaned closer. "Please don't deny us both this pleasure and please do not give the bishop and council any reason to doubt our union."

She knew he was right. They had already deceived the bishop and council once. If word got out they had not joined, they could be torn apart.

Something she couldn't even think about. It would destroy her, she was sure. Being without Maximilian now would break her soul in two.

"But..." she said, her heart squeezing as a new thought popped into her head.

"Do not fear. I will make this work. You can count on me."

"It is just..." She touched his cheek. "I'm worried that..."

"No worries," he said as he brushed his lips over hers.

"But what if our marriage becomes the same as our parents'? And we have no affection and you are never here and..."

He stilled and looked into her eyes.

"What if we prefer to be apart rather than together? What if we run out of things to talk about?" She paused. "Already, I don't think I could live a life like that."

"And neither could I." He stroked his hand over her hair. "Let's promise to always be honest with each other."

"Yes, let's always be honest."

"And you have to admit, thanks to our parents, we've witnessed how *not* to be married." He smiled. "So all we have to do is the opposite."

His simple solution made her smile. "I think we can manage that."

"So do I." He set his lips on hers, a firmer press than she'd been expecting. And then he was laying her down onto the cape, the grass springy beneath the material as her back and shoulders pressed onto it.

She squeezed her legs together as her heart rate picked up.

The kissed deepened, his tongue touching hers as he lay half over her and half at her side. His long, hard body was touching hers and the feel of him was thrilling.

He stroked her cheek then slid his finger down her neck to the rise of her chest.

Her nipples tightened beneath her clothing. She thought of the feather gently stroking them, then his mouth sucking, licking, laving. A small moan caught in her throat and a lovely warmth spread through her breasts.

"You are the most desirable woman I have ever seen," he murmured against her cheek. "And I will make you feel that way."

"But…"

"There's a *but*?" He lifted his head and looked down at her.

"I don't want to disappoint you, but I really don't think this will work."

"You could never disappoint me. And this will work." He ran his hand to her left breast and squeezed over her gown.

She hitched in a breath, a sudden longing for the material to not be there. She wanted flesh on flesh.

He smiled, then kissed her again.

His caress moved to her other breast and he pinched her nipple through the material.

She squirmed and arched her back. Heat was growing in her belly and seeping down to her pelvis, gathering between her legs.

"My penis is hard for you," he murmured. "I want to claim you as mine so badly."

"So do it."

"When you are ready."

"I thought you said it was time?"

"It is, but not quite the perfect moment." He rucked up her gown, over her shins, her knees, her thighs until it sat at her hips. "We must remove your riding undergarments, but you should keep the gown on, as we are outdoors."

She nodded, then wriggled as he pushed her underwear down to her feet and off.

When he lay up and half over her again, she trembled and bit on her bottom lip.

"Be calm," he said softly. "And close your eyes. Imagine the blindfold is there again and you are just feeling."

She did as he'd instructed and let blackness steal her vision.

He stroked up her right leg, then her left, running his fingers over the soft fuzz of hair at the juncture of her thighs. Everywhere he touched was so sensitive.

"Open up. Let me into your virginal womanhood."

She parted her legs a little.

"More, my love."

She did, cool air washing over her cunny.

Instantly, his finger was there, smoothing over her tender lower lips, exploring and caressing. He was kissing her again, filling her with his taste as his finger found her sensitive bud and rolled over it.

A moan caught in her chest and rumbled upward. A memory of the pleasure he could drag from her burst into her mind. Suddenly, she felt greedy for it again, for the cascade of bliss that had spread over her body in a quivering, delicious wave.

He rubbed and circled her nub over and over, until she was squirming with the pleasure of it and the mounting pressure. When he stopped and dipped his finger lower, to her entrance, she whimpered in complaint.

"You feel amazing," he murmured. "And utterly perfect."

"Maximilian." She opened her eyes and stared into his. "It just feels so…so… Oh…"

He'd slid his finger into her cunny, the heel of his hand catching on her nub.

"Oh, for the love of…" She gasped.

"Just feel," he murmured, gently rocking inside her and on her bud.

She pulled his face closer and kissed him, finding his tongue with hers. She canted her hips, wanting more. Her cunny was wet—she was sure of it. There was a definite sensation of dampness.

After a few minutes, he broke the kiss. "You are ready."

"Oh, please, don't stop." She grasped his ear. "It... The feeling, it's growing again. I want it again..."

"And you'll have it again." He lifted his hand from her cunny and fiddled with the flap on his breeches. "I promise you'll have it again."

He positioned himself over her, his legs between hers and his weight on his elbows. "We will enjoy this even more when we are utterly naked," he said, giving her an impish grin.

Mary didn't reply because at that moment, the domed, wide head of his cock found purchase on her entrance. She tensed.

"No, my love, relax." He curled his hips a little, pushing against her tightness. "Think of the pleasure you will soon have if you relax and take me." He gave a little more of himself, his way eased by her wetness.

For the first time, it didn't seem like an absolute impossibility to take his big cock into her cunny. So she gripped his shoulders and stared up at him. "Maximilian...oh..."

"Please, my love, relax. I don't want to hurt you."

"You're not. It's not hurting."

"Are you sure?"

"Yes, it's just new...oh...and big...but it's..." She drew up her knees, clamping him to her. He slipped in another inch. "Oh, yes..."

He fluttered his eyes closed and drove into her, one long, slow glide that stretched her and filled her. When he reached full depth he groaned—a sound that came from deep within him and sounded so primitive, primeval almost.

She arched her neck, her cunny fluttering around the invasion. "Ah...oh... That's it. No more."

"There is no more to take." He kissed her neck and up to her ear. "We have joined. And...oh, you feel better...than I could ever...have imagined."

She clasped his head and looked at him. "Give me that feeling," she said, firmer than she'd intended. "And spill your seed, into me, high into me."

He raised his eyebrows. "Your wish is my command."

For a moment, she wondered what she might have let herself in for, but then he slowly, seductively, began to roll his hips in a way that ground against her bud.

The delicious pressure was there in an instant, building with each rub of his body on hers. Her cunny tightened around his cock and she concentrated on the rising pleasure growing inside. It had started off as a small spark, but Maximilian had stoked it and now it was growing into wild, big flames. It was almost too big to contain.

Her breaths became hard to catch. Her heart was thudding. She forgot where she was. All that existed was her husband.

"My love, take your pleasure," he said against her lips. "Take it." There was an urgency in his tone. "Now."

"I am... Oh... It's there... I..." She held her breath and gripped his tunic so tight, her fingernails hurt. The bubble inside her was about to burst, release its magic.

He groaned and thrust into her, harder, deeper.

The action sent her over the edge. She cried out and let bliss carry her on a wave of ecstasy. Her cunny spasmed and clamped around Maximilian's cock and her body lifted to meet his.

"Ah, give me strength." He straightened his arms, elbows locked, and buried deep inside her. He stilled.

With gritted teeth and closed eyes, he groaned. His cock pulsed, once, twice, three times and heat spread through her pelvis.

She'd taken his seed, taken him, all of him. Joy rushed through her, mixing with the pleasure of her magical moment.

"Husband." She pulled at him, wanting his mouth on hers.

He gave it, a breathless, fervent, almost-delirious kiss. She barely knew where her body ended and his began. They were so as one, so connected.

"That was…" he said after a few moments. "Are you…?"

"I am quite well." She pushed his hair back from his perspiring brow. "I have a skilled husband who made my first time truly wonderful."

"I did?"

"You know you made it wonderful for me." She giggled. "You could tell, I'm sure."

"Yeah." He raised his eyebrows. "You're right, I do know that. I just wanted to hear you say it again."

CHAPTER TWELVE

A FTER A FEW minutes, Maximilian pulled out and flopped heavily at Mary's side.

Quickly, Mary pushed her gown down to her knees, to cover her nakedness. Her heart was still thumping and she was even wetter between her thighs now, as though his seed were seeping out of her.

She clamped her legs together, hoping to keep it in and secure an heir.

For a moment, she wondered if her husband had gone straight to sleep, but then he pulled her into an embrace with her face nestled in the crook of his neck. Her sigh of contentment took with it weeks of stored-up tension.

"You are sated," he said, though it didn't sound like a question, more of a fact.

"Yes, and also glad."

"Glad?"

"That you are who you are."

"What do you mean?"

"We sent letters of betrothal many months before we met, which left lots of time for my imagination to run riot. I had no idea what you would be like."

"You must have had *some* idea. Otherwise, you wouldn't have written to me to begin with."

"I had only hearsay to go on. Margaret said you were a fine warrior, a skilled horseman, and from a good family. When she talked of you, I felt excited to meet you and sure that I'd made the right decision."

"And who else spoke to you of me?"

"Councilors, courtiers… I heard rumors."

"Rumors?"

"They weren't all favorable." She linked her fingers with his and rested both their hands on his chest.

"What do you mean?"

"That you were a dirty brute, illiterate, rude, uncouth." She giggled. "I'm sorry to say it, but that is what I feared on some days."

"So you had Jeanne come and examine me before we even met, before I even entered your castle, just to be sure of my cleanliness and ability to do sums and to read."

"I'm sure you value my sensible nature now that I am your wife."

He laughed softly. "It is true, and I will confess that there were days I told Lars of my fears about you."

"You did?" She lifted up and frowned at him. "How could there be any doubt of my nature? I am Mary of Burgundy. This is my land. I am famed within it."

"Indeed, but I was in Vienna, don't forget. My days filled with tournaments and my nights filled with…"

"With what?" She tipped her head.

"Reading, obviously." He raised his eyebrows. "How else would I be so well versed on the classics?"

"Mmm." She tapped his nose. "What were these fears about me? What kept you awake at night on your journey here?" She paused. "What made you nearly turn around? I'm sure you thought about it."

"I expected and feared the worst things, actually." He pulled a face and shook his head, appearing to shudder.

"The worst things?"

"Yes, and I couldn't have gone through with the marriage if it had been true, not for all the gold or all the land in the world."

"What things?" She shoved his shoulder. "Tell me."

He laughed. "I will tell you. I will tell you." He straightened his face. "I feared you would have smelly feet and warts."

"*Smelly feet and warts!*" she shouted. "Of all the boldness, never ever have I…"

Suddenly, he tipped her over, laughing, and caught her mouth in a kiss.

She melted against him, looping her arms around his shoulders. It seemed Maximilian had the ability to bring her laughter, pleasure, surprise, shock, and desire, all in one afternoon.

Eventually, they mounted the horses and made their way from their secluded spot on the riverbank up the hill toward where they'd left Lars and Jeanne.

"We should journey to the palace of Coudenberg soon," she said.

"It is a place you are fond of?"

"Yes, I have missed it during my time in Ghent. But more than that, my father kept many scrolls in locked chests in his bedchamber. Lots of information for you to peruse now that you are Duke of Burgundy."

"Then we will go."

"I'm glad you are willing."

"Is there more you wish to say?" He looked at her, squinting in the sunshine.

"It was a hard winter here, losing my father, the uprising of my people and the pressure from the council. Plus, I didn't know if you were going to ever arrive."

He frowned. "I am sorry it was so hard for you. This coming winter will be different, though, I promise."

She smiled. That wasn't a promise he could make, but she was grateful for the sentiment.

"We will make plans to travel soon," he went on. "I am keen to see Coudenberg, and you are right, I must now turn my attention to stopping the French invasion of Burgundy territories."

Did he mean that now he had planted his seed in her, he could devote his time to warfare? She wasn't sure, but she was grateful she had him as her duke to protect Burgundy. She knew already he had a sharp mind and would be a great asset.

"Before we travel," he went on, "we must ask the Estate of Flanders for money."

"They will not be happy."

"It is not my job to keep your councils and estates happy." He scowled. "It is my role to defend Burgundy from the French and to do that, we need money. I am afraid I do not bring much of that to the table."

"They refused my father last year when he asked for money."

"I am not your father." He raised his eyebrows at her. "I will persuade them."

She thought of the tangles of treaties that would bind Maximilian's arms. Some he knew about, some he did not. "How much will you ask for?"

"Five hundred thousand riders."

"That is a princely sum."

"That can be raised with taxes. All they have to do is agree and I will ensure Louis retreats."

"I hope it is that simple."

"It is if they want to win this war."

Maximilian was asking for a lot from men who not only didn't see him as a friend of Burgundy, but didn't trust him, either.

"Look over there," he said, his mood suddenly lightening. "It seems our friends are enjoying close conversation."

Lars's and Jeanne's horses were tethered to a couple of saplings, and under the shade of a larger tree, the couple sat on Lars's cloak. Jeanne put her head back and laughed, the sound catching on the breeze.

"Scandalously close," Mary said, smiling. Jeanne, like her, had been through difficult times. If she was enjoying the company of a hand-some man on a sunny day, Mary was pleased for her.

When the couple saw the duke and duchess, they jumped up. Lars shook out his cape, then held Jeanne's horse as she mounted.

"I trust you enjoyed your alfresco dining," Lars said.

"Very satisfying," Maximilian said with a curt not. "Let us head back to Ghent. We need to pack."

"Oh?" Jeanne studied Mary.

"Yes, we are going to Coudenberg." Mary smiled.

Jeanne sighed. "At last."

ONE WEEK LATER, Mary looked upon her newly inherited palace rising grandly on the mount of Coudenberg Hill. Her heart filled with warmth despite the name given to the lavish palace: Cold Mountain.

It was the first time she'd been here knowing her father wouldn't appear at any time, day or night, fresh from battle, exhausted and full of tales. It was a sharp and painful emotion, but it was softened by the fact that her new husband was accompanying her.

Behind them rattled an entourage of courtiers, cooks, servants, councilors, and bishops. Carts carried chests of precious documents, food, and clothing. Philip rode with Jupiter on his arm. Aymer, tired now, lay upon a cart of soft hay.

"It is quite something," Maximilian said, adjusting the sword that sat against his thigh as he stared at the regal building in the distance.

"I'm glad you approve."

"Very much so. It is spectacular. I am looking forward to arriving."

"Some time ago now, my grandfather ordered new wings to be built, and the Aula Magna also."

"Which is?"

"A grandiose hall for receptions, weddings, and state meetings. The gilding is quite something. The most elaborate and admired in all of Europe, I am told."

"Perfect."

"What do you mean?" she asked.

"Perfect for the christening I hope we'll be celebrating in the spring." A grin spread on his face, rounding his wind- and sun-kissed cheeks.

A little spark of desire flickered to life in Mary. Since their first time joining, Maximilian had entered her each night. Always slow and tender, his kisses sincere and adoring. What he said was true. She may well produce their first child within nine months of their marriage.

Soon they were dismounting and handing their horses over to be fed and watered.

"Show me our home," Maximilian said, holding out his arm for Mary to take. "I am happy to be here."

"As am I." She slipped her hand into the crook of his elbow. They started walking on the stone path. Legs stiff and behinds saddle sore.

Aymer bounced down from the hay cart and circled Mary and Maximilian as they went, yapping and sniffing, then cocking his leg against an urn holding a glossy, round bay tree.

A peacock strutted from behind a rhododendron, elaborate tail feathers fanned and glinting in the sunshine.

"In God's good name." Maximilian came to a halt. "What is that?"

She smiled up at him. "You have never seen a peacock?"

"No." He peered at the shimmering bird. "What a magnificent beast."

The peacock shook its tail, a rippling, whispering dance.

"Impressive." Maximilian blew out a breath.

"Indeed, but it is not you whom he is trying to impress, it is the peahen, who is likely to be around here somewhere.

"His feathers." Maximilian shook his head. "The colors...they're unreal, like nothing I've ever seen before. It's as though they have lots of eyes on them."

"When he loses one, you shall have it."

He laughed and kissed her cheek. "Are you sure, my love? I have some unique uses for feathers, as you well know."

She trembled. A lovely little tightening of her muscles at the memory of him teasing her with a feather. She cleared her throat. "I will show you our chambers."

"I am looking forward to this very much." He paused and side-stepped as Aymer almost tripped him up. "This dog!"

They stepped into the entrance of the palace. A huge vase was set on a table; it was full of summer flowers and a butterfly had flown indoors to flutter between the stems. On either side of the table stood iron sconces, the candles unlit as the day was bright and sunlight poured in.

Maximilian looked up at the lofty ceiling that was thick with beams. "I like it already."

"Good." She squeezed closer. "Come, this way. The Aula Magna will be at your disposal." She turned. "Lars, see that all of the chests are brought in here. And ask for the ones in my father's chamber to be brought down also."

"Yes, Your Grace."

Mary hesitated. Her father's chamber. It was his no longer. He'd never sleep in that bed again, use his comb, bathe, or enjoy the view from his window. She pulled in a deep breath. So much had happened since his death, yet still, grief was as fresh as a tart apple sliced in two and placed upon her tongue.

A courtier opened the huge oak doors to the vast room. They stepped in.

Three fireplaces were set along the east side, and to the west, some of the largest glass windows in the land let the sunlight stream in. A long, oak table and sturdy benches that could comfortably seat one hundred people extended centrally in the room and was laden with bowls of fruit and nuts, candles and blank scrolls, quills and inkwells. At the head of the room, on a plinth, two ornate, golden chairs with scarlet upholstery watched royally over proceedings.

"Your grandfather spent handsomely on this room." Maximilian gestured around. "Even the walls are gold."

"I told you it was grand." She stepped away from him, arms held out, and spun a circle. "I am so glad to be here. Ghent was becoming oppressive."

"And far too close to Louis for comfort." Maximilian strode to the right and studied a portrait of a woman, pale, small-chinned, and reading a Bible.

"That is my mother, Isabella of Bourbon." Mary came to stand next to him.

"I can see where you get your beauty from." He touched Mary's cheek, a sweet and delicate gesture. "Your mother was very fair of face."

"She was. I wish I'd had her for longer. You must feel the same way about your mother."

"I do. But let us not look back. We are not going that way and our loved ones would wish us to be victorious on their behalf." He strode to the table, his moment of tenderness quickly replaced with purpose and energy. "I have lots to do, scrolls to pore over, plans to make, treaties to make and break." He threw his head back and shouted at the ceiling. "A king of the worst sort to defeat!"

Mary tensed, not at his passion or the sudden raising of his voice, but at the word *treaty*.

At that moment, the first of the chests of documents were brought in by courtiers.

"Place them along there," Lars said, directing the chests toward the wall beneath the windows. "Maximilian, I think we should make a start. We have wasted many days since our arrival. There is work to be done—Louis is gaining upon Burgundy."

"I do not consider spending time with my wife a waste of time." Maximilian scowled at Lars but then sent his gaze over the chests. "Though you are right, my friend. We must give the most serious of matters our attention. Where is Melchior, and our nobles? We must have all the good brains working together and be overseen by God."

"I will ensure they are with us." Lars squeezed Maximilian's shoulder. "Know the place you will lay your head tonight, for later, you will likely be too exhausted to find it in this maze."

"Good thinking. Though when I return, I expect us to get straight to work."

"We will." Lars poured wine into several goblets, splashing blood-red drips as he went. "And we will not stop until we have a plan."

"And a winning plan at that." Maximilian set his attention on Mary. "Show me to your bedchamber."

She stepped up close, her fingers linking with his. "Do you mean *our* bedchamber?"

"Ah, yes, that would suit me well."

"I do not wish to be without you," she said. "The nights are long and cold if you are not beside me, even in the summer months."

"It is my will to be beside you every night. I have no need of my own bedchamber, other than for bathing and dressing."

"It is unusual. The courtiers will talk."

"Do we care?"

"No." She smiled. "We don't."

She led him up a wide, stone staircase that had been swept so much, it gleamed. At the top, she took a right turn and after passing the entrance to the bedchamber her father had used and that Maximilian would now set his wardrobe in, she opened the door to hers.

Aymer ran in, nose to the floor, tail wagging, sniffing, exploring, reminding himself of the scents of home.

Despite the warm day, a blazing fire was the beating heart of the room, and a large, indulgently soft four-poster bed was positioned to allow for both warmth and glorious, rolling hillside views.

"Ah, Philip has been swift." Mary nodded at the corner of the room.

Jupiter was perched on his wooden stand tearing at a strip of meat. It was his usual spot, between a walnut table and a tapestry of four gowned maidens meeting with four knights on horses.

"Do we really have to have the dog and the bird in our bedchamber?" Maximilian asked with a sigh. "Here as well as in Ghent?"

"You know we do. They are my friends." Mary watched as Aymer leaped onto the bed, turned a circle, then flopped down as though completely exhausted from the journey and preparing for a long nap.

"But...really?" Maximilian pointed at the dog. "I don't think I can do this forevermore. A dog. On the bed. A screeching, raw-meat-crunching bird in the corner. How is a man to sleep? How is a man to concentrate on creating heirs?"

She frowned at him. "They were here before you."

"But I am here now." He patted his chest.

"And I am glad." She paused. "But are you asking me to choose?" She cocked her head and squinted her eyes. "Between you and my beloved pets?"

The look he gave her had her breath hitching and her heart rate picking up. Had she pushed him too far?

"No." His jaw clenched. "But we do have to have some boundaries."

He flipped open a chest and snatched out a checkered, red, woolen blanket.

"Aymer!" he snapped, striding to the fire.

Aymer lifted his head.

"Aymer, come here." Maximilian laid the blanket on the floor in a cozy spot near a stack of logs.

Aymer ignored him.

"I mean it." Maximilian pointed at the blanket. "Get your hairy doggy behind here. Now."

Aymer appeared to think about it for a second, looked at Mary, and then jumped down from the bed. He sniffed the blanket, turned a circle, and then sat.

"Good boy." Maximilian ruffled his ears. "Stay there. It's just as warm as the bed, if not more so."

"But I will miss his warmth." Mary pouted at her husband.

"You will be very warm, my love." He pulled her close. "For my blood is hot for you, my cock hard for you, and I cannot help that I want you all to myself." He glanced at Jupiter. "And hoodwink him before I retire each night. His screeching when you find pleasure is quite off-putting."

"He does not screech when…" She looped her arms around his neck. "Does he?"

"Yes, and it scratches my ears the way you scratch your nails down my back."

She gasped. "Maximilian! To accuse me of such a thing…"

He chuckled and kissed her. "Dog on the floor, bird hoodwinked, that way I can concentrate on giving you everything you deserve, my Grand Dame." Suddenly, he released her and stepped away. He winked as he held up his arm and turned. "I have much work to do. But I will come to you. Later."

And then he was gone.

CHAPTER THIRTEEN

MAXIMILIAN BIT INTO an apple and frowned. A pile of scrolls sat shoulder height on the table to his right and he'd made notes and calculations on parchment to his left. "We need men," he said. "Many, many more men."

"It will cost a great deal to hire an army." Lars shook his head, candlelight flickering over his worried expression.

"Money we do not have." Melchior adjusted his clergy gown and studied the sums.

"It is a shame you brought so little wealth with you." Hugo sniffed and folded his arms.

Maximilian's frown deepened. "Why are you here?" He pointed at Hugo with the apple still in his hand.

"I am of Her Grace's ducal council. It is only right that I am here to represent her interests."

It irked Maximilian that Hugo thought Mary's interests wouldn't be foremost in his, her husband's, mind. He stood and strode to the fire. The hour was late, his bones were weary, but his mind couldn't switch off. "We will not buy an army." A sudden tumble of thoughts came to him, like rocks falling down a mountain and forming a new hill. "We will create our own."

"I do not understand," Lars said. "How will we create our own army?"

"The good men of Burgundy want their land back, do they not?"

Maximilian turned and swept his gaze around the room. "So it stands to reason they will fight for their future, a future without French aggression, without French oppression."

"They are poor farmers," Hugo said. "Simple men. What use will they be on the battlefield?" He rolled his eyes.

Maximilian fought the urge to draw his sword on the weasel-like, little man once again. Instead, he strode to the table, sloshed wine into a goblet, and drank. "Farmers are strong and clever. With training, they will be fine soldiers. I'd wager my best armor on that fact."

Melchior fiddled with his rosary and appeared deep in thought. He nodded slowly.

Lars stood, finger pressed over his lips, as though holding in words he wasn't ready to say. He strode the length of the table, his footsteps heavy on the stone floor.

"It is a crazy idea." Hugo tutted. "The Estates General will never go along with it."

"The Estates General"—Maximilian pointed at Hugo—"will have to understand that my specialty is warfare, and if I have been brought to this land to defeat Louis, then I must be given free will." He marched up to Hugo, enjoying the way the man took a step backward and paled slightly. "And my ideas and recommendations must be considered."

"I am sure they will be considered." Hugo nodded, rapid, little movements of his head.

"No." Lars came to a halt.

"No?" Maximilian turned to him, surprised. He'd thought he could rely on Lars for support.

"No, there is no time for consideration. It is an excellent plan that should be put into practice as soon as possible. France is encroaching, ever more daring. The sooner farmers are trained as pike bearers, archers, riders, and fighters, the better."

"And what, pray, will happen to their farms while they are gone?"

Melchior asked. "And I only mention it because it is what the council will argue next." He raised his eyes at Hugo.

"Women and children can plow and sow," Maximilian said. "And let's face it, if they don't work, their land will not be theirs to farm. It will belong to the French devil-man Louis."

"I will put the idea to the council first thing in the morning." Hugo dipped a quill in ink and wrote on a scroll. "And I will let you know their decision as soon as possible."

"Thank you," Lars said quickly before Maximilian snapped anything derogatory. "And it is late of hour, Hugo. We will all be going to our beds soon. Why don't you seek yours?"

Hugo had bags under his eyes, but he sat, hands on his knees, and leaned forward. "I am not tired."

Maximilian was tired. They'd been going through figures and letters for days. He'd barely seen his wife and all he'd done in their marital bed was sleep. And now the moon and stars once again filled the sky as they worked.

"We will write to Louis," Maximilian said, finding a new lease of energy. "This night."

"I beg your pardon?" Hugo said.

"We will write to him, formally. It is essential he knows whom he is dealing with now that I am Mary's husband, now that I am the duke." Maximilian sipped his wine. "And it is also essential that he knows what I want. What my demands are."

"Which are?" Hugo asked.

"That he return the Burgundian lands he has taken."

"It is a good idea." Lars sat and spread out a scroll, picking up a quill. "He must know that he is no longer dealing with Charles, that now he is dealing with Maximilian of Austria, a fine young Habsburg warrior, expert strategist and brave defender." He dipped the quill in ink. "Unless we state what we want, how can we achieve it? How can he give it?"

"You might not get what you want," Melchior said, "but he may meet you halfway."

"Halfway?" Hugo scoffed. "Give half the lands back?"

"He may agree to ceasing the invasion, which would stop the killing of God's good people." Melchior set his soft, intelligent gaze on Hugo.

Hugo pursed his lips.

"And that would give us time to prepare our army. It will take a year, I'd guess." Maximilian felt his spirits rise. A plan was forming, and it might just work. Especially if his new archenemy, Louis, was sensible enough to know that he would soon be spreading his French army thin in a region that did not want them there.

"Would you like me to begin?" Lars asked.

"Yes. The sooner, the better." Maximilian sat, picked up a handful of nuts, and after throwing one into the air and catching it in his mouth, he dictated the letter to Lars.

When it was written, Maximilian signed it as Melchior heated the red wax for the seal.

"I hope this is successful," Hugo said when the scroll was ready to be handed over to an envoy for immediate delivery to France.

"Failure is not a word I understand." Maximilian stood, hooked his thumbs into the waist of his breeches, and pulled in a deep breath. "Or intend to ever have associated with my name."

And with that, he bid Lars and Melchior goodnight and made his way to his wife's bedchamber.

When he arrived, the moonlit room was quiet.

Jupiter was hoodwinked and still. Aymer was curled up on the blanket beside the smoldering fire.

Maximilian added another log, tickled the dog's ears, then set his sword upon the table, being careful not to wake Mary.

She lay angel-like, her hair spread on the pillow and her features soft in sleep.

For a moment, he stopped and took in the wonder of her. God had been kind and generous when He'd sent Mary into his life. She was everything a man could ever want or need. Beautiful, clever, witty, and constantly challenging his mind to think in new ways.

Yes. He was indeed blessed.

He took off his tunic and breeches, laid them beside his boots and sword, then slipped into bed.

She stirred but didn't wake. He pulled her close and kissed the top of her head. For the first time in days, he had a sense of action. A plan was unfurling, and he'd defeat Louis…he had to.

When he woke, Mary was gone, as were Jupiter and Aymer. He glanced at the window. The sun was high. He'd slept late. A rise of disappointment grew within him. He hadn't had a chance to speak to his wife and tell her of his plans and ideas. He knew she'd be interested.

And now she'd gone out hunting by the looks of it.

Something he didn't have time for.

Quickly, he dressed and readied himself for the day, then he marched from the room, down the long corridor, descended the vast staircase, and strode to the Aula Magna.

When he reached it, Lars already sat reading.

"Good day to you," Maximilian said, nodding at a courtier holding a jug of mead.

"And to you, Your Grace." Lars didn't look up.

"There is much to read today again?"

"Yes." Lars pushed the scroll to one side and reached for another. "There is a great deal about a convening of the estates last year."

"There is?"

"Yes, it seems there was quite a division between them and the council."

"About what?"

"Money, of course."

"Ah, yes, I should have known." Maximilian sat and tore off a chunk of bread from a fresh loaf.

"A divide in opinion between north and south," Lars went on. "When it came to supporting Charles the Bold's battle endeavors, it created a lot of distrust between Estates General and council."

"That is interesting…" Maximilian chewed slowly. "And it means we can assume them not to be as closely aligned as Hugo might have led us to believe."

"Yes, and the more cracks there are, the stronger you will be."

"No cracks in me." Maximilian banged his chest and grinned. "This is good. Keep reading. Tell me the important bits and I will make a start on these treaties."

"And long may we have peace to do it." Lars nodded at the door. "I don't mind Melchior helping—his words are wise—but councilors like Hugo hanging over us, and the other day the bishop, too. I just can't concentrate."

"Should we lock the door?" Maximilian raised his eyebrows.

"And then how would the courtiers bring us luncheon and wine?" Lars chuckled.

"Very true."

They sat for several hours reading, making notes, and stacking scrolls to be scrutinized further. Melchior joined them, as did Hugo and one of his aides.

When the shadows began to stretch like long fingers over the floor, Lars suddenly stood. He picked up a scroll, slotted it beneath his arm, and walked over to Maximilian. "Your Grace, there is something I wish to show you."

"So show me." Maximilian looked up at him.

"Not here," Lars said quietly. "In private."

Maximilian frowned and glanced around. "I would like the room," he said, clenching his fists and putting them on the table. "To discuss a private matter with my chief advisor."

Lars puffed up his chest, clearly pleased with his title.

Melchior stood, scroll in hand. "Yes, Your Grace."

"But we are all studying together," Hugo said, not raising his head from where he was peering at some very small script.

"Are you refusing my order, man?" Maximilian asked slowly.

"No." Hugo looked up and stood, gesturing to his aide to do the same. "Of course not."

"I would advise you to take some air," Maximilian said, flicking his wrist at them. "For the day is pleasant." He looked at a courtier. "Please leave us, but bring us wine soon."

"Yes, Your Grace."

When the vast room was empty and a heavy silence descended, Lars sat next to Maximilian and unrolled a scroll.

"What is this?"

"A treaty."

"Go on…"

"A treaty signed by Mary in February year gone that contains clauses regarding the man she was to marry."

"I was not aware of such a treaty." Maximilian frowned. "What does it say?"

"I fear you will not like it, which is why I wanted you to peruse it in private, away from the prying eyes of the council."

"Do you think they know about it?" Maximilian read the first few lines of a document titled *The Great Privilege*.

"Yes. I would bet my life on it."

"In the name of…" His mouth fell open. He could hardly believe what he was reading. "This is… This…"

"Carves you out of the duchy so everything goes to your children and not you should Mary die."

"Heaven forbid. I do not like to even consider the thought of my wife dying." He crossed himself.

"But these things need to be considered."

Maximilian looked at his friend. His mind was spinning, emotions rattling around.

"You love her," Lars said, not as a question, but as a fact.

He swallowed. Was it that obvious that he was obsessed with his wife? Enchanted by her, enraptured, would spend the rest of his life making her happy, God willing.

"I can see it," Lars said, "and I am happy for you."

Maximilian nodded curtly.

"I know you had hesitations on our journey here," Lars went on, "as I'm sure she did as she waited for you to arrive."

"She finds me pleasing, or so she says." Maximilian rubbed his temples. "So why would she not tell me of this?"

"I do not know." Lars paused. "But perhaps she presumed you knew, or maybe she didn't know of its existence, either."

"She has signed it...here."

"Ah, yes, there is that."

Maximilian sighed, the ramifications of the clause extending. "How will the Burgundy people ever respect me as their duke? Word of this will get out. They will see me as weak, with no sway or power. Simply a cock to produce an heir for Burgundy. I am as good as a nobody to them. No wonder Hugo and his cronies eye me with such derision."

"I agree. Something must be done."

Maximilian read the treaty again, every word seeming to scorch into his brain. When he reached the end, he rolled it up and stood.

"Where are you going?" Lars asked.

"To speak to my wife."

"Shall I come with you?"

"No, I need to do this alone. I need to see her face when I first speak of it."

CHAPTER FOURTEEN

ARY SAT READING her Bible beside the window, a cup of
rosewater and a saucer of sweet marzipan at her side. Aymer
slept by her feet.

The room was quiet, other than the occasional shifting log in the
grate. She missed her husband. He'd been so busy for what felt like
weeks, appearing only late at night to fall exhausted into bed.

Suddenly, the door burst open.

Maximilian filled the frame, scroll in hand, face dark.

"My love." She stood and set the Bible to one side.

"We need to talk." He shut the door not with a hard bang, but not
as gently as he usually would.

Jupiter, without his hoodwink today, flapped his wings and
squawked. Aymer jumped up to greet Maximilian.

Maximilian ignored the animals. "I have come across a treaty."

"You have?" Instantly, her heart rate picked up. She knew exactly
what he'd found.

Maximilian came up close, so close, she could see the frustration
searing over his blue eyes. But what was worse was that she also saw
the fear of deception lurking in their depths.

"It is a treaty with a most displeasing clause about your marriage."

She said nothing but held his eye contact.

"*Our* marriage." His jaw clenched and a muscle flexed in his
smooth cheek. "What do you know of this?" He was unblinking as he

stared at her. "Tell me. Tell me now."

Her pulse thudded in her ears. Her knees felt as though they might give way. Her mind raced with denials and explanations. Should she fake surprise at its existence?

"Mary." His voice was low and dark. "I need the truth from you."

"I know of it." She swallowed. "And I know what it sets out. Because it was my idea—I was pressed into a corner. My signature is on it, as you have no doubt seen for yourself."

"*Your* idea?" A flash of pain crossed his face and he turned, slinging the scroll to the floor. It rolled beneath the table. "It was *your* idea?"

"Maximilian." She reached for his arm, but he stepped away with a shrug. "My love," she said. "I did not know it would vex you so. And I believe our fathers also discussed, even planned, a similar arrangement in a similar treaty all those years ago when they met, so it is not the first of it... I mean... Please do not be hurt. I beg you."

"You knew I would be hurt this way." He spun to her again, redness coming to his cheeks. "That is why you said nothing of it."

"It will only be relevant if I die before we have children." She rubbed her belly. "Hopefully, one is already on the way."

"I do not wish to think of your death." He frowned. "God forgive me for even saying such a thing, but how do you expect me to go on as your duke while this treaty is in place?"

"'Go on'?"

"Yes." He reached for her hands and squeezed them. "I am planning a war with France. I am preparing to go to battle, to be maimed, to die, all in the name of Burgundy, yet I am not seen as a Burgundian. I am merely an outsider brought in to give you and your people an heir."

"You know that is not true."

"How do I know that?"

"Because... Because we are not a typical marriage. We might be joined to create stability and progression for our people, our land, and families, but we…"

"We what?"

"We… We're fond of each other. Good friends, as you'd hoped."

"'Fond'? 'Friends'?" He dropped her hands and reached for her face, cupping it in his big, warm palms. "I am not *fond* of you, Mary."

Her heart sank and tears pricked her eyes. The treaty had ruined everything. Just when she'd thought they'd had something special. She'd been such a fool to keep its existence from him. To never mention the deal their fathers had made, but he'd clearly been kept in the dark about.

"I am more than fond of you," he said, coming closer, his body heat radiating onto her. "I am in love with you. You are my one love. My true love. Don't you see that? Can't you feel it?"

The deep timbre of his voice and the passion in his eyes filled her with a warmth she'd never experienced before. It was comforting and honeyed and seeped into every vein, every corner, of her body and soul.

"I love you. I love you, Mary, with all of my heart." He pressed his mouth down on hers.

She whimpered and clung to him. Relief flooded her and her heart seemed to expand in her chest.

His tongue stroked against hers and he wrapped her in his arms, pulling her close and holding her as though he'd never let her go.

When he pulled back, she ran her fingers into his hair. "I love you too, Maximilian. I love you so much, it frightens me."

"Don't be frightened." He rested his brow on hers. "We are to-gether, and together, we can achieve anything."

"Yes." She made a sudden decision. "And the first thing we will achieve is changing this treaty. I was never comfortable with it. It was made with haste and I was practically held hostage in Ghent at the time by council and my people. So I apologize from the depths of my soul to you."

"I forgive you. I would forgive you anything." He paused. "But yes, let's change it. Not that I want inheritance from you—that thought is unthinkable and I pray God takes me first so I don't have to live without you…" He paused and closed his eyes.

"Let's not think of death." She touched his cheek.

"I can agree to that." He opened his eyes again. "But I need to have the support of our people if my plan to defeat Louis is to succeed and if I have no claim on these lands, no vested interest, they will neither trust nor respect me."

"You have come up with a plan? What is it?"

"To train farmers to fight." He stepped away and retrieved the scroll. "It will be cheaper than hiring an army and our funds are limited, taxes hard to raise."

She nodded slowly. "It could work."

"It *will* work."

Mary reached for her bell and rang it. "The Estates General will not be happy, nor the council."

"I will deal with them, my love."

Within a minute, Jeanne appeared.

"Could you get the dowager, please?" Mary asked. "Tell her she is needed in my chamber on a matter of great import."

"Yes, Your Grace." Jeanne glanced at Maximilian then rushed off.

"Margaret can bear witness to the change in the treaty," Mary said, opening her bureau and reaching for a quill. "And we will sign it, and seal it."

"Keep it secret?"

For a moment, she was deep in thought, weighing her options. "What is the point in angering the Estates or council further? Especially when this change will be a moot point, hopefully." She paused. "I do not care for those interfering old men with their fat chins and pie- and ale-filled bellies. I am Mary of Burgundy, duchess and governor of these lands." She tipped her chin. "It is I who makes the rules and treaties and decisions, and I decide this, that you should be my heir if we have no children. Burgundy would be safe in your hands. I know this in my heart." She pressed her hand to her chest. "Deep in my heart."

He chuckled and gave her a long, smoldering look. "You might be little, but you are fierce when you decide to be, oh, dear wife of mine."

"You had better believe it." She smiled at him, fired up, her blood hot and her body tingling. Her husband looked fine today, and with his clothes off and lying on their bed, he'd look even better.

"Mary, you called for me?" Margaret appeared at the door.

"Ah, yes. Come in, Dowager." Maximilian smiled and bobbed his head respectfully. "It is good to see you."

⭑⭑⭑

THE NEXT MORNING, after training Jupiter and two new young falcons with Philip, Mary entered the main foyer, her bird on her arm. Philip was at her side talking about grouse seen on the eastern hill.

Maximilian came rushing from the Aula Magna, his cape flying out behind him. He strode up to her, glanced at Philip, then clutched her shoulders. "Mary!" Excitement flashed over his face and his muscles were tense.

"What has happened?" she asked.

"I have had an idea."

"Another one?" He was often excited by his thoughts on many subjects.

"Yes, we are to hold a tournament. A lavish tournament. Give the people a spectacle to behold."

"A tournament?" Philip echoed. "Why?"

Maximilian ignored him. "I am their duke and they know nothing of me, nothing of my skills as a warrior, a leader. We will show them." He banged his chest. "I will show them the man who has come to lead them against the French and defend this land."

"It is a grand idea," she said. "When will this be?" She smiled, enjoying the enthusiasm on his face rather than the worry that had been there of late.

"Soon, very soon. I will set Lars to the task immediately."

"Won't it cost a lot of money?" Philip asked.

"Money well spent." Maximilian tilted his chin. "Or do you disagree with the idea, Philip?"

Philip hesitated, then, "No, not at all, Your Grace."

Maximilian flicked his eyebrows. "And you and I shall joust, Philip of Cleves. You can show me what skills you have, though do not expect to win." He laughed. "For I am most accomplished."

Philip set back his shoulders and he held Maximilian's eye contact. "I will look forward to it."

Mary noticed he didn't add "Your Grace" onto the end of his sentence as usual and wondered if Maximilian's words had antagonized her gentle cousin.

"As you *should* look forward to it." Maximilian laughed harder, then kissed Mary full on the lips. "You will have the best seat in the arena so you do miss not a thing, my love."

ONE WEEK LATER, the sun shone brightly and a light breeze caught the first leaves that were falling from the maple trees surrounding the palace.

A lavish jousting arena topped with flags had been built and word had spread, enticing a large crowd of eager spectators. They were keen to witness their duchess's new husband in action and the excitement was palpable amongst their chatter.

For the local landowners and nobles, the fighting, racing, and jousting were only part of the exhibition. There would be a banquet and a masquerade dance for those with energy after all the sporting events—and mead.

A helmet show had been set up in the arena and guests were allowed to study the elaborate adornments up close.

Mary, dressed in a brown, velvet gown with detailed, golden embroidery, sat with Margaret and Jeanne in a box covered with a red, silk canopy in the event of inclement weather. She sipped from a goblet of wine and studied the crowd. Aymer lay at her feet, gnawing on a lamb bone.

Her nerves were rising, not just because she wanted Maximilian's event to be a success, but because she hoped desperately that he wouldn't get hurt. He was very excited about his racing joust with Philip. Maybe too excited.

"There are a lot of people here," Jeanne said.

"Many have traveled from far away." Margaret nodded. "Your husband's reach has been expansive."

"I never doubted that it would be." Mary sat up a little straighter as the helmets were taken away, ready to be worn. "He is a very determined man, not least when it comes to showing off his prowess in combat and bravery."

"Louis should be wary of him," Jeanne said.

"I believe he is. He has not advanced since Maximilian sent him a letter of warning."

"This is good news." Margaret nodded. "Long may it last."

Mary sat quietly until Philip rode out on a gray horse covered in equine armor and the red-and-yellow Cleves coat of arms upon his cape.

"Oh, I hope he doesn't get hurt." Mary locked her fingers and sent a prayer heavenward.

"You would prefer your husband lose to Philip?" Jeanne asked.

"No, of course not, but I care for Philip. He has been a good friend to me for many years."

"I fear Maximilian suspects him of more," Jeanne said.

"Whatever do you mean?" Mary turned to her with a frown.

"He told Lars he thinks Philip is in love with you." Jeanne down-turned her mouth, knowing she'd said something troubling.

"In the name of the good Lord!" Mary stared at her friend with wide eyes. "What would make him thing that?"

"Men's minds work differently to ours," Margaret said, tapping her temple. "They are much simpler than us. War. Power. Heirs. Wealth. That is all they think of."

Mary frowned at her stepmother. She didn't agree with her. Certainly not where Maximilian was concerned. She found him to be a complex and devoted man with many original thoughts and much appreciation for the arts and scholars. The new ideas coming from Florence and Milan fascinated him. But she didn't wish to argue a point. Not now. Not here.

Maximilian rode out into the arena, his feather-adorned helmet under his arm. He galloped around the edge, waving wildly, beaming, and whisking up a raucous frenzy of excitement in the crowd.

He came to a halt in front of Mary's box. "Do you wish me victory, Grand Dame?"

"Of course, my love." She leaned forward, hands curling over the wooden edge of the box. "I also wish for you both to walk away in a condition that will allow for dancing later."

He laughed. "Never a straight answer from my dear wife." He spun his horse around, arm in the air. "My people, show your appreciation for your beautiful and wise duchess."

The crowd was on its feet, clapping and cheering.

Mary's heart filled with pride and a sense of duty as she dipped her head, hiding a broad smile. She didn't want to come across as conceited.

"They love him," Jeanne said.

"Most of them." Margaret nodded to her left. Several Estates General members and councilors sat steely-faced and stiff.

"But they are here," Mary said quietly. "They know they have no choice but to back Maximilian. To do as instructed. They have no other alternative if they wish Louis to retreat. They must accept their new duke."

"I have faith in Maximilian," Jeanne said firmly. "And in all the men who arrived with him. They are good men." Her gaze settled on Lars, who was in the arena securing a piece of armor on Maximilian's horse.

Mary reached for Jeanne's hand and squeezed. It was heartening to see her friend finding happiness after years of loneliness.

Maximilian had his helmet on now, the eye slits thin and the jaw pointed. Sunlight bounced off his heavy armor as he took hold of his lance and settled it into position.

Philip did the same, his black horse eager to start the race and hopping on the spot.

"Let the games begin!" Lars shouted.

A drum banged in the corner. The horses uncoiled like springs, racing toward each other with just a thin, flag-adorned fence between them. The sound of their hooves competed with the drumming and seemed to shake the ground.

Mary's heart raced as the lances were angled forward and over the fence, each ready to take a rider down.

"Oh, dear Lord." She gasped. She could barely imagine the strength required to hold such a heavy weapon when wearing unfathomably weighty armor. And she certainly couldn't imagine the fear at being faced with such a thing.

"I can't watch," Jeanne said breathily, tightening her grip on Mary's hand.

Suddenly, Maximilian's lance caught on the fence, but he righted it quickly. The action seemed to confuse Philip, whose lance glanced off the armor Maximilian's horse wore.

This gave Maximilian the advantage and he shoved at Philip, sending him toppling to the ground with a hard bang and a puff of dust.

The crowd cheered. Many people were on their feet. The drum banged harder and a horn blasted.

Maximilian rode around the end of the fence, then came to a halt beside Philip, who was dragging himself heavily to his feet and shaking his head within his helmet.

"Philip is unharmed." Mary jumped up, clapping so hard, her palms stung. "Oh, how does Maximilian do that? Such skill. Such strength." She was filled with pride. Her husband was a fine and talented man.

Maximilian threw down his lance and pulled off his helmet. He raised his hand and punched the air in victory.

"Good people of Burgundy!" he shouted.

The drumming and trumpeting stopped, the crowd quieted.

"Prepare yourselves," Maximilian bellowed, "for many such spectacles and acts of bravery and skill. And know this…" He kicked his horse into a jog. "I am here now, as your duke and at your service. Know me and know that you are in good hands." He came to a halt beside Mary. "My wife and I will not bow to King Louis's demands. He is unreasonable, pompous, and greedy, not qualities any country should have in a leader."

Mary tipped her chin and stood. "My husband, your duke, speaks wisely. God shines the light of victory on those who are pious, brave, and of impeccable morals, and I am pleased to inform you that that is the man I, your duchess, got when I married Archduke Maximilian of Austria." She paused and swung her gaze around the crowd. It was important that they see her face and know her sincerity. "That is what you, my people, were also blessed with when I married. Because this man"—she pointed at her husband—"will be seen and known from this day on as your noble leader, your prudent guide, and your brave warrior.

"I know in my heart that he will lay down his life for you, for your children, and for your lands and as such, I demand he is respected." She shot a look at the generals and council. "Do not be fooled by our youth. For we have the lineage of great judiciousness and knowledge to rule our good people. It is what we were both born to do." She raised her arms, slowly, fingers spread. "Now tell me, who is your leader? Who will save us from the devilish King of France, who is waiting and plotting our downfall as I speak to you on this day?"

"Maximilian! Maximilian! Maximilian!" The bellows of the crowd made Mary's ears ring.

Aymer barked and ran in a circle around her legs.

She clasped her hands beneath her chin and bent her head. The tournament was going to be a great success. How could her people not love Maximilian now that they'd met him in person and seen his prowess? And what was more, she had assured them of his authority, meaning he would get the respect he deserved.

"And now," Maximilian shouted, "let the tournament festivities continue!"

CHAPTER FIFTEEN

T HE RACES AND games and jousting went on for several more hours with pauses for displays of floor combat and archery and a free tourney. Philip brought out his new falcon and demonstrated his mastery in the air, much to the crowd's delight.

When the sun began to slip into the western horizon and the air chilled, Mary stood.

Margaret and Jeanne did the same.

"I am ready to depart," Mary said. "We have had quite the entertainment all day, but now I will leave my people to enjoy themselves."

"Very good, Your Grace," Jeanne said, holding up a furred cloak for Mary to put around her shoulders.

Along with Margaret, they headed back to the palace. The peacock strutted around, tail spread and squawking, no doubt cross that his territory had been invaded so thoroughly and by so many.

After climbing the sprawling set of stone steps to the front entrance, Aymer bounding ahead, they entered the dim foyer. Candles had been lit and a fire was coming to life in the huge hearth.

"Yes! Yes! We will do it now. This is the perfect time!"

She heard Maximilian's booming voice before she saw him.

"Perfect time?" Jeanne repeated. "For what?"

"I have no idea." Mary came to a halt. She'd thought he'd gone to the stables with Lars to check on the horses.

"While the good people of Burgundy are here, so many of them.

Gather the horses, gather the weapons, tell the nobles..." Maximilian stormed from the Aula Magna, his boots banging hard on the stone flooring with each footstep. "Ah, Mary, good. I need to speak with you on a matter of great import."

"I am supposing you have had another great idea when in the Aula Magna, dear husband. It is clearly a suitable environment for your thinking."

He tapped the side of his head. "Indeed I have." He was highly charged, like a storm cloud brewing up energy or a wild stallion preparing to break free. "And this idea will be put into immediate action."

"Pray tell me this idea," she asked, watching him pace, his sword bouncing off his thigh.

"Yes. Yes. Of course." He seemed preoccupied, as though thoughts were tumbling into his brain and he was sorting them as they arrived. "We are going to war. Now. We will defeat Louis with a swiftness that will leave him dizzy." He turned to Philip, who had walked out behind him, along with Lars. "The way you were left, when I struck you from your horse, Philip. So fast, you knew nothing about it."

Philip bobbed his head. "Yes, Your Grace."

"And we will strike when he least expects it, now, when he likely believes a tournament is taking up all of our attention."

She'd never seen him so excited about something—about something that really *wasn't* a good idea. In fact, it was horrifying. "But, Maximilian, you said it would take time to train the farmers to fight."

"They will know what to do when the time comes. It is not that hard to point a pike or wield a dagger." He gestured to Lars. "Don't you think?"

"Yes, Your Grace."

"Don't just say, 'Yes, Your Grace' because you don't want to contradict my husband." Mary pointed at Lars. "I know you to be stronger than that."

Lars folded his arms. "King Louis must be defeated. Now is as good a time as any." He tipped his chin. "As Maximilian has suggested."

"This is madness." Margaret shook her head. "Utter madness."

"Indeed it is." Jeanne kissed her rosary and then clasped it and sent a prayer heavenward.

"Now is not a good time to go to war." Hugo rushed forward, Melchior at his side. "Adequate preparations have not been made. They really haven't. There is still so much to do."

"I beg to differ," Maximilian said haughtily. "It is all I have been doing for weeks. Preparing."

Tension filled Mary's shoulders, tightening her neck and jaw. It felt as though her blood were heating, anger and frustration a hot, toxic mix. It would be a slaughter, she was sure of it. It couldn't be allowed to happen.

But how could she stop it? How could she make her husband see sense?

She pulled in a deep breath and willed herself calm.

"You can go," she said quietly to Maximilian, a plan forming in her mind. "But you must come and say goodbye to me."

"I bid you farewell, my love." He stepped forward, arms held open.

"No." She dodged out of his way, glancing at Hugo and the cleric as she did so. "Privately, in our bedchamber. You must bid me farewell there."

"Why?" Maximilian raised his eyebrows at her.

"I wish to say goodbye to you in private before you go to battle. Without curious eyes upon us." She paused. "Would you deny me that?"

"No, I will never deny you. Not a single thing." He grinned. "Go ahead. I will be there in but a few heartbeats."

Maximilian strode into the Aula Magna once again—a whirlwind of energy and purpose.

"Your Grace," Hugo said quietly with his hands clasped. "Please, you must make the duke see sense. I beg of you. I pray to God that you will stop this madness."

Mary looked at Philip. "You can't really believe this is a good idea, Philip."

Philip shook his head. "No, Your Grace, I fear it will be a bloody massacre. Louis's men are strong after a restful and plentiful summer and are ready and waiting on the front. I have heard they have congregated in great numbers."

"But it is what he wants." Lars frowned. "And he is the Duke of Burgundy, is he not? You have just shown off his prowess to the people. He must have what he desires, even if that is war."

"Even a duke can't always have what he wants." Mary bit on her bottom lip and frowned.

"Please help us, Your Grace," Melchior said. "He will listen to you, I am certain. Allow God to lead us with common sense." He flattened his palms together and closed his eyes.

"I think you should listen to the advisors," Margaret said, gently touching Mary's forearm. "We do not wish to have the blood of our people on our hands."

"I *have* listened," Mary said, lifting up her gown an inch so that her feet were free to climb the stairs. "And do not fear, Hugo, I, your duchess, will manage this situation *and* my husband."

"Yes, Your Grace." Hugo nodded, his cheeks wobbling. "I hope that you can."

"Do not doubt me." She narrowed her eyes at him.

"I am sorry, Your Grace." He looked at the floor. "I do not doubt you. As God is my witness, I do not."

Mary walked to the staircase.

"Let me come with you," Jeanne said. "Your husband is in a most fractious and excitable mood. Goodness knows what he will do."

"No, Jeanne. I wish you to go outside and stand beneath my window."

"I beg your pardon?" Her eyes widened.

"You heard. Now please, go. Take Aymer and await me. Right beneath my bedchamber window."

"Yes, Your Grace." Jeanne bobbed her head, then rushed for the main entrance, clicking her fingers for Aymer to follow.

"Do you know what you are doing?" Margaret fretted as she climbed the stairs a step behind Mary.

"I know my husband. So yes, I know exactly what I am doing."

"Then I wish you luck and will be at your disposal if you need me."

"I suggest you see that the banquet is prepared for our honorable guests."

"You mean…?"

"The feasting and dancing will go ahead, Margaret. So yes, that is exactly what I mean." Mary stopped, took her stepmother's hand, and squeezed. "Do not be surprised to know that I can take care of things when necessary. I have learned from the many strong women who came before me and who surround me now. I am quite capable."

"I do not doubt you for a second, my strong and wise daughter." She kissed Mary's cheek. "For that is what I see you as, my daughter, and you should know you are one of the dearest people on God's Earth to me."

"As are you to me." Mary held her stepmother's hand for a moment, then made her way to her bedchamber.

Once there, she was relieved to see Jupiter hadn't been returned yet. Philip likely had stored him with the other falcons.

She stoked the fire and then removed her headwear, allowing her hair to tumble free the way she knew Maximilian liked it. Quickly, she added a dab of rosewater to her wrists and neck, then slipped off her shoes.

The door flew open. "My love. I am here to bid you farewell." Maximilian strode into the room, his footsteps heavy and his arms wide for her embrace.

"Oh, husband of mine, I pray it is not our last goodbye... a goodbye forever." She rushed past him to the door and closed it. "For war is a dangerous game." She turned the key, locking them in. "Battle is bloody and bitter."

"It is not a game. I fear you have spent too many hours watching displays today."

"Perhaps you are right." Quickly, she moved past him, to the window, clutching the long key in her hot hand.

"You wish for a memory of my body joining with yours?" he said, watching her. "Is that why you insisted on private time in the bedchamber?"

"You know me so well, dear husband." She opened the window and peered out.

Jeanne stood beneath, staring up, the breeze catching the lace hanging from her hennin.

"What are you doing?" Maximilian stepped toward her.

She didn't answer him. Instead, she held the key out of the window at arm's length, hesitated for a second, and then released it.

Jeanne caught the key just as Maximilian reached the window.

"What in God's name are you doing?" he demanded again as he looked outside.

But he knew—she could see it in his eyes. He knew exactly what she'd done. What her very devious and calculated move had been.

"You've locked us in." He stormed to the door and yanked on it, rattling it on its hinges. "I can barely believe your brazenness, wife."

"It is for the best." She straightened and pulled in a deep breath.

"For the best?" he roared. "I have a war to win. A battle to march to." Again, he yanked at the door.

But it was no good. It was solid and strong, designed to prevent intruders entering a duchess's bedchamber and, as it turned out, just as good at locking a duchess and her husband within.

"Lars! Hugo! Philip." Maximilian hammered on the door with his fist. "I demand you let me out. Find that key. Now!"

Mary undid the buttons on her gown, her movements quick and deft.

Maximilian shouted louder, then removed his sword as though it were hampering his efforts. He slammed it onto a nearby table and a vase clattered to the floor, spilling the flowery contents in a puddle of water.

Mary allowed her gown to slip free of her arms, then pushed it so it pooled around her feet.

"There must be someone out there. Go and find the key, I command you," Maximilian shouted. "Whoever it is who can hear me. I command you to unlock this door."

Mary removed her undergarment and let it also land around her feet. She then took a step forward, the cool air washing over her flesh and tightening her nipples. Her heart raced and her breath hitched. She felt small and vulnerable and hoped she hadn't underestimated her husband's desire for her.

"Maximilian," she said as calmly as she could.

"Mary, I implore you, go and tell Jeanne to…" He spun around.

He froze, as though a spell had been cast on him. His eyes widened and his jaw hung slack.

"Maximilian," she said again, pushing her hair back over her shoulders. "Can you think of something more interesting to do this very evening other than marching to war?"

"You…You…" He leaned back, hard, against the door and stared at her like a man seeing an angel sent from heaven.

His attention was like a heated caress and her skin goosepimpled. "I what, Maximilian? What are you trying to say?"

"You are utterly naked."

"You have seen me naked before."

"Not like this, unexpected, in the middle of the bedchamber, with night not yet upon us."

"Are you complaining?" She cupped her right breast and flicked her thumb over her nipple. Jutted her hips to the left.

"No, I am not complaining," he said quickly and then he glanced at the window. "So you locked me in and disposed of the key so you could..."

Slowly, she stepped up to him, close, and touched his cheek. "So I could what?"

He stared down at her, his eyes flashing and his breaths coming quick.

"So I could seduce you?" she whispered, then she brushed her lips over his.

He didn't answer. He didn't kiss her back.

"It has been an exciting day, Maximilian." She ran her hand from his cheek down his neck to his abdomen, feeling the taut muscles beneath his tunic. "And you have dazzled me with your prowess and strength." She slipped her fingers over the waistband of his breeches. "I do not want you to leave me for war. I want you to stay with me. Can you blame me for wanting you after your daring performance and show of skill?"

"I have a war to fight and win," he said, his voice gritty and dark. His eyebrows pulled low. "As you well know."

"And do you think you can fight in this state?" She slid her hand lower and cupped his groin. "With this?"

His cock was semi-hard and she squeezed it gently.

"Lord, help me," he said. "You are a most devious wife."

"I simply adore my husband and wish for his pleasure, not pain." She went onto her tiptoes and kissed him again, tracing the shape of his cock with her fingers as she did so.

He groaned and kissed her back. In that moment, she knew she had him. Thoughts of war and marching and gathering his army were seeping from his mind like sand through his fingers.

With a sense of triumph she pushed at his tunic, rucking it up his chest. He clutched it in his fist and tore it off. It landed beside his sword.

Cupping his groin, she peppered kisses over his neck, his stubble scratching her lips and his heavy scent filling her nose. Her nipples grazed his warm chest.

He groaned and his cock grew harder still.

"My dear husband," she said, smiling up at him as she slipped her hand inside his breeches. "You could take a man clear off his horse with this big lance."

CHAPTER SIXTEEN

MAXIMILIAN GRIPPED HIS wife's left buttock and held it firmly. "Dear Lord, I have never seen you like this. Never heard you speak in this brazen way."

"You have stoked a desire in me even I did not know existed." She squeezed his hard length. "I want you. I want you now, my big, brave warrior."

Maximilian's heart was racing and lust raged through his veins. His wife was more beautiful in this moment than he'd ever seen her. Her pupils were wide, her lips pink and glossy, and a rise of red upon her cheeks glowed like apples. But it was more than that. It was the confidence in her hold on his cock and her unabashed *need* for him that had really gotten him riled up for her.

She stroked his length—a long, firm slide of her hand, her small fingers warm and dexterous.

He groaned and let his head fall back to the door, closing his eyes. It was tempting to grab her, throw her to the bed, and take them both to a wild, wet, screaming pleasure. But he didn't want this moment to end. Her slight, naked body pressed to his and her sweet kisses peppering his neck was a fantasy he hadn't known he'd had.

Until now.

"You like that?" she murmured, caressing the tip of his cock.

"Yes…"

"Then I'm sure you're going to love this."

He felt her sliding downward and watched as she sank to her knees, her pale shoulders so delicate below him. "My love…?"

"Shh… Just feel." She'd repeated words to him that he'd once said to her as she'd pulled at his breeches, lifting the waist over his erection and pushing the material to his thighs.

"Oh, dear Lord," he whispered as her sweet breath washed over his cock. Surely, she wasn't going to do what he thought she was. She was his wife, the duchess, a God-loving woman.

And then she looked up at him with the most sinful smile he'd ever seen upon her, licked her lips, and swiped her tongue up the length of his cock.

He gasped, locking his knees and running his fingers into her hair, holding the strands tight. She was going to do what he'd thought…hoped.

"Relax, Maximilian, I want to do this," she murmured, cupping his balls. "Let me taste you the way you taste me."

"Mary…I…" He lost the ability to form words as she opened her mouth and took him into the warm heat, sliding him onto her tongue and pursing her lips.

He groaned and his buttocks clenched, his abdomen tightening to stone. But still, he watched as his cock disappeared into her graceful mouth, slowly, deliciously, erotically.

He fought the urge to push deep and feel the back of her throat and instead let out a long, low groan. "My love…"

When he felt like he was filling her, she sucked gently. It was almost his undoing and he released her hair, splaying his fingers on the door, for fear he would take control and hurt her with his enthusiasm. "Mary…oh…yes…"

She pulled back, keeping her lips tight and her tongue hugging his length. But she didn't withdraw completely and within a few seconds was sliding back down, taking him again. Playing with his balls, rolling them, teasing him.

Pressure was building fast, his cock needy and solid, but he remained perfectly still, taking it, taking what she was giving him the way he'd demanded of her.

Until he began to leak his pleasure into her mouth.

"My love," he managed through clenched teeth. "You are making... me feel... too good."

She pulled back, catching his cock in her hand. "Is there such a thing?"

"There is when you are not in the same moment of bliss as I am." He reached for her, cupping her underarms and dragging her to standing. "We will find pleasure together."

He caught her mouth in a needy kiss, urgency suddenly gripping him. And when he pulled her close, he kept going, lifting her up, his hands slapping onto her buttocks.

She locked her legs around his waist and clasped her arms about his neck. And then he found himself walking to the bed, barely hindered by his breeches, even though they'd fallen to his knees. He stroked his tongue against hers, a wild dance that had him breathless.

The breath puffed from her as he dropped to the bed, her beneath him, but she didn't break the kiss. She moaned and arched upward, toward him, offering her cunny to his cock.

And his cock was there. He found purchase on her sweet, wet entrance and drove into the tightness. She felt so good, he was sure he was losing his mind. Hot and gripping, delicate yet strong.

"Oh, Maximilian," she gasped into his mouth.

"You said you wanted me," he managed, "that I had stoked your desire."

"Yes. Oh, yes...please... I want you."

"As I want you, today and always." He groaned and hit full depth. A full body tremble went through him and he caught her right breast in his palm, squeezing it.

She groaned and fluttered her eyes closed. Her cunny was quivering around his length.

"Find your pleasure quickly," he said against her lips. "Because you have me on the edge. Seeing your pretty mouth full of my cock has me on the brink of ecstasy."

"I want my pleasure," she said, rolling her hips and connecting their bodies in a circular motion.

"Yes. Like that." He caught her rhythm, knowing he was stimulating her little bud. "You are the most beautiful and giving woman I could have ever hoped to marry. I love you so much."

"Oh…oh…yes, oh, I love you…" Her breaths were quickening, her body slick with perspiration against his.

"That's it…like that…" he said, gritting his teeth and willing his release to hold off for a little while longer.

"Oh! Maximilian…I…" She slapped her hands onto his buttocks and gripped tight, bucking up to meet him as a long wail left her mouth.

"In the name of…" He closed his eyes as her first spasm of bliss contracted around his cock, finally allowing his own pleasure to release.

With a gruff cry and an unholy shout to the Lord, his seed burst from him. The relief and satisfaction was instant and he rode with it, working Mary through her orgasm.

She gasped and moaned his name, then found his mouth for a desperate and intense kiss.

Still, he ground into her, her ecstasy seeming to extend as her body jerked against his.

"Oh, my…" she managed, panting and dragging her nails up his back. "I… That was…"

"Very scheming of you." He stared down at her, his hair hanging forward and his chest grazing her peaked nipples.

She stilled and stared up at him. Pushed a lock of hair back from his right eye. "I did not hear you complain."

"You will never hear me complain about seeing you naked, or bedding you any time of day or night."

She smiled, an almost smug smile, definitely one with a hint of triumph. "I believe even if we have ten, or twenty, children, we will still join whenever we can. This is about more than creating heirs."

"Yes." He ducked and kissed her chest, from one breast to the other. "This is about love and adoration."

She ran her hands into his hair and sighed as she let her legs slip from the backs of his. "Is it so wrong that sometimes I wish the rest of the world would disappear and we could just live here, in this room, alone? Just you and I."

"It is not wrong to wish problems away."

"But it's more than that, sometimes…"

"What?"

"I know you have much to discuss with your advisors and aides, that we have a large and noble land to protect, but I wish we spent more time together."

"You do?" He stared down at her again, searching her eyes.

"It is selfish of me. I am sorry." She looked away.

"No, don't be sorry. We promised to always be honest with each other. That is all you are doing." He gently turned her to face him again.

She smiled. "I do remember that day."

"Yes. I need to know how you feel, and if you feel like we should be together more, then that is what will happen."

"It is?" She cupped his face.

"Yes, that is my promise to you."

"Good." Suddenly, she grinned. "Can we start now?"

"Now?"

"Yes. Let us feast and dance the night away. Side by side. In a room full of many, but with eyes only for each other."

"You wish to *dance*? After the way you have just tricked me?" He raised his eyebrows.

"It was not a trick. Simply a way to give you time to realize what you really wanted to do this night."

"Which is?"

"To be with me."

He chuckled. It was impossible to be mad at his wife, despite her deception. She was his everything.

"Maximilian, my love." She brushed her lips over his. "Please say we can go and dance. No more talk of war, not tonight."

He was quiet.

"While you organized the tournament, it was I who planned the banquet," she said. "Is it fair that while I have watched the tournament, you do not then feast and enjoy the music and dances I have arranged?"

Suddenly, a chuckle caught in his throat and he pulled out and rolled to her side. He reached for her hand and kissed her knuckles. "You have an answer for everything, my Grand Dame, and a logical one at that."

"So we can go dancing?" She kissed his cheek.

"Yes. Yes, my love. We will go dancing. But first, you must dress. Only I am allowed to see you naked, today and tomorrow and forevermore."

>>><<<

MAXIMILIAN DANCED AT his wife's side enjoying how she laughed and moved and gripped his hand so tightly, he thought she'd never let him go.

He feasted on suckling pig and applesauce, salted bread, and mustard. Figs, almonds, and walnuts were washed down with wine. Mary ate modestly though inconspicuously, a habit she hadn't been able to break, for she feared looking greedy.

When the sky had lightened to pink and lilac and the birds had begun to sing, the band stopped playing.

All around them, guests lolled and talked, their voices a little slurred by tiredness and wine.

Lars had disappeared some time ago. Maximilian noticed Jeanne was also absent.

"Do you think they are together?" he asked Mary after pointing this out.

"Do you?"

"I know he is very fond of her. Though I can't say I am after she had a hand in your plot to trap me."

Mary laughed. "She was quick to open the door upon my instruction."

"But not upon mine."

"Perhaps she is more *my* friend."

He chuckled and refilled their goblets of wine. "It is a blessing to have good friends. I am always grateful for mine."

"I agree." She turned to the door. "Here is Lars, after we were just talking of him."

Lars strode across the room, his strides purposeful. He was holding a white scroll with a scarlet seal.

"What do you have?" Maximilian stood.

"It has just arrived by envoy." Lars was slightly breathless. "I saw him coming at great speed and stopped him at the palace steps."

"Whose envoy?"

"He stated the King of France."

"Louis?" Mary stood at his side. "What does it say?"

"It is unopened." Lars handed the scroll forward. "It is addressed to Maximilian of Austria, the Duke of Burgundy."

Maximilian snatched it and tore at the seal. Flakes of cracked wax dropped to the floor. Quickly, he pushed aside a tray of cheese and pickles and spread the scroll out.

Lars and Mary crowded on either side of him as he read the words.

"It is a cessation in hostilities," Mary said after a few moments. "He wants to stop the fighting."

"And the advance." Lars pushed his hand through his blond hair, sending it sticking up in all directions. "But why?"

"It is because of the letter I sent him." Maximilian pulled in a deep breath, his chest puffing up. "He knows I am not to be underestimated. I am not Charles the Bold. I am Archduke Maximilian of Austria and the new Duke of Burgundy."

"He is scared," Lars said. "You are a new, young and brave adversary. He is retreating and seeking time to plan his next move and to see what you do."

"And time is what we need," Mary said. "If our army is to be funded and trained." She squeezed Maximilian's hand. "This could not have come at a better moment."

He nodded and thought of his plan only hours ago to gather his men, and the farmers, and storm to the front. It was a good twist of fate that he had not, for this letter might have gone unseen. Lives could have already been lost. Good men sent to heaven.

Mary ran her fingertip over his name on the scroll.

"Thank you," he said to her.

"For what?"

"You know for what, my love. You know exactly for what."

CHAPTER SEVENTEEN

MARY LOOKED OUT of the window at the sparkling hills and frosty forest. "It has snowed all night." She turned to Maximilian, who was drinking hot mead in bed. Aymer lay over his feet. "We should go out. The first snow of the winter is magical. Before all the hoof and cart trails and the slushy, muddy puddles have arrived."

"I think I would rather stay in the warm." He nodded at the fire, which had been recently restoked and was blazing happily.

"We can return to the warm."

"I have scrolls to read, and I must write a letter to the States of Flanders once again asking for money to fund our army."

"Yes, yes, you do that." She picked up her bell to ring for Jeanne. "You do that and I will go out." She paused, a wicked, little voice prodding her. "And I will skate with Jeanne, Margaret, and Philip if the lake is frozen. We always enjoy skating. It is somewhat of a tradition each winter."

"Philip?"

"Oh, yes, he is rather good at skating." She rang the bell.

"Then I will also come. I should become good at this skating too." He paused and studied her. "If it is something you enjoy."

"I do, and you did promise to spend more time doing things with me." She rushed up to him and pressed a quick kiss to his lips. "Hurry, we do not have the luxury of many hours of daylight."

He went to grab her but was hindered by his drink and the dog.

"Hey."

She skipped away, snatching up a fur hat as she went and plonking it on her un-brushed hair. "Come, my love. I am sure you will be most talented on the ice the way you are at everything else you do."

"You should believe it."

An hour later, Mary stood with her stepmother, Margaret, as well as Jeanne, Philip, Lars, and Maximilian by the east lake. It was partially surrounded by fir trees and their branches hung resignedly under the heavy weight of snow.

A skein of geese flew overhead, honking loudly. In the distance, smoke rose from the palace chimneys.

"Do you think it is solid enough?" Jeanne asked, tapping the icy surface with the curled, iron toe of her skate.

"I will test it," Philip said, gingerly stepping onto the gleaming, white surface.

Mary held her breath. Once Philip's brother, John, had fallen in when testing it. He'd been quite blue by the time they'd returned to the palace and he'd shivered for the rest of the day.

"It is solid around the edge," Philip said, pushing off on his skates. "I will check the center."

"Be careful," Mary called after him.

Aymer barked and rushed onto the ice, his feet slipping and sliding, but he didn't seem to care as he raced after Philip.

"He is going quite fast," Lars commented, then he worried on his bottom lip.

"It's easy once you have your balance." Jeanne smiled at him. "Come, I'll hold your hand."

"I do not wish to pull you over."

Lars was so tall next to Jeanne, with his broad shoulders and heavy cape, he would surely squash her should he fall and land on her.

"You won't," she said, stepping onto the ice. "Here."

Mary watched as they moved, with both grace and no grace, onto the slippery surface.

"How hard can it be?" Maximilian huffed as he watched Philip shoot from left to right, examining the ice as he went and avoiding Aymer, who was scampering around and having a wonderful time.

"It is not difficult once you have been doing it for a few minutes." Margaret stepped onto the ice, arms held slightly out, then slid into a dance-like rhythm.

"Are you ready?" Mary asked.

"Of course." Maximilian stepped onto the ice, his big feet clumsy in his new skates.

"Be careful," she said, following him. "It does take getting used to."

"If Philip can do it, I can." He pushed forward, concentration etched on his face. His brow furrowed.

"Yes, but Philip has been skating since he was a child and... Oh...be careful."

Maximilian had lurched to the right and his arms were windmilling as he attempted to keep his balance. His hot breath puffed in front of his face.

Mary rushed up to him and took his hand.

He gripped it tightly and steadied himself. "Who in God's good name made ice so slippery?"

"God Himself." She giggled.

He huffed. "I am sure I will not need to hold on to you in just a moment."

"Of course. Look, just move your legs like this and let your feet glide." She pushed forward but kept hold of him. "Like walking but without stepping."

He attempted to follow her but once again became unbalanced. This time, he couldn't right himself and as his feet flew out from under him, he released her hand so as not to drag her down.

He landed with a hard thump, the air knocking from him in a loud grunt.

"Maximilian." She rushed to him.

"Is he hurt?" Philip was suddenly there.

"No, I am not hurt." Maximilian snapped and maneuvered to his hands and knees. "I will master this skating presently." His knees skidded to the right and he struggled to stay on all fours.

"Let me help you," Philip said, reaching for his arm.

"No." Maximilian pushed his hand away and got into a crouch. Tentatively, he stood again, his torso wobbling as he battled to maintain the upright position.

"Do you have your balance?" Mary asked.

"Naturally." He pointed forward. "Come, we will skate to the other side of the lake."

"Are you sure?" Philip said. "You are just learning and it is a long way."

"Do not seek to tell me what to do." Maximilian frowned at Philip. "Mary. Let us go."

Once again, he pushed forward. This time, his landing was even more spectacular. He seemed to lift into the air before slamming onto his buttocks, legs akimbo, and arms spread wide like a star. He grunted loudly and his palms slapped onto the ice.

"This is a imbecilic pursuit," he shouted, his cheeks red and his cloak hanging at an angle. "I will not give it any more of my time."

"But, my love, you will soon be able to do it."

"I will not, and it is not because I cannot learn, it is because I do not *want* to learn." He brushed ice from his breeches. "I am returning to the palace. I have things of much import to attend to. This"—he gestured to the skating figures—"is clearly a whimsical pastime."

"Shall I help, Your Grace?" Philip asked, again holding out his hand.

"I do not need your help." Maximilian managed to get to his feet. He then proceeded to slowly shuffle, arms outstretched to the shoreline.

"I will dine with you later, my love," Mary called after him.

He didn't answer. When he'd reached the shore, he adjusted his cape and cap and began to stomp toward the palace. A courtier rushed behind him, along with Aymer, who'd clearly had enough of the cold on his paws.

"He is frustrated," Philip said. "That he isn't able to skate with confidence on his first try."

"It is not his fault," Mary said, wishing he'd had a little more patience in learning a new pursuit. "He's used to being not just proficient at everything he does, but also talented."

"He doesn't have natural talent for skating, it is true, but still he was a wise choice for a husband." Philip held out his arm. "Shall we?"

"Yes, thank you." She slipped her hand into the crook of Philip's elbow. "I was not sure if you would approve, when I took him in marriage."

"He is very suitable, if not financially. I believe he will be a strong leader of your country and people. King Louis has already requested to lay down arms. That would not have happened were it not for Maximilian and his standing."

"Yes, I agree."

"And whatever you did to persuade him not to go to war that night of the banquet, after the tournament... You are owed a great debt by many."

Her cheeks flushed, not from cold, but at the memory of kneeling before her husband and utterly distracting him. Quickly, she changed the subject. "It will be Christmas soon. Will John join us?"

"Yes, I believe he is traveling to Coudenberg as we speak."

"Oh, I am pleased to be seeing him. And he will be an enormous help with the new birds."

"Indeed."

They skated past Lars and Jeanne. Lars was doing surprisingly well.

"Maximilian should have tried for a little longer," Jeanne said. "He couldn't have been on the ice for more than five minutes."

"But he is also right to return. He has much to attend to," Philip said. "The weight upon his shoulders is large for a man so young."

"You speak in his favor despite his short temper with you earlier," Mary said.

"Of course, I am loyal to Burgundy and he is duke." He smiled at her. "I am loyal to *both* of you and I hope that one day, he will see me as a friend and ally. I wish to help him in war and trade. I believe I have local knowledge that he could make use of."

She sighed. "I am sorry he picked you out to be in the first game at the tournament."

Philip laughed. "I am not. It is what he wanted."

"And so if it pleased him, it pleased you?"

"If I'd had a chance to knock him from his steed, I would have. I wanted to win, don't get me wrong. I am a competitive man also."

"That would have made him angrier. If you'd won."

They'd reached the end of the lake so turned and started on their way up the west shore.

"Is he often angry?" Philip asked.

Mary said nothing.

"I am sorry. I should not speak to you this way about your husband. You are a married woman now. It is not as it was when we were growing up. When we laughed and shared jests and told each other stories about our dreams."

"Do not apologize, dear Philip." She squeezed his arm. "And in answer to your question no, he is not an angry man. Maximilian laughs more than he frowns. His words and deeds are kind and thoughtful. I have been blessed with a devoted and loyal husband I not only care for, but admire and love."

"That has made me very happy." Philip smiled. "To hear you say that. Really. I cannot tell you how happy I am for you, for him too."

"It is a truth." She nodded at the palace. "I am getting cold. I think it is time to return."

"Of course. I will accompany you if that is agreeable."

"Yes, thank you."

He helped her onto a waiting sleigh, then handed her a fox fur with which to cover her knees. "Back to the palace, driver," he instructed.

On the journey, Mary admired the snowy landscape. It never failed to thrill her, and now with the sound of bells jingling on the horses' reins, she was transported back through time to many happy childhood moments with Margaret at her side and riding through the frosty trails spotting eagles, bears, and deer just for the sheer delight of it.

When they arrived at the palace, they changed into their boots and Philip walked with her up the steps and toward the main entrance. It had been swept clear of snow and two blazing outdoor fires burned on either side of the door in iron caskets.

When she stepped inside, onto a rug, she stamped her feet to rid them of the snow.

Philip laughed. "That is your habit, Duchess, but there is no snow on your boots."

She looked down and also laughed. "You are right. I am remembering our days playing outside and coming in through the side entrance. We were often covered from head to toe."

His grin broadened. "They were fun times. Always. Always with you."

"What in God's name is going on?" Maximilian suddenly appeared before them. He'd removed his cloak and in his dark clothes in the dark hallway, he seemed to loom larger than life from the shadows. Broad-shouldered, and his face marred with frown lines, he appeared tense and irritated. "Tell me. This instant. What. Is. Going. On?"

CHAPTER EIGHTEEN

"MAXIMILIAN," MARY SAID, her laughter fading.

Philip's laughter also stopped, though he stayed standing closer to her.

Maximilian's attention wasn't on Mary—it was concentrated solely on Philip.

"What is going on?" he demanded again, each word carefully enunciated.

"Whatever do you mean?" Mary asked, her heart rate picking up. She'd just described her husband as a jovial man, yet here he was before them with an expression that could only be described as thunderous.

"I want to know," Maximilian said, his jaw tight, "why this man"—he pointed at Philip—"believes it is acceptable to laugh and joke with my wife. To touch you, to enter our bedchamber and—"

"'Enter our bedchamber'?" Mary said, looking between the two men.

Philip had raised his chin and puffed up his chest. He didn't look at all intimidated by Maximilian and she feared that would anger her husband further.

"He is always back and forth with Jupiter and if you recall, I expressly said no man other than I was to cross the threshold."

"But he is doing his job and—"

"Enough!" Maximilian clenched his fists. His cheeks had reddened.

Lord Ravenstein, Hugo, and Melchior stepped up behind Maximilian.

Hugo was holding a quill aloft as though he'd been midway through writing and come to see what was going on.

"Is there a problem?" Melchior asked, stepping from one foot to the other and back again in an anxious, hopping motion.

"Yes, there is a problem." Maximilian took a step closer to Philip. "I believe this man wishes to take my wife as his own."

Philip held Maximilian's steely eye contact. "I promise you, Your Grace, that is not the case."

"You were a potential marriage match, were you not?"

"It is true," Lord Ravenstein said, coming to stand at his son's side and studying Maximilian. "But it was not to be. The duchess chose you, Your Grace."

"I think that Philip…" Maximilian jabbed his finger on Philip's chest.

Philip didn't move, didn't even blink, though a tendon flexed in his cheek.

Maximilian went on. "That you have plans on wheedling your way into Mary's affections more than you already have."

"*Maximilian*," Mary said. "Philip and I grew up together. When his father married Anne, he and John came to—"

"Exactly," Maximilian said. "They lived here, with you, and so Philip thinks you are his." He sucked in a breath. "And I am here to tell him you are not. You are mine. You are my wife. My lover. And you will be the mother of my children. I will not have other men sniffing around you like wolves in heat."

"'Wolves in heat'?" Philip repeated. "Your Grace, that is not the case. I wish only to serve, to assist, and to convince you of my loyalty."

"You are a scheming weasel who—"

"I am *not* a scheming weasel." Philip clenched his fists. "And I will ask you to take that back because it is unfounded."

Maximilian made a strange, throaty, growling sound. "You dare to order me what to do?"

"I would ask that you not slander my name."

"Please, Maximilian, let us go beside the fire." Mary touched his arm, but he shook it off.

"No. Not until Philip apologizes to me."

"For what?" Philip's eyebrows were pulled low. His eyes narrowed.

"For being too familiar with my wife. For entering our bedchamber. And for presuming you can order me, Maximilian of Austria, your duke, to do your bidding." He took a step even closer, their chests almost touching. "Apologize. Now."

Philip said nothing, just stared steadily at Maximilian.

They were almost exactly the same height, Maximilian being a fraction taller. Anger and pride radiated from them, seeming to shimmer off their big bodies in waves.

"I am waiting." Maximilian growled.

"I will not apologize," Philip said, his voice steady and calm, "for maintaining a friendship with my cousin. I will also not apologize for caring for her animals, as she has entrusted me to do so."

Maximilian's fists clenched tighter. "You refuse me? Your disrespect is…" He didn't finish the sentence. Instead, he drew back his arm and punched Philip square in the face.

Philip reeled backward, but only for a second because then he threw his own punch, hitting Maximilian across the jaw.

Mary let out a squeal and rushed away from the explosion of energy, only to have Hugo steady her when she bumped into him.

Maximilian stared at Philip in what seemed to be disbelief, and then he swung a right hook into the side of Philip's face. But Philip was ready and managed to partially dodge it, retaliating with a thump to Maximilian's chest.

Air rushed from him in a wild, animalistic growl, then he ducked his head like a charging bull and rushed at Philip.

He took him to the floor at full speed. Arms flew. Legs kicked. Grunts. Gasps. The sickening sound of flesh on flesh.

"Stop! Stop this!" Mary shouted.

Lord Ravenstein rushed to the brawling men. He grabbed Philip, preventing him from delivering what would have been a teeth-cracking punch.

Melchior was also in the fray, tugging at Maximilian. Two courtiers jumped in to help drag Maximilian away.

Philip went much easier, with just his father's hand around his upper arm. He swiped at his bleeding bottom lip.

"I haven't finished." Maximilian tried to shake the hands and arms pulling him away from Philip. "Let me at him." His right eye was already swelling and a drip of blood trickled from his nose. His tunic was torn at the neckline.

"No." Mary rushed between the two men, her palms held out as if to stop them from coming close again. "This is preposterous. What are you doing?"

"Reminding this man who is your husband," Maximilian said, his eyes flashing.

"He knows full well you are my husband. Don't you, Philip?"

"Of course, Your Grace." He dipped his head. "And I would never come between a man and his wife."

"See…" She turned to Maximilian. "You have got the wrong end of the stick. We are friends, Philip and I, nothing more. And I had hoped…" She scowled. "That you would be friends with Philip instead of knocking him off horses, snapping rudely at him, and now starting a fight with him."

"Get off me." Maximilian growled and shook like a dog, easily flicking the holding hands from his arms and shoulders.

"Philip could actually be an asset to your future plans," Mary went on, tilting her chin. "If you could just see past your jealousy."

Maximilian sniffed loudly. "I am not jealous."

"Oh, no?" She tipped her head and studied him. "That's not what I see."

"I will tell you what you see." He stepped up close to her. He was breathing fast, his eyes flashing dangerously. "You see a man who loves his wife and will not have any other man thinking that they may take her."

"Philip does not wish to take me. He told you that—I, oh…"

Suddenly, Mary found herself upside down, butt in the air, and staring at the floor. Maximilian had hoisted her over his shoulder and set his palm firmly over her bottom.

"Oh, dear Lord, put me down!" Her furred hat dropped to the ground and she gripped his thick, metal belt.

He didn't answer and he didn't put her down. Instead, he strode to the wide, stone staircase and started to climb them.

"We do not wish to be disturbed," he called in a low, commanding voice. "By any person or any animal."

A few seconds later, Maximilian kicked the bedchamber door closed behind him. The bang bellowed around the room. He marched to the bed.

"Put me down. I demand of you." Mary gasped the words. Her husband had never behaved with such gruff determination and such unwarranted jealousy before. "Maximilian. Now. Put me down."

"As you wish."

For a moment, Mary was in the air, then she landed on the mattress with a soft *whump*. Her hair fell over her face, the cape fell to the floor, and her gown rucked up. She pushed to sitting.

"You are mine," he said, crowding over her. "Not Philip's. You are not anyone else's wife. You are mine."

Before she could answer, he kissed her, hard, his lips slightly tangy with sweat and blood and his breaths storming against her cheek.

She gripped his tunic, anger and frustration warring inside her as she kissed him back. She was furious with him but could not deny his kiss.

"Say it," he said, his nose touching hers. "Say that you are mine."

"I am yours, but—oh…"

He'd tipped her over, onto her stomach, his movements deft yet urgent. His big hands and strength made her feel like nothing more than a ragdoll. "There are no *buts*, Mary. You are mine and that is the end of the discussion."

"This is a discussion?" Breathlessly, she tried to push up to sitting, but he held her firm.

"No. Stay like that. I am going to prove to you that you are mine. That only *I* can give you everything you need."

"I don't know what you mean. Please, I…"

"You will." He pushed her gown up, higher, higher still, until it reached her bodice. The material bunched around her waist, her bare buttocks completely exposed.

His belt landed on the floor with a loud clatter, then he gripped her hips and pulled her to her hands and knees. "I am the only man who will ever enter your body," he said gruffly as he leant over her, his mouth by her ear. "Only me."

She gasped as his thick cock nudged at her entrance. "Oh!" Her eyes widened and she gripped the blanket beneath her. So this was what he'd meant by proving that she was his.

"Lord, give me strength." He grunted as he pushed in.

Unlike his usual, slower entry, this time, he drove in determinedly. Stretching her, taking her, not stopping until he reached full depth.

She let out a cry of need that mixed with a nip of discomfort at being invaded so unexpectedly, so thoroughly.

"You have made me a fool for love," he ground out. "A lunatic obsessed with his wife."

"Oh, Maximilian…" She arched her back as her cunny clenched around his hard length. "Oh, please…"

"You want me?"

"Yes. Yes. Always."

"Even like this?"

"Yes. I want you. Yesterday, today, and forevermore."

"Right answer." He pulled halfway out then surged back in.

"Oh...yes..." She moaned. He felt so good inside her. Hard and dense. But it was more than that for Mary. Knowing how much her husband loved her, *needed* her to the point of foolishness and wildness, made her blood run hotter than ever for him. "Oh...please...more." She sought out her nub and rubbed over it, the way he did sometimes with his fingers or tongue. "I want to...like this...I want to find pleasure."

"You will. We. Both. Will."

Over and over, flesh slapped on flesh, his hips beating to a wild tempo as he gripped hers. Air was pushed from her lungs with each thrust. Still she worked herself, the pressure building and the need for release growing.

"Oh, my love...my wife..." He gasped. "My cock is so hard for you."

"Don't stop...please...don't stop..." She arched her back, taking him deeper still, and stared at the window. But she barely noticed the snow clouds forming on the horizon or the single crow flying above a pine tree, because her vision was blurring. Her climax was almost there. Her arm ached, her spine was taut, her toes curled in her boots. Her body was a bow about to fire its arrow. "Yes. Yes. Oh..."

As she spiraled into bliss, Maximilian did the same. His fingers were pincers on her hips, holding her firm and exactly where he wanted her. His cock plundered deep and he let out a roar of satisfaction as it pulsed, releasing his seed.

Her breath caught in her throat as ecstasy burst through her nerves. She shook and trembled, her cunny squeezing and releasing around his cock, each flutter of her muscles sending new fingers of satisfaction winging over her skin. She was glad he had hold of her—it felt like pleasure might tear her apart, send her skittering into every corner of the room.

"Oh…my love." He bent over her, his cock buried deep, his balls pressing up against her cunny. "That felt…incredible. You are…"

"A very…forgiving wife," she said, twisting to press her cheek to his. She was breathing hard. Her pulse was loud in her ears.

"You think I must apologize for hoisting you over my shoulder and then ravaging you in the privacy of our bedchamber?"

"No."

"Then what?"

She wriggled forward, his cock slipping from her, and then turned to face him.

He grinned and crawled over her, pressing her to the bed.

"You must apologize to Philip. You were wretched to the poor man."

"There is nothing *poor* about him." He huffed.

"He is my friend, nothing more. And you"—she cupped his cheeks and frowned up at him—"have behaved abominably to him, from the moment you arrived."

"Is that what you really think?"

"Yes. I really do. It is most ungentlemanly."

He chuckled, his eyes sparkling. "Then, of course, if I have been ungentlemanly, I will apologize."

"And you will be courteous to him from this point on?"

"I am sure we will become the best of friends."

"Don't mock me." She scowled up at him.

He kissed her. "I would never mock you. I will make amends with Philip just as soon as I have come up with a plan to defeat King Louis once and for all."

"No." She shoved his shoulder.

He didn't budge.

"That might take a while. You will do it today. I insist."

"Will it make you happy if I do?" He raised his eyebrows.

"You know it will."

"Then consider it done, my sweet wife." He brushed his lips over hers. "That really was wild, huh? If we have just made an heir, I'd imagine he'll be quite the handful."

She laughed and pulled him close, enjoying the weight and heat of his body, and knowing that their love had so many levels, it would never get stale the way other marriages she'd seen had.

CHAPTER NINETEEN

MAXIMILIAN OPENED THE freshly delivered scroll and studied it. "Whom is it from?" Mary asked as she carefully laid glossy strands of holly along the mantel in their solar—the private room in which they were spending more and more time during the long, dark, winter evenings.

"On examining the seal, I'd say it's from the States of Flanders."

"Hopefully, it will be good news." She smiled at him, the shadows of the firelight dancing over her pale and delicate features.

"Good news at the beginning of the Christmas celebrations would be most welcome." Maximilian was quiet as he read the information contained. "Well, I never."

"What is it?" She came and stood beside his chair.

"It *is* good news. Finally, they have agreed to cooperate and my financial demands will be met." He pulled in a long breath, then blew it out. "This is a good start, is it not?"

"Yes. It really is." She ran her hand over his hair, then kissed his brow. "I am pleased. Sticking to their word is a sign that they are respecting you as their duke."

"Which pleases me greatly, but more than that, I can really start to arm our men. I believe the truce will melt with the winter frosts."

"I will pray that it does not."

He rerolled the scroll and set it down, turned to her, and placed his hands on her waist. "There is something else I predict will happen when the spring arrives."

"There is?" Still, she toyed with his hair, brushing the strands this way and that, something she was fond of doing when they were alone together. "Are you going to tell me?"

He leaned forward and kissed her belly, over her embroidered, red bodice. "A baby, perhaps?"

Her eyes softened and her lips curled in that demure way he loved so much. "And what makes you predict that?"

"You tease me so."

"I am just curious as to how you have come to this deduction, dear husband."

"You have not had menses for nearly three months now."

"You keep track?"

"It is not hard to count days." He paused. "Wasn't that something you demanded I could do before I even entered Ghent? Count?"

She laughed softly. "You are quite right that I wanted you to be numerate."

"And still, you avoid my question." He slid his hands up her waist and cupped her breasts.

Her breath hitched and her lips parted.

"You are tender here." He didn't say it as a question. "And you have had nothing for breakfast other than a few pieces of crystalized ginger this last two weeks."

"You know my appetite is not big."

"And now it is barely there at all." He stood and slipped his arms around her, pulling her delicate frame close. "You must have had the same thoughts."

"I will confess that I have."

"And have you spoken to Margaret? Jeanne?"

"Yes."

"And?" He searched her eyes, wanting desperately for his suspicions to be true.

"They have come to the same conclusion as you. That we will have an heir come the summer."

"Summer. That is good. Nice and warm for a babe." As he'd spoken, reality set in. His wife was pregnant. They were to become parents. Burgundy would have an heir. A son, if God was smiling down on them. "So you are…" He paused and shook his head. "You…are…"

"Pregnant." She raised her eyebrows.

"Yes, that." He swept his lips over hers. "But you are amazing. To think that our child grows and sleeps in you right now as we speak." He pulled back, holding her at arm's length, and directed his attention at her belly. "Our child, made by us and nurtured by you and you alone for these long months."

"I am sure I, in turn, will be well cared for."

"Yes, my love." Once again, he pulled her close. "You will want for nothing. You will have the best care, the best food, and all of my love and attention."

"That is kind, but I know you must give attention to the politics and troubles of our land."

"It is true, but you should know that my first love is you. You and our child." He pulled her close, wrapped her in his arms, and closed his eyes. How precious she was. How lucky he was.

He was so happy, he felt like he'd burst with it, that his heart would overflow.

Which terrified him. Because great joy could be taken away, and without Mary, without his child, he'd suffocate. Breathing would be impossible. Life would be unbearable.

⋙⋘

CHRISTMAS FESTIVITIES AT Coudenberg were an elaborate affair with many traditions Mary, Margaret, and Jeanne insisted upon. And as the twelve days rolled along, Maximilian enjoyed the break from matters of much import and relaxed into the feasting and dancing.

On the sixth day, he sat with both Lars and Philip before the fire. The hour was late. The women had retired. Aymer lay at his feet, hoping for scraps of meat from Maximilian's plate. He never should have started feeding the wiry dog that way.

"Has the money from Flanders arrived?" Lars asked.

"Yes." Maximilian drank from his goblet. "I find it frustrating, though, that I had to ask at all."

"I agree." Philip nodded and sat back, crossing his legs. "As duke, you should have been able to just take it."

"Exactly." Maximilian raised his goblet Philip's way, glad of his company now that the storm between them had blown itself out.

"And I fear you will have to ask again." Lars shook his head. "We will need more men, mercenaries, if we are to be victorious over France."

Maximilian frowned and thought of the farmers willing to fight for their land. "I fear you are right."

"Swiss and German," Philip said. "It will be our best hope."

"I agree with you." Maximilian nodded. "And if King Louis drives troops into Ronse, we will need all the soldiers money can buy."

"And all the money we can get our hands on to buy them." Lars drummed his fingers on the arm of the chair. "When should we ask the Estates for more?"

"As soon as possible, but not too soon," Maximilian said. "They have just given us much-needed funds. We don't want to appear greedy or make it seem that we need an endless amount."

"Yet we must be honest with them if they wish to be defended by you, their duke." Philip stood and poured more wine into his goblet. He then topped up Lars's and Maximilian's drinks. "I hear Crevecoeur has defected to King Louis's cause and is leading a section of his army."

"I heard that too." Lars worried at his bottom lip. "He is a knight of the Golden Fleece."

"He shouldn't be," Maximilian said. "He has turned his back on Burgundy and its friends. He is treacherous and if I ever meet him in battle…" He paused and fought down his anger. "I will slice off his head."

"A fitting end," Philip said, sitting once again.

A courtier appeared. "Your Grace, visitors beg your attention."

"At this hour?" Lars exclaimed.

"Yes, and they have journeyed from afar. Shall I send them in?"

"Who are they?" Maximilian stood.

Aymer also jumped up.

"They have traveled from Florence," the courtier said. "Scholars, they tell me."

"Ah, they have finally arrived." Maximilian set down his drink and clapped. "Yes. Yes. Send them in. And fetch them sustenance too."

"You were expecting scholars?" Philip said.

"Yes, somewhat of a festive present to myself." Maximilian grinned.

"Whatever for?" Lars appeared bemused.

"To talk to. To learn from. These are wise men who have been at the forefront of all the exciting things happening in Florence and Milan. It is a wonder their skulls can contain their big brains." He laughed.

"Are we not sufficient conversation?" Philip raised his eyebrows at Maximilian.

"For all things concerning war and trade." Maximilian squeezed Philip's shoulder. "Yes, you are. But I have many interests. My head buzzes with thoughts on occasion, as if there are bees inside." He tapped his head. "Scholars are the way forward. They are not good for battle, but they are good for thinking and progression. They are a torch to light the way to a more learned future for us all."

"And how much will these big brains cost?" Lars asked. "For I suppose they will command a salary for all of this wisdom."

"Oh, just a few coins here and there." Maximilian wafted his hand in the air. "Ah, here they are. Come and take the weight off your feet, gentlemen."

He caught the look between Lars and Philip but decided to ignore it. Spending money on scholars' salaries, paying for their journey and keep, wasn't the best use of finances. But he had his eye on the bigger picture. Burgundy needed to keep up with the times and clever thinkers from Italy would help him ensure that was the case.

WHEN THE TULIPS rose from the ground and cherry blossoms sprung on trees, Maximilian found himself on the front line and ordering troops to battle with the French. King Louis had reached Ronse, as predicted, and a bitter fight broke out.

The fight had drawn him away from home and his pregnant wife, something that made his hatred for Louis all the greater.

He'd also received a letter from Adolph of Cleves.

Archduke Maximilian of Austria, Duke of Burgundy

I write to you in a time of dire need. The chivalrous Order of the Golden Fleece has been decimated in the chaos of 1477 and now stands without sovereign and with much depleted members due to death and defectors.

It has been decided that as Charles the Bold held the previous title of sovereignty and by marriage you are protector of his lands, that this esteemed title should pass to you.

So it is with a sense of urgency, in order to avoid King Louis XI of France taking over our illustrious order, that I ask you to attend a public ceremony in Bruges so that you can be both ordained and inaugurated.

Prayers be to God that you agree and that you send word to in-

form us of such in this worrying time.

    God's speed.

Adolph of Cleves

He read the letter again and then handed it to Lars, who quickly took it in, with Philip and Melchior reading over his shoulder.

"Louis is trying to make a claim to the Order?" Philip said, wind flapping the canvas at his side. "We should not be surprised."

"Indeed." Melchior frowned and set his hand on Maximilian's shoulder. "This is a great honor for you."

Maximilian nodded. His mind was whirring. Yes, it was an honor, but also with it would come power and influence, things he needed more of. Not only that, but it would give him the chance to forever link the distinguished order with the Habsburg lineage. His father would be most pleased. "I will of course accept."

"You are the rightful successor," Lars said, folding his arms, his lips a tight line of thought. "Yes."

"It goes without saying." Maximilian puffed up his chest. "And I will of course expel Order members who have defected to France and reward those who are loyal." He paused. "And when the opportunity presents itself, I will invite foreign rulers to join ranks. Rulers who can bring benefit and stability. That is something my father would do and I will follow his lead."

"You are very wise, Your Grace." Melchior clasped his hands beneath his chin and closed his eyes. "Very wise."

"Indeed I am." Maximilian waved his hand in the air. "So the sooner I take on the role, the better. Fortunately, I have good men here who can oversee the front." He looked around the tent at each of his friends and aides in turn. "I trust you are glad to do so."

"Honored, Your Grace," Philip said, dipping his head.

"You can count on us." Lars nodded seriously.

"And I shall write to inform the duchess of such wonderful news," Melchior said. "If that is what you wish."

"Yes. Thank you." He stroked his chin and thought of how this title could change things dramatically. He'd be seen on a public stage in a grand ceremony. No one would be able to question his entitlement to Burgundy. As a knight of the Golden Fleece, he would command respect. As the Order's sovereign, he'd have power to evoke change, influence the masses, grow his name.

And it would be a splendid affair, a celebration—after the traditional mourning ceremony for Charles the Bold's loss—it would be a chance to show people, ordinary people, that it was time to live normally again. Under his rule, they could be happy, celebrate, and enjoy festivals.

Yes. This would be very good for him, and for his son.

CHAPTER TWENTY

MARY SWATTED A fly from in front of her face as she rode toward Coudenberg on her favorite gray mare. The early summer day was warm—the air filled with the scent of sunflowers and alive with fluttering butterflies. Above, a charm of finches swooped and earlier, she'd been treated to the splendid sight of a goshawk moving silently through the trees.

As always, she rode side-saddle and even though her belly was rounded, this was still comfortable. She was glad to be outdoors, filling her lungs with fresh air, and feeling the sun on her face.

Aymer loped along beside the horses' hooves. He was tired now that they'd circled the lake and weaved through the forest. Jeanne rode at her side and Margaret and Lord Ravenstein followed behind talking about Maximilian's recent and lavish inauguration to The Golden Fleece in Bruges.

"I do miss him," Mary said to Jeanne. "Probably much more than I should. And I worry about things that might happen when he is at war."

"Why shouldn't you worry?" Jeanne replied. "He is your husband."

"Yes, but wives of husbands who are knights and sovereigns and warriors should expect to spend a great deal of time apart, and accept worrying into their lives."

"Forgive me for saying too much..." Jeanne paused. "But from what I see, your marriage to Maximilian is not like other royal marriages."

"Please go on." She knew full well she and Maximilian were different and was proud of the fact.

Jeanne glanced over her shoulder at Margaret and then, "Your father and the dowager were content to live apart. From what I recall, they rarely spent time together when he was home and having a break from organizing and fighting battles. There did not seem to be a considerable deal of worry or indeed love there despite her grief when he died."

"It is sad but true."

"I think it is good that you love your husband and that you miss him. Surely, that is what God would want."

Mary sighed and nodded. "Yes, but loving him does make it hard. I am carrying his child, yet he's been gone for weeks—months now."

"I shall pray that he returns soon, Your Grace."

"And will you also pray that Lars returns soon?" Mary raised her eyebrows at Jeanne.

Her cheeks flushed almost instantly.

"I am sure you miss him," Mary said. "Even if just as a friend."

"Yes." Jeanne nodded. "Just as a friend. I will pray that he too returns safely."

"We shall have a banquet when they do," Mary said decisively. "Roast a swan for the occasion."

"How marvelous. And we should have honey and aged cheese and waffles."

"Honey, most certainly." Mary licked her lips. "I really cannot get enough of it at the moment. I fear my child might come out buzzing." She laughed.

Jeanne laughed with her but then stopped suddenly. "Look. Over there."

Mary followed her line of sight. In the distance, approaching the palace at a different angle to their trajectory, was a line of dark horses. Some pulled carts and some had riders atop. Leading the procession was a horse and the outline of an upright, broad figure wearing armor that she recognized well.

"Oh, thank the Lord," Mary said on a gasp.

"It is them, is it not?" Jeanne said.

"I believe it is." Relief flooded through Mary.

"Look," Margaret called from behind. "The duke has returned."

"Yes. I see." Mary urged her horse into a trot—anticipation and excitement winging through her. How she longed to feel her husband's arms around her. Hear his voice and taste his kisses. Her heart rate picked up and when she reached the lawn before the palace steps, she called out. "Maximilian. My love."

He turned and saw her, and in an instant had kicked his horse into a canter. Within seconds, he had drawn up beside her and leaped from his horse, the sunlight glinting off his armor. "Mary, I have missed you so."

"And I you, dear husband."

He reached for her—Aymer yapping excitedly around him—and carefully helped her down from her horse.

She set her hands on the hot metal covering his chest and studied his face. For once, he wasn't clean-shaven—his jaw was dark with stubble—and he had a streak of grime over his forehead. But his eyes shone with the same love and intelligence she adored.

"I am thankful that you are here safe," she said, reaching up for a kiss.

He gave it, a long, deep kiss that told her he'd missed her as much as she him. When he pulled back, he cupped her cheeks. "I am glad to see you, but…"

"There is a *but*?"

"But I did not expect to see you out riding, not in your condition."

"It is a beautiful day for a ride, you cannot disagree."

"On the day no, but on having my pregnant wife upon a horse, I am afraid I do disagree."

"You cannot expect me to stay indoors throughout my pregnancy, surely."

"Not at all." He slid his hand to her swollen belly. "But on your own two feet, closer to the ground, that I do expect."

She frowned. "You are forbidding me to ride?"

He hesitated, then, "I am asking you to enjoy safer pursuits while you carry our child."

"But really, I—"

He touched his brow to hers and closed his eyes. "Do you have any idea how utterly terrifying it is for a man when his wife is pregnant? Not only do I risk losing the love of my life, but also my child. The two people for whom my heart beats and without whom I cannot imagine life. In all honesty, I would rather face an enemy cavalry both naked and without a weapon."

"Maximilian. What a thing to say."

He smiled. "It is a truth. And now you understand how serious I am about my request."

She pouted up at him.

"Say you will agree."

"I will be so bored. Life will be utterly tedious."

"Do you really think so? Now that I am here?"

She shivered in anticipation. "I hope not."

He kissed her again and then whispered against her lips, "I can find plenty of ways to keep you entertained. You should be in no doubt of that."

"I HAVE ORGANIZED for our portrait to be painted," Maximilian announced, striding into the solar a few days later.

LOVED BY THE LAST KNIGHT

"You have? By whom?"

"Hans Memling. He's the best, apparently."

"Will it be awfully expensive?"

He waved his hand through the air. "Hardly anything. Certainly not worth thinking about."

"We do need to think of money." Mary frowned.

"You mean, *I* do?"

She hesitated. "A little more, perhaps, here at home." She rubbed her belly, a habit these days. "The scholars were complaining that they had not been paid yet?"

He clicked his tongue on the roof of his mouth. "I will see to that shortly."

"Good. They were not happy." She dipped a tiny piece of bread into a pot of honey and popped it into her mouth. "When is this Hans person coming to paint?"

"Next month."

"Oh, Maximilian. I shall be the size of a castle by then. Hardly an ideal image to be captured for all of time."

"You will be beautiful."

"Can he not come sooner? Before I get a puffy face?" She blew up her cheeks. "Bags beneath my eyes?"

"I will tell him not to paint such things."

She sighed and sat back.

"What is the matter?" He stooped before her and took her hands. "Are you not happy?"

"Of course I am happy. You are here, and soon, our child will be here. You have amassed an army and found a general for that army and…"

"Go on."

"It feels almost sinful to say, but I am bored. You have been discussing the new offensive for what feels like every hour of the day with your aides and—"

"And neglecting you." His jaw tightened. "You are well within your rights to feel overlooked because I promised you would be entertained and I will remedy it at once." He stood.

"You will?"

"Yes, I have noblemen and many soldiers hard at work. I can take an afternoon with my wife, whom I have barely seen of late."

She smiled. "I would like that very much."

"What shall we do? Read, take a walk, fly Jupiter?"

She thought for a moment, luxuriating in the choices. "How about, as you have put it into my mind, we paint? Paint each other. The light in here is perfect today. Pure and clear."

"Unfortunately, I am no better at painting than I am at skating on the ice, but if it pleases you for us to paint, then that will make me happy." He straightened. "I will absent myself and call for easels and paints." He nodded at the honey and bread. "Would you like more?"

"Yes, thank you, and some candied spices too."

"Your wish is my command, Grand Dame." He kissed her cheek. "We will have a fine afternoon together."

Two hours later, Mary sat before an easel directly opposite her husband. She'd captured the outline of his face and the strands of his hair and was just starting on his eyes.

"How is your portrait of me?" she asked.

"It will be fought over by the world's greatest galleries." He laughed. "And sell for thousands of gold coins."

"Really?"

"No." His laughter deepened as he reached forward and squeezed her knee. "Not in this century, anyway."

"Can I see it?"

"Not yet. When it is finished."

She dipped her brush into a vivid shade of red. "Tell me about the ceremony in Bruges."

"I have already told you about it."

"I want to hear again." She smiled. "I wish I could have been there."

"I never met your father," he started as he dabbed his paintbrush on his easel. "But I'm sure he would have cherished the sight of the Order mourning his death. A beautiful, white horse carried the golden collar he'd worn as sovereign through the streets of Bruges to St Savior's church. There, it was laid at the altar while everybody changed from mourning clothes into ceremonial garb, myself included." He paused and looked at her as though deciding on a color or shape. "The sovereign chain and collar was then placed around my neck, Adolph of Cleves leading the inauguration."

"What is he like?"

"Old." Maximilian smiled. "But wise."

"Did your father, Ferdinand, attend?"

"No, he was fearful of leaving Vienna." Maximilian sighed. "I worry he is becoming even more reclusive in his old age."

"Would he visit us here?"

"No, I don't think so."

"Then perhaps we should visit him, when Louis is defeated and the baby is born."

"Only two small things to do first, then." Maximilian smiled, then leaned forward. He pinched the end of the lace that held her gown together at the collar. Slowly, he pulled, releasing it inch by inch and allowing the material to gape.

"Maximilian?" she whispered, aware that his mood had flicked from conversational to something else entirely.

The right side of his mouth twitched, but he didn't speak. Instead, he undid her gown until it was completely loose and put the rise of her breasts on show.

She hitched in a breath and a tremble went up her spine.

"I want to paint all of you," he said, carefully lifting the material away from her swollen breasts to expose them.

"That would be quite improper," she managed. Her nipples tightened as the cool air washed over them.

"But I am your husband. You are mine." He raised his eyebrows and looked at her steadily.

"As you are mine."

"From this day until my last." He eased her gown lower still, so her expanding belly was uncovered.

Her skin was so pale, a few veins could be made out through it.

"You are even more beautiful like this. Heavy with my child." He picked up his brush again and swirled it in lapis lazuli blue until the rich, royal color coated the tip. He then leaned forward and set it at the hollow of her throat.

The tip was cool and she sat very still as he drew it downward and over her sternum. "What are you doing?"

"Painting you, in the literal sense."

She swallowed, her nipples twisting to even harder points as he swept the brush over her right breast.

He then paused and re-dipped his brush.

She looked down and watched as he very carefully, and very precisely, drew a neat circle around her nipple. The blue was so startling against her white, full flesh that a new wave of excitement gripped her. "Maximilian."

"You are a much better canvas," he said, adding more paint to his brush and then circling her left nipple several times.

She let out a small sigh as heat traveled between her legs and a need began to grow.

Next, he painted from her sternum to her abdomen, not a hard line, but in little fans of color.

"I want to paint you," she said.

"You do?"

"Yes." She reached for his tunic. "Take this off."

"For such a small woman, you are a very demanding wife."

"You should know by now that my stature has little to do with my will."

He laughed softly. "That is something I do know." After putting down his brush, he removed his tunic, then pulled his chair closer to hers.

The sight of his broad, hair-speckled chest stoked her desire. She wanted to touch him all over. Feel his heat against her flesh, have her breasts pressed to his chest.

"What color do you choose for me?" he asked.

"Vermilion red." She dabbed her brush in paint the color of the darkest-red rose. "Love, beauty and glory."

He smiled and took a deep breath, his chest expanding, as though offering himself as a canvas.

A canvas Mary made good use of. She swirled the paint around his nipples, over the rounds of his shoulders, then from his sternum to his navel. Coating him in a series of lines that highlighted his strength, his power, and his masculinity.

When she'd reached his belt, she held her brush tip still. "Will you let me paint lower?"

"Oh, wife of mine, and you said *I* was improper." He raised his eyebrows at her.

"That was before I knew what fun this game was."

He chuckled. "I am pleased to be entertaining you on what would have been a boring afternoon." He cupped her breasts, flicking his thumbs over her nipples. "I *am* entertaining you, am I not?"

"Yes." She fluttered her eyes closed. She was so sensitive there, as if all her nerves had gone to her breasts.

But then his touch lifted and he pulled at his belt, letting it clatter to the floor. In another second, his breeches were down and off and his cock, semi-erect, was exposed.

Mary caught her breath and her cunny clenched. She didn't speak. Instead, she dipped her brush into the red paint again. This time, she painted from his right knee to his hip crease, very slowly, almost a full breath per inch. With each delicate, sweeping motion of her brush, his cock hardened, stiffening until it stood proud. By the time she'd reached the dip in his groin on the left side, he was at full mast, his cock tip round and glossy and veins standing proud on his shaft.

Once again, she dipped her brush, loaded the end, then angled it at the root of his cock, where the hair was thickest.

He caught her wrist. "Not there."

"But it would look so good." She tipped her head. "Don't you think?"

"I think not." He took the brush from her hand, setting it aside. "Stand."

She did as he'd asked, her gown floating downward, over her hips, to land at her feet.

Maximilian took his cock in his hand and massaged it from the base to the top. His gazed traveled from her breasts, over her swollen belly, to her feet and back. He bit on his bottom lip.

"Now what should I do?" she asked quietly.

"Sit on me."

She didn't answer.

"Sit on me," he said again. "On my cock. I do not wish to crowd the baby with my weight."

"So I should just…while you're sitting…there…on the chair?"

"Yes, my love. No sitting side-saddle today." He grinned, reaching for her hand and pulling her closer. "Trust me, you will enjoy it."

"I would trust you with my life, and I have always trusted you with my pleasure."

His smile dropped and his breath hitched, as though he were having to hold tight to his male instincts.

This thrilled Mary more, that she could still have her husband on the edge of his desires, even while carrying his child. He clearly wanted her for more than just heirs. He wanted her…his wife…his lover.

"My knight," she said, straddling his legs and her dampening entrance hovering over his cock. "I will never want another."

"And neither will I." He cupped her face and kissed her. "You are truly my grandest of loves."

As their tongues tangled, she lowered onto his waiting cock. She took it slow, not sure how it would feel with a baby in her belly, but it felt no different and soon she was seated.

"Oh, how I have missed you," he said, his voice tight. "Missed being in your hot, tight cunny."

"It is one of the things I longed for when you were gone. Even though there was a time I dreaded it. Our joining. Feared it." She gripped his shoulders, her palms smudging the red paint there.

"Didn't I promise to make it right, to have you desiring it?"

"You did. And I didn't doubt you. I have never doubted you."

He smiled and ran his hands down her back to cup her buttocks. "Move, like this." He tugged her forward, her hips rolling and her sensitive nub connecting with his body.

"Oh!" She gasped, her mouth hanging open. "Oh, Maximilian."

"Like that. You set the pace." His voice was as tight as a viola string. "I don't want to hurt you."

"It feels incredible. Oh, I love you."

"As I love you." He kissed her and their chests pressed together, red and blue paint smearing in smudgy, rainbow arcs.

Mary had never felt so desirable, so utterly feminine, or so loved unconditionally. And this gave her all the confidence she needed to ride her husband. She worked her needy nub into a frenzy until she was gasping and constricting around him.

He hissed in a breath around his teeth and cupped her breasts, squeezing gently. "You are so beautiful like this. So perfectly feminine."

She didn't reply but caught his face in her hands, coating his cheeks in bright paint. She stared into his eyes and saw into his soul. Love. Desire. Respect. Everything she would ever need.

"My love." He held her buttocks again, pulling her close, urging her on. "I cannot contain my pleasure much longer."

"Mine is…here." She tipped her head back and closed her eyes. For a blissful moment, she kept all the pleasure in her cunny stored up, anticipating the rush of pleasure about to release.

And then it was there. It tumbled through her, shaking her limbs, rattling up her spine. She folded onto him and he surged his hips upward, spilling his seed in urgent, frantic pulses.

His cry of ecstasy mixed with hers. Filling the room, filling her ears and mind.

On and on, she moved, rocking her hips, finding every last shred of satisfaction.

Eventually, she opened her eyes and stilled. He was staring at her, his face a streaky mess of paint and his pupils wide. He was breathing hard and perspiration shone on his forehead.

"We must do it again like this," he said. "You are incredible atop me."

A surge of delight filled her heart. "To be truthful, you are like riding a wild stallion."

He laughed, a big boom of a noise. "Oh, how funny you are." He found her mouth and kissed her, holding her close, sweat and paint sliding over their flesh.

"How absolutely dirty you are," she whispered.

"As are you." He stroked her hair. "And I wouldn't have it any other way."

CHAPTER TWENTY-ONE

"A RGH!" MARY CURLED forward, the pain in her belly like a thousand knives stabbing at her.

"You are doing so well," Jeanne said, dabbing Mary's brow with a damp cloth.

"Soon, it will be over," Margaret said from her other side as she held Mary's hand. "And your babe will be in your arms."

"I can't… I can't…" Mary was breathless, her heart racing. It felt like she was being torn in two.

"Your mother is right. The babe will be here soon." The midwife peered between Mary's legs. "I can see the head now."

Mary closed her eyes. The next contraction was coming—the agony starting as a whisper that would soon become a deafening scream that rendered her body hostage.

"Good. Now push when you need to," the midwife said. "Your body will tell you when."

"I need to push!" Mary yelled, her voice hardly sounding like her own.

"Yes. Push. We are here with you," Margaret said. "And God is watching over you. He will care for you and the child."

A primitive grunt vibrated through Mary's chest as she put all her strength and effort into expelling the baby from her body. The labor had been short but intense and she felt if it didn't end soon, she wouldn't survive the pain. It was red-hot, all consuming, a wicked, blinding torture.

"You're doing so well, Your Grace," the midwife said, excitement lacing her voice. "Keep going. Keep pushing. Keep pushing. Not long now."

"I can't. I can't."

"You can," Margaret said sternly. "You can and you will!"

"Lord, have mercy," Jeanne said. "Oh, my dearest friend, please, you can do this. He is with you."

Mary dragged in another deep breath then worked with the contraction. She was stretching, opening, and then there was wriggling, slithering, and it was like something hot and wet had fallen from her. "The baby!" She opened her eyes, fearing it had slipped right to the floor.

"It is out," the midwife said, lifting up a shiny, blood-streaked bundle of limbs with a tiny body and a large head. "He is out. You did it. Your son is born."

"A...A son." She gasped, happiness flooding her. The pain was forgotten and in its place pure joy.

"A boy. Oh, you have a boy. I knew you would produce a male heir for Burgundy." Margaret kissed Mary's brow. "You are so clever. So wonderful, my beautiful girl."

"Is he well?" Mary asked, peering at the baby as a second midwife cut the cord.

She didn't answer but laid the baby on a towel and rubbed him.

"Is he well? What is the problem? Tell me, I—" Panic gripped her.

A loud wail filled the room. High-pitched and indignant, it was nonetheless music to Mary's ears.

"He has good lungs." The midwife smiled and picked the baby up. "Congratulations, Your Grace, and God bless you both." She passed the baby to Mary.

The moment Mary held her son, she fell in love. He was the wailing bundle her arms had been aching to hold, her heart waiting to love.

"Oh, my beautiful, perfect son," she said, utterly mesmerized by his tiny face, pink gums, curled tongue, and screwed-up eyes.

"He is perfect," Margaret said, tears making her words catch. "Perfectly perfect. Thank you, God." She held his tiny hand as if counting his fingers, then moved to the next, then to his little feet.

"I am so proud of you," Jeanne said, kissing Mary's head and then the baby's. "And Maximilian will be too."

"Yes, Maximilian. Where is he? I want him…" She glanced at the door, sure that he'd be pacing outside the bedchamber and no doubt driving everyone to distraction with his concerns. "Please, get him at once."

"This is no place for a husband, Your Grace." The midwife was still between her legs.

"Oh…Oh, what is…?" Another hot, slithering sensation seemed to gush from her.

"The afterbirth, Your Grace." The midwife set the large, dark blob to one side.

"Is there anything else?" Mary was alarmed. What else was to come from her poor, exhausted body?

"No, that is all." The midwife smiled and took the warm, white cloth the other midwife handed her. "Soon, we will have you all cleaned up."

The baby was still crying and Mary rocked him gently. "Oh, little one, is it too bright in here? Have you had a fright, suddenly landing in the world?" She kissed the tip of his nose. "You don't need to be afraid. I will love you always, as will your father, and God is shining on you as I speak, filling you with His love."

"Why don't you send him away to a wet nurse?" Margaret suggested. "He's sure to be hungry."

Mary's heart lurched. Send him away? Her newborn baby, whom she had been waiting months to meet? "A wet nurse?"

"There are two waiting in the nursery," Jeanne said. "Both from good families and of placid disposition."

"No. I don't want that."

"It would be for the best," the midwife said, efficiently switching a sheet beneath Mary. "The poor little mite has had a busy morning too."

Mary held him tighter. "Have you finished…down there?"

"Yes, Your Grace." The midwife nodded and covered her over with the blanket. "You will be tender for a while, but you haven't torn, so you'll recover quickly."

"Torn? What… I mean… Oh, dear…" Mary shook her head. Being torn sounded awful. "Please, can someone get my husband? I want to see him. I want Maximilian. I need him with me."

"You should wait a few days," the midwife said, wiping the baby's face.

"*A few days*! No. I demand to see him. Now." She turned to the door. "Maximilian! Come in. My love, come in and meet your son."

"Mary, no, I must implore…"

"Maximilian. I need you!"

The door suddenly flew open, bashing against the bedchamber wall.

The baby cried louder.

"Mary!" Maximilian strode into the room, his tunic flapping and his hair sticking up wildly, as though he'd been dragging his fingers through it over and over again. "I heard you call for me, and…" He stopped beside the bed and stared down at the crying child. "You said 'son'?"

"Yes. God has blessed us with a son."

He smiled, a slow smile at first, but it turned into a big beam. "How fortunate we are." He bent and kissed the babe's head and then set his lips over Mary's. "How clever you are."

"Our child of imperial seed is perfect in every way."

"I have no doubt. He is of noble blood, double noble blood, for us to take pride in." He tenderly kissed the baby's head. "Are you well?" he asked, seeming to study her body through the covers before setting his attention on the midwife who was wringing out towels.

"Your wife is young and healthy," the midwife said, "and she coped incredibly well with childbirth, Your Grace."

"As I knew she would, but a husband cannot help but worry and pace and fear the worst."

"My love." She touched his cheek. "Do not fear another moment. Our son is here now, in my arms."

"And making quite the noise," Jeanne said. "I really think it is time for the wet nurse."

"I said *no*." Mary scowled.

"Perhaps she could come to the room," Margaret suggested. "So that you are not parted from your baby."

"He would still be out of my arms." She looked up at Maximilian. "I don't want a wet nurse. I want to feed our son myself."

Maximilian considered her for a moment, then, "You are a duchess. Naturally, your milk is far superior."

"It is most untoward," Margaret said.

"And word is sure to get out." Jeanne looked aghast.

"That I have nurtured my child from my own bosom?" Mary frowned. "Let word get out. As long as my husband is in agreement, I have no care for others' opinions."

"You will exhaust yourself," the midwife said. "It is too much."

"You just told me that I was young and healthy. How can it possibly be too much for me to feed my own child with my own milk?"

The baby's wailing reached a new level.

"It is a decision that must be made soon," Maximilian said. "Before our new son starves or our ears break."

"I will feed him." Mary stroked the baby's mouth and he instantly tried to latch on to her finger.

Margaret looked steadily at Maximilian. "You should leave. This is women's business."

He narrowed his eyes. "With the greatest respect, Dowager, my wife and child are my business every moment of every day for as long as I live." He looked at Jeanne. "Please, everyone, leave, but for one midwife. Mary might need some help that I am ill advised to deal with."

"You cannot stay. That is beyond scandalous." Margaret's mouth fell open and her eyes widened to saucers.

"And what would you have me do for the next months while the babe is fed? Sleep outside on the floor?"

"No, but in order to be proper and—"

Maximilian pointed at the door. "I wish to be alone with my wife. But I thank you from the bottom of my heart for your support and love during her labor. Truly, I do."

Jeanne sucked in a deep breath, then stepped away from the bed. Margaret followed her.

Mary stared at her son's tiny face. He was sucking her finger now, greedily, and his eyes were open, staring up at her.

"Maximilian," she said quietly. "His eyes are the same color as yours."

Maximilian sat on the bed at her side. "And I believe as you are beautiful, he will be handsome." He held the baby's tiny hand on the tip of his index finger. "He's so small, so very precious."

"What will we name him?"

"Philip."

"After my cousin?" She turned to her husband. "How your opinion of him has changed so."

He laughed quietly. "No, after one of his grandfathers. Philip rather suits him, don't you think?"

She studied the child even more intently. "Welcome to the world, Philip. You really are going to have quite the life and your father and I will be at your side every step of the way."

〰〰⧫〰〰

TWO WEEKS LATER, Mary had acquired the skill of breastfeeding and was enjoying every moment with Philip. She hadn't left the bedchamber, not even to visit Jupiter, who was living with the other birds for the present time—upon Maximilian's insistence.

She looked forward to the day when she could teach Philip to ride and hunt. He had fine-shaped legs and already, his arms were gaining strength, she was sure. He'd be strong and powerful, a force to be reckoned with, just like his father.

Philip's baby smell and his downy hair were intoxicating to Mary and she constantly thanked God for her good fortune. She'd never known love like it. It was different to how she loved Maximilian. It was raw, feral almost. She'd never hurt another person—it was not her nature—but she knew she'd kill for Philip. One night, she'd dreamed she was a wolf protecting him, the growl in her throat a warning, her heart pounding with instinct and rage, not a care for herself, just for her child.

"What are you thinking?" Maximilian asked as he removed his tunic and breeches.

"Truthfully?"

"Yes, of course." He walked to the bed, naked, the way he always slept in the summer months.

"I was thinking that I would kill anyone who tried to hurt our son."

"Mary, that is not like you." Maximilian got into the bed next to her and stroked Philip's head; he'd just begun to feed. "You are the most gentle soul I know."

"Perhaps, but becoming a mother has changed that." She paused. "It's quite frightening, actually, the depth of my love for him and how far I would go to protect him. I feel like it is endless. That I could be pushed to do anything."

"Please, don't be afraid." He kissed her cheek, then wrapped his arm around her shoulders, being careful not to disturb the baby. "I am here to protect you both. And do you not recall what a skilled fighter I am?"

"Yes, of course, and I am grateful for you every day. That you are my husband."

For a few minutes, Mary sat content, husband at her side, baby feeding. Her left breast had been aching with milk but now was becoming more comfortable. The right was leaking onto a small, linen cloth.

"He likes it," Maximilian said. "And he is growing strong on your milk. I can tell each day that he thrives."

"Yes. He does."

"Have Margaret and Jeanne forgiven you for feeding him yourself?" he asked. "They were here earlier, were they not?"

"Yes, and Jeanne has. Margaret still thinks I should make use of a wet nurse."

"Do you want to?"

"No, of course not. Feeding my baby is almost magical, and to know that he is flourishing on what I give him, the same way he did when in the womb, fills me with pride."

"I am proud of you for doing as you wish. People should never doubt your strength of conviction, Mary of Burgundy. It is one of the things I love the most about you."

"Even if at times it drives you to distraction?"

He chuckled and touched Philip's cheek as it sucked in and out. "Will he be finished soon?"

"Yes. Sometimes he seems to feed in his sleep." She smiled.

"It is incredible to see."

"That is what Margaret cannot forgive," Mary said. "You being with us, like this, with him so young and me feeding him in front of you."

"She thinks it is wrong for a father to see his son growing strong on the food God has naturally provided?"

"She thinks that a husband and wife shouldn't be as familiar as we are. Some things are sacred, for women's eyes only."

"Just because she was distant from your father doesn't mean that we should be." He spoke softly. "We agreed a long time ago to do it differently to our parents. To be friends and lovers, as well as husband and wife."

"I am glad we did."

"As am I."

The baby stopped feeding and released Mary's nipple, his lips puffy and with a drip of milk at the center. He sucked a few more times on nothing.

"He is sleeping," Mary said. "And his swaddling is fresh. I'm hopeful for a few hours of rest myself."

"Shall I lay him in his cradle?" Maximilian asked, pushing the covers from his legs and standing.

She nodded and carefully passed Maximilian his son.

He held him close, his hands looking even bigger than usual against the tiny child.

For a moment, Mary studied her husband's naked body. His long, strong legs, his taut abdomen and the bulging muscles on his arms. It was hard to believe that he had been a baby once. That Philip would one day, God willing, have the size and strength of his father.

Very gently, Maximilian laid Philip in his cradle, a richly decorated, wooden cot with gilded coats of arms on either end.

"Shh," Maximilian whispered. "Sleep well under God's watchful gaze, my cherished son."

The baby stirred momentarily. Maximilian seemed to hold his breath. But when no high-pitched wail came, he climbed back onto the bed with Mary, the mattress dipping a little with his weight.

"If Aymer barks now, he'll be spending the night in the courtyard," he said, throwing a glance at the sleeping dog, who lay on his rug beside the fire.

"He won't. He seems to understand to be quiet when the baby is."

"Clever dog."

Mary removed a soft pad from her left breast. A pearly drop of milk sat on her nipple.

Maximilian leaned close. He took the pad then very gently swiped his fingertip over the milk, catching the drop on the end.

Mary held her breath. Her breast ached. Her skin heated.

He placed his finger in his mouth. Tasting her. Tasting her milk.

He looked steadily at her and sucked his lips in. "It's warm from your body," he said, leaning close and touching his lips to hers.

"Maximilian," she said breathily. "I…"

"I want to show you how much I love you," he said, then he glanced at her breast. Another bead of milk had formed. "But I can see you are not ready, so just believe me, deep in your soul, when I tell you I adore you and love you with everything I am."

"As I do you." She stroked his hair. A need was growing in her, but she knew she wasn't ready to give him her body. Not yet. "The midwife said we should wait at least two moons."

"I can wait." He dipped his head and with the tip of his tongue licked her nipple, taking the next milky drip onto the end. Then with his eyes closed, he drew it into his mouth and suckled once, twice, three times.

He raised his head again, his eyes sparkling. "It is sweet, like dew." He set the pad over her nipple. "No wonder he thrives."

"He does." Her breath hitched. "The midwife also said while I am feeding, it will be harder to fall with child again."

"I hope we do have another child, and another." He pinched her chin and held her face to his. "But when we lay together, it is about more than procreation, don't you agree?"

"Yes." She smiled. "I feel like we are one person, that our pleasure, when it comes at the same time, is almost heavenly." She blushed. "That is probably quite a blasphemous comparison."

"God smiled on us when we wed." He kissed her gently. "And every day since."

Within minutes, Mary was lying in her husband's arms. His breaths became slow and steady as sleep stole him and she stared at the shadows from the fire and was thankful for all that she had.

CHAPTER TWENTY-TWO

MARY STOOD AT the head of a crowded Aula Magna holding baby Philip, who was swaddled in a cream, lace shawl and sleeping peacefully. His fair hair was fluffy, his mouth a little rosebud, and his cheeks held a hint of pink—he was the most beautiful baby boy ever born.

·A harpist played and the sun shone through the large windows, the streaks of light dancing with dust motes.

Maximilian set his hand on the small of her back and leaned down to speak quietly into her ear. "We have gathered practically every nobleman, scholar, and clergyman in the land here." He paused. "That makes me nervous. Very nervous, indeed."

"Why on Earth would it make you nervous?" She frowned up at him. "I don't understand."

"Removing all of the powerful men of Burgundy would be a great victory for King Louis, no bloody battle needed. Chaos would ensue. Our lands would be for the taking, like a blanket from a babe."

Mary studied the familiar faces on the front row. All were men who owned land, wielded authority, and held wealth. "Yes, we are like the stories of congregations locked in churches when the Norsemen arrived. They had nowhere to hide, nowhere to go. They'd trapped themselves. Easy prey."

"Yes, and now here we are, conveniently circled by our walls, we are but an archery target," Maximilian said. "We really should get the

Christening under way."

"I agree." She held her baby a little closer and looked nervously at Margaret, who stood close at her other side.

"Bishop," Maximilian said with a nod at Melchior. "If you would begin."

The bishop cleared his throat and opened his Bible. "If I could harness your attention, lords, noblemen, gentlemen."

The vast hall quieted. The harp stopped playing.

"First, I would like to welcome you all," the bishop said, "in joining Archduke Maximilian of Austria, Duke of Burgundy, and his wife, Duchess Mary of Burgundy, on this special day to mark the christening of their son, Philip."

A few people turned to each other, eyebrows raised, silent words passing between them.

"A christening," the bishop went on, "is an important and sacred event and before we start, I would like to read several passages from the Bible that—"

"Please, Bishop, if you could just..." Maximilian circled his finger. "Get on with it."

"Oh, er, yes, of course." He paused. "No passages?"

"No, just the baptism, if you would be so kind."

"Oh...er. Certainly, Your Grace." He passed his Bible to a contemporary. "If you could step this way with baby Philip." He moved to a large, stone font that had an ornate base and was filled with holy water.

Mary's attention was still on the crowd. There were whispers now too, a little ripple of quiet conversation.

"If you hold the baby like this," the bishop was saying, "with his head over the font."

"Yes, yes, of course." She did as instructed and Maximilian circled his arm around her waist. She was glad of him there, his body heat and his strength. She had an uneasy feeling that wasn't entirely caused only by Maximilian's comment about them being a target.

"People of God," the bishop said loudly, "will you promise to welcome this child and uphold him in his new life with Christ?"

"We will," said the crowd in a low hum.

"I baptize you." Melchior dipped his hand into the water and scooped some into his palm. "In the name of the Father, of the Son, and of the Holy Spirit." He let the water fall on Philip's head.

The child opened his eyes, staring straight up at Mary, clearly surprised to have been woken this way.

"Shh, little one," she cooed, rocking him. The last thing she needed was for Philip to start wailing for milk.

"What is going on?" Maximilian's attention had been harnessed by the crowd. "What are they saying?"

Once again, Mary looked at the sea of faces. They were huffing, rolling their eyes, nodding at each other, as though colluding in some great secret.

"I do not know," Mary said. "But it is most untoward on this, Philip's most sacred day."

"I know," Margaret said from behind them. "I know what is being said."

They both turned to her. "Pray tell," Mary demanded, swallowing, her emotions beginning to get the better of her, the way they'd been prone to of late.

"They are saying Philip is a girl."

"They are *what*?" Maximilian said, his mouth hanging open.

"A girl?" Mary repeated. "But he is not."

"I have been told," Margaret went on, "reliably, that just before the service, a rumor was started that you are concealing the true gender of the child because of your need for a male heir."

"We would never lie to our people," Mary said. "They should know that."

"I know that," Margaret said. "But perhaps doubters believe you are waiting to have a boy on your next pregnancy and will then disclose the truth."

"That is preposterous and downright insulting," Maximilian snapped. "We must rectify this."

"Yes. I agree." Margaret held out her arms. "Give the babe to me."

Mary hesitated for a moment, then handed him over to his grandmother, whom she knew loved and adored him almost as much as she did.

Margaret held Philip close, then quickly and expertly un-swaddled him until he was naked in her arms. She handed the blanket to Mary.

"You will see," she called loudly across the hall. "That there is no substance to these vicious rumors you all seem so intent on circulating and believing." She held Philip up high, his small legs dangling, and his tiny penis on full display. "My grandson, Philip, is very much a boy."

There was a collective gasp cut short by Philip's indignant, high-pitched wail that threatened to burst eardrums.

"Please, Margaret," Mary said, reaching for Philip. "Let me take him." She pulled him tightly to her chest and kissed the top of his head.

Maximilian laid the blanket over his son, then turned to the crowd, hands on hips, sword banging against his leg. "Who said this lie to begin with? I demand to know."

Nothing. The crowd went silent.

"You deny your duke?" he boomed. "You deny me the name of the man who all but committed treason?"

"We do not know," a nobleman from the border said. "Other than it was said with surety."

"A lie said with surety." Maximilian laughed stiffly. "How very...French."

A few members of the crowd laughed awkwardly.

"We are sorry, Your Grace, for any untoward angst," a scholar said, dipping his head respectfully. "Collectively sorry."

That seemed enough to satisfy Maximilian and he strode forward and pointed at the feasting table. "Now that this matter is resolved, for you all know my son is truly a son, we will begin eating."

He walked up to a tower of candied spices that glistened with sugar. It was set on a round, silver tray and spread with tiny blueberries. It had been perched on the end of the banqueting table, like a late addition to the feast.

He took the top berry, and as he was prone to doing, tossed it into the air and caught it in his mouth.

Mary wished he wouldn't do that in public. It was somewhat crude.

But it had barely touched his tongue, chewed perhaps once, and he spat it out. "Yuck!" he exclaimed and circled his hand around his throat. "That was…" His words cut off and his face paled.

"Maximilian!" Mary passed the baby to Margaret and rushed to her husband. She reached him at the same time that Lars, Philip, and Melchior did. "My love, what is it? Pray tell me. What is it?"

He didn't answer. Instead, he sank to his knees and placed one hand on the floor, arm locked.

Aymer ran a circle around him, barking. Mary hadn't even realized he'd been in the hall.

"Oh, my goodness," Mary said, stooping and resting her hand on his back. "He…He has been poisoned. The duke has been poisoned! Help…someone…" Her voice broke as she stared around the crowd. "Oh…" She wailed. "Someone, help us."

"Take those candied spices away, the whole tray!" Philip ordered. "And find out who put them there. Find out what is in it. Immediately."

Mary's head was spinning. Panic flooded her system. Poison. Who would do such a thing? And what could she do to help? "Water, get him water," she commanded of the nearest nobleman. "Now."

Maximilian was breathing heavily and noisily, his body tense and his arm shaking. He didn't appear capable of speaking.

"Oh, my love, be well! I beg of you, be well. You didn't swallow it, did you?"

His arm gave way and he collapsed to the floor, his face twisted in pain and his lips swelling.

Mary screamed and flung herself on him, not caring about the sea of watching, curious people. "No, no! My love."

"Your Grace, Mary, please, let us get him to his chambers." Philip gently pulled her away. "He won't want prying eyes in this moment."

She spun to Philip, sobbing, her heart breaking. In this moment—the moment of her dear, beloved husband taking his last breaths—she was broken.

"Send for a surgeon," Lars called, hoisting Maximilian up by the arms. "The best surgeon. Get him this instant."

Two courtiers grabbed Maximilian's legs and he was quickly carried from sight, Melchior and Aymer in close chase.

"I must go with him," Mary said. "I must."

"No, wait here," Philip said. "It is not something you want to see."

"I cannot be parted with him when he needs me most. And do not try to stop me." She pushed away from him. "Margaret, please, care for baby Philip for me, and…watch out for traitors to our realm." She swung an accusing look at their audience. "I give you my word, I will find out who has done this and I will have them hung." She gathered her hem and rushed through the parted crowd.

With her heart thudding and tears streaming down her cheeks, she raced up the stairs. Lars had moved quickly and already, Maximilian was on the bed, tunic removed.

"Where is the surgeon?" she demanded, running into the room. "Go. Go and get him quickly and tell him to run to us. That is a direct request from his duchess. A life is at stake."

"Yes, Your Grace." One of the courtiers sprinted from the room.

"Maximilian." She grabbed his hand and sat on the bed. "Please, do not die. Please, I beg of you."

He didn't answer. His eyes were closed, his face blotchy, and his lips puffy.

"Lars," she said, looking up at her husband's best friend and ally. "What will happen?"

"I do not know, Your Grace." He wrung out a cloth then set it on Maximilian's brow. "I fear those berries were belladonna."

"Belladonna... Oh, dear Lord."

"They are lethal."

"Oh...who would do such a thing?"

"But he didn't eat it, only chewed it," Lars said. "He had the good sense to spit it out."

"Yes. Yes, he did." A sliver of hope grew in her chest. "Perhaps he will just be sick for a while."

"That is what we must pray for." Lars took another cloth and pressed it to Maximilian's lips.

"Here, I can do that. I can care for him." She took the cool cloth and tenderly wiped his lips and face. "Where is that surgeon?"

"I am here..." The red-faced, rotund surgeon, Benedict, rushed in. "What has happened to His Grace?"

"I fear belladonna poisoning," Lars said.

"Oh, in heaven's name." The surgeon dropped his small leather bag. "There is no tonic for that. We must perform bloodletting."

"Yes, anything, do what you must," Mary said. "But be quick. I fear he will never wake up."

The surgeon leant his head over Maximilian's. "He is breathing. Shallowly, but breathing. That is a good sign."

"I will pray and pray," Mary said, raising her face to the heavens. "Lord, please do not take my husband. He does not deserve to die this way."

"Somebody, please take this dog out of the room," the surgeon said. "Bloodletting will excite him and be quite distracting."

Lars nodded at the remaining courtier, who quickly escorted Aymer outside.

"This won't take long." The surgeon rolled up his sleeves then removed a small, silver knife with a wickedly sharp blade from his bag. He also retrieved a small, clay bowl. "Hold his arm like this."

Lars did as instructed.

The sight of the blade pressing into her husband's flesh sickened Mary and she turned away, not wanting to watch his blood flow from his body. "Please, Maximilian, get well." She kissed his hand, the one she was holding. "I beg you."

The metallic scent of blood filled her nose. She prayed this would work. That the surgeon would be able to remove the poison that had rendered Maximilian in a state of stupor and swollen his face.

"When will we know if he will recover?" Lars asked.

Mary studied the surgeon's face for signs of hope or despair.

"With luck, by tomorrow morning," the surgeon said. "It will be a long and dangerous night for him."

"What can we do?" Mary asked. "I will do anything for him. Anything at all."

"Keep a watch over him and keep him cool," the surgeon said. "And do not try to feed him. His system needs to rest." He set a bandage over Maximilian's arm. "I will remain close by, should you need me."

"Thank you, sir."

Jeanne rushed into the room. "How is he? Please, tell me he is not dead."

"No," Lars said, taking her hand. "He is not dead, but he is currently choosing between staying on Earth or moving on to heaven."

Mary swiped at a tear rolling down her cheek. "Jeanne, will you stay with me?"

"Of course."

"And Lars." Mary sniffed. "I wish you to go and help my cousin

Philip. Find out who did this. Find out who poisoned Maximilian and who started the rumors about our son being a girl. It is one and the same person, I am sure, and I am also sure the King Louis has a hand in this." She frowned. "Do not fail me. Do not fail Maximilian, for when he wakes up, I wish to tell him the culprit is swinging from a tree."

"*Mary!*"

"I have no room for mercy, Jeanne, not today. Do you understand, Lars?"

"Yes, Your Grace. Perfectly."

Mary sat beside Maximilian all night, wiping his brow, wetting his lips and adjusting his pillow. A few times, he murmured and moved his head and her heart skipped, thinking he was waking.

But he didn't.

He remained pale and puffy, his breathing shallow. Blood leaked through the bandage on his arm and she changed it with Jeanne's help.

"I fear for him," Jeanne said. "And I fear for you."

"For me?" Mary asked.

"Yes, for if something happens to Maximilian, I do not think you will ever be able to smile again."

"That is true." She pressed her lips together. "He is my true love. I cannot imagine a life without him at my side."

"And he feels the same about you. I see it in the way he looks at you. How he is possessive over you, how your smile makes him smile. You fill his heart to bursting point."

A fresh set of tears spilled from Mary's eyes and dampened her cheeks. "I have prayed every day of my life, and if only this one is answered, I will be content. Please, God, let him get well. Don't let him leave me."

Outside the window, a blackbird started singing, a chirpy melody that signaled dawn.

"It is morn," Jeanne said. "The dead of the night is over."

"I am thankful." Mary sat and clutched his hand again. "And I am thankful for your company, Jeanne."

"I am always here for you. But..."

"But?"

"But I must go and use a chamber pot."

"Of course, go."

When Jeanne had left the room, Mary lay at Maximilian's side and rested her head on his shoulder. She could hear his heart beating steadily and the sound gave her comfort. She closed her eyes.

After a few minutes, she sensed Maximilian's fingers moving, just a little. She raised her head, watched them pulling at the sheet, and then looked up at his face. "My love?"

"Mmm..."

"Maximilian. Are you awake?"

He opened his mouth a little, then grimaced.

"Here, let me get you water." Quickly, she reached for a goblet and wet his lips. A trickle ran down his chin and she caught it on her fingertip.

"More..." he managed, his voice scratchy.

She gave him more and he took several big swallows.

"Oh, Maximilian, you are awake. All will be well." Joy filled her. Her prayers had been answered.

"My love..." He looked at her with bloodshot eyes. "What...What happened?"

"Belladonna, on the candied spices. They weren't blueberries at all."

"But...who...would?"

"Lars and Philip are hunting down the culprit. I know they will be successful."

He sighed as though still exhausted.

"Rest, my love. You need to rest."

He closed his eyes.

Suddenly, the door opened. Lars and Philip strode in, along with Jeanne.

"We have news," Lars said.

"So do I," Mary said, standing with her hand on Maximilian's shoulder. "He is—"

"Awake," Maximilian said.

"Oh, what mercy He has." Jeanne clasped her hands beneath her chin. "What a relief."

"I am glad." Lars blew out a breath and some of the tension went from his shoulders.

"What news do you have?" Maximilian said.

"We found the traitor."

"You did? Who was it?" Mary asked.

"An assassin sent by King Louis and dressed as a courtier," Lars said. "He confessed to starting the rumor about baby Philip being a girl as well as dotting the candied spices with belladonna berries."

"He could have killed so many people. The berries were numerous," Mary said, pressing her hand to her chest. "Where is this evil man now?"

"He is hanging from a great oak, to the right of the palace," Philip said.

"Good," Maximilian said. "The ravens can have his eyes."

CHAPTER TWENTY-THREE

MAXIMILIAN GRIPPED HIS pike. He was horribly hot and sweaty in the August sun. Armor was not good for a summer's day. He stood on the outskirts of the small village of Guinegate and in the center square gathered eleven thousand Burgundian troops.

He was ready for battle.

They were ready for battle.

Mounted cavalrymen flanked the infantry, who halted, alert, at the center of the square of armored horses. "Are you absolutely sure about this formation tactic?" Maximilian asked Jacques of Savoy, who stood at his side also holding a long, sharp pike.

"In God we trust always," Jacques replied, sunlight glinting off his helmet, "but in this case, trust me too, my friend."

"It is the Swiss way." Maximilian nodded, as if confirming the information to himself. "The Swiss do this."

"Yes, it is the way your predecessor, Charles the Bold, was swiftly defeated by the Swiss. I studied it carefully," Jacques said, his voice gruff. "Louis will not be expecting this formation, this style of attack. I believe it to be our best chance to defeat him."

"Well, we have discussed this much, and I have lain awake at night thinking through the scenarios…" Maximilian nodded, a drip of sweat rolling down his temple. He was unable to swipe it away.

"I believe it is good sense." Philip, his wife's cousin, shifted impatiently from one foot to the other and spun the base of his pike into the damp earth. "To attack this way. I like it."

"As do I." Lars nodded, his eyes peering from the slit in his helmet. "We must be victorious."

"Though it is most unusual for a man of your standing, Archduke, to be going into battle with so many nobles," Jacques commented. "And here, on the ground, in what will be the thick of the fighting. Are you sure you do not want to mount a steed?"

"I am a knight and a warrior." Maximilian banged his hand on his metal-covered chest. "What would my men think of me if I were not also on the battlefield, at their side, on this land, and wielding a weapon?" He huffed at the very thought. It was acceptable to have generals take the lead when he wasn't in attendance, but when he was, he, Maximilian, would not just give orders, he'd also fight, no matter the risks.

"Prepare to give the signal to the archers and crossbowmen," Maximilian said, raising his chin and taking a deep breath. "We will attack the French and be triumphant. God be with you all."

Within minutes, the battle had commenced, arrows sung through the air, and cannons fired overhead. The panicked horses the cavalry rode added to the chaos. Hooves stamping. Blood spraying. Yells of effort and agony. Soon, Maximilian found himself fighting face to face with the relentless French.

A pike jabbed at him and he dodged, only to be faced with another. He struck out, landed it with good aim, then swiped at a Frenchman about to deliver a deathly blow to a young Burgundian infantryman— he killed the enemy instantly. Quickly, he dragged the wide-eyed young soldier to standing, patted him on the shoulder, then continued fighting.

Somewhere in the onslaught, he registered the left flank of his cavalry falling into a perilous state. They'd scattered and captured artillery was being used against them.

He spun around, pike held out, and spotted a Burgundian knight, one of their own, heading into the forest at a full-stretch gallop. It appeared to be Philip. His loyal advisor and friend, who had only moments ago been fighting at his side. Hot on his heels were a great chase of French knights whooping and shouting, weapons at the ready.

"What on Earth...?" He gaped for a moment but then had to direct his attention to fighting hard and long and skillfully as his infantrymen pushed forward. There was no time for thinking. Each second required his full concentration to stay alive.

Which he had to do. He'd promised his dear wife he'd return home to her with all four limbs and his head on his neck. A promise he fully intended to keep.

MARY LAY WATCHING the curtains shifting in the breeze from an open window. Since Maximilian had been gone, she'd been lethargic but restless, a horrible combination that had left her so exhausted, she'd taken to resting on top of her bed each afternoon.

But she couldn't concentrate, not even on her Bible studies, because her mind wouldn't stop racing through all the terrible scenarios which might befall her husband at battle.

She feared the pike and the arrow, the sword and the dagger. His precious blood, she prayed would stay in his veins, and she prayed his big, kind heart would beat strongly.

He'd recovered quickly from his near death after the poisoning and she knew his strength of body had stopped him from being taken from her.

Security at court had been tightened upon Hugo's insistence and no one had disagreed. King Louis, it seemed, was prepared to stoop low to get what he wanted.

"Your Grace, can I get you anything?" Jeanne asked from the corner of the room. She was sitting embroidering.

"No, thank you." Mary sighed. "Is little Philip still sleeping?"

She stretched her neck to see into the crib. "Yes, not a peep. He is very content."

"I have been blessed with a child of gentle nature."

"As he has been blessed with strong and kind parents."

"I thank you." Mary paused. "You may leave now. I will sleep while Philip does."

"Yes, Your Grace. Call if you need me." Jeanne left the room.

All Mary really needed was her husband to come home. Her soul felt empty without him. He was the pulse in her veins and the very beat of her heart.

Oh, please, God. Let him be well.

She turned over and closed her eyes, willed for sleep to give her a reprieve from the anxiety. They'd had no word from the front for over a week and if it weren't for the fact that Maximilian would be furious if she did it, she'd mount her horse and go to Guinegate herself.

This very minute. As fast as the wind.

After pulling in a deep breath, she let it out slowly, trying to force her body into a state of relaxation and letting her limbs go heavy.

It must have worked because before long, she found her thoughts scattering and sleep stealing her away. Vivid dreams came almost instantly—Maximilian's handsome face hovering before her. Horses, pikes, arrows, and cannons around him. The sky a dark, angry, blood red and full of sharp bolts of lightning.

She reached out for him but couldn't harness his attention—his mind was elsewhere. She also couldn't touch him, her dreaming hands going straight through his body as though it were thin, misty air.

Panic gripped her. She sensed death all around. A creeping, chilling sensation tightened her core. She was cold. Her body numb. Dread permeated every fiber of her being.

She tried to call his name, but no sound came out.

She tried to run to him, but it was like moving her limbs through treacle.

Frustration clawed at her and she tossed her head from side to side.

A pike was flying straight at him, the sharp end mean and deadly.

"Maximilian!" she shouted, her eyes flying open as she sat bolt upright gasping for breath.

"Shh, my love. I am here."

She blinked. Blinked again in the daylight. Her mouth opened and she fought for breath as a sob tightened her throat.

Sitting in front of her, on the bed, was Maximilian. His hair was mussed up and a streak of dirt marred his left cheek. The collar on his tunic was ragged and ripped.

He took her hands in his big, warm ones. "My love, you were dreaming." His deep voice echoed through her mind.

"Are you... Are you really here?" Her eyes filled with tears and her heart thudded. Disorientation made her dizzy.

"Yes." He drew her hands to his lips and kissed her knuckles. "I have returned, as I promised I would, my love, and—"

She let out a whimper and flung herself forward, wrapping her arms around him and burying her face in his neck.

"Oh!" He laughed and held her close. "Do I need to ask if you missed me?"

"You know I did. Every minute of every day." She breathed deeply, inhaling his outdoor scent that was tinged with leather and soap. "I prayed constantly for your safe return." She pulled back and cupped his face, studying him. "You are unharmed?"

"Nothing a few nights' rest in my own bed with my wife won't cure." He kissed her.

It was a wonderful, deep, familiar kiss that told her without words how much she meant to him, how much he needed her, how much he'd missed her too.

When he pulled back, he tucked a strand of hair behind her ear.

"Tell me. It went well? The battle?" She searched his eyes for clues as to the outcome.

"Yes. We were victorious in pushing the French back. Louis is storming around his palace as we speak. No doubt breaking things, bellowing at courtiers, kicking his dogs, but he had no choice but to concede. We had strength and skill on our side, as well as great numbers of passionate loyal men."

"I knew you would be victorious. I never doubted you or our brave, brave soldiers."

"I appreciate your confidence." He smiled and his eyes sparkled in the way she loved so much. Had missed so much.

"I hardly dare ask," she said quietly and thinking of Jeanne, "but Lars...Philip... How did they fare?"

"Lars is well. He is with Jeanne. I ordered him straight to her, knowing she would be anxious for his return and his news."

"You are as thoughtful as always." She swallowed and touched the cross at his neck, dreading the worst about her dear cousin Philip. "And..."

"And Philip..." Maximilian paused. "I feared I would have to tell you of his passing, but..."

"But what? What happened? Please tell me." She straightened.

"He realized that the French knights had mistaken him for me."

"They did? How did that happen?" She frowned.

"We had on similar armor and when he leaped up onto a black horse like mine to circle back around the infantry, a Frenchman shouted my name at him. He turned, raised his sword, and they presumed from that moment on that he was me. That he was the grand prize they wished to take to King Louis."

"And where were *you*?" she asked, aghast. "While this was happening." She didn't like the thought of her husband being a macabre prize the way her father had no doubt been.

"I was fighting with the ground infantry, with a pike in my hand. It was crazy...brutal, bloody, and..."

She held her breath, waiting for him to go on.

He shook his head as though to rid ghastly images that had suddenly appeared. "And so Philip galloped away, leading the French knights into the forest and away from a weakened area of our attack."

"My goodness, what desperate peril. Poor Philip."

"Indeed. And as the battle commenced, the peril increased, though because so many knights had chased after Philip, we found our compromised left flank had a chance to recover, and with it, the infantry moved onward in strength and..."

"And you were victorious." She held his cheeks and kissed him. "And Philip now?"

"We presumed him dead, but then, as we re-grouped, poured ale, and started to... Well, never mind... He appeared. Dirty, exhausted, bloody—but alive."

"I am so pleased." She blew out a breath. "What a relief."

"Yes, he served you and your people well. You should be proud of your cousin, as indeed I am. He fought well, singlehandedly, and came out the other side having done a great service to the cause as a lone warrior."

"I always knew he would have his day of glory."

"He certainly claimed that." He paused and raised his eyebrows. "As did I."

"Oh, my love." She gripped her shoulders. "I will give thanks to God every day for an entire year for your safe return and for your victory."

"Our victory. And it was for you, I returned." He leaned forward and pushed her gently with his body until she was lying flat beneath him. "For you, my love. I do everything for you, each breath, each heartbeat, each victory."

"And my heart beats for you too." She cupped his face, enjoying the solid weight of him above her. The heat of his body, his scent, his warm breath. "Show me, my brave knight. Show me how much you love me."

"It is all that is going to happen next." He pulled up her summer gown, exposing her legs to the cool air. "Let me into your body. Let me remind you how it feels to be loved absolutely by me."

"Maximilian. My love." She sighed as he settled between her legs and pushed his hand between their bodies. He took his weight on one arm and released his cock.

"My beautiful wife," he murmured as he nudged her entrance. "How a man misses his true love. You will never know. It is as painful as any wound."

"I know, for I have missed you with every beat of my...oh..."

He pushed into her, stretching her delicate entrance. A determined, heavy invasion that felt so good.

"Be gentle." She gasped and stared up at him. "For I believe I am with child again."

He stilled and his eyes widened.

"A baby," she whispered. "Your second child lives inside me. I am sure of it."

His lips curled upward. "You could not make me a happier man."

"I only want to make you happy."

He kissed her softly. "Perhaps a girl this time, a lady who is just like you."

"God will decide."

"And I will be happy with His decision, but the world should have more beauty in it, and that beauty should be yours."

She wrapped her legs around the backs of his and arched to take him deeper. "I will not break."

He groaned softly. "Though still, I will be very gentle."

Mary hugged her husband, the man, the leader, her first and last love. No other would ever live in her heart. And the future... It would likely hold turmoil and testing times, but if they had each other, and their beautiful children, they would not only be successful, they'd also be as happy as anyone on God's glorious Earth could be.

THE END

Don't miss ADORED BY THE ARCHDUKE
and find out how baby Philip's life pans out.

Book Club Questions

Loved by the Last Knight

1. Maximilian I is credited as starting the trend of giving a diamond ring as a promise of marriage. How relevant is a symbol like this today?

2. Which scene stuck with you the most?

3. As the only daughter of Charles the Bold, Mary inherits great power. How do you think she handled the uprising of her people at the beginning of the book?

4. Would you like to live in the world Mary and Maximilian existed in?

5. If you could ask the author anything, what would it be?

6. It is revealed in Chapter One that Maximilian was mute until the age of nine. How confident do you think he is as an adult and how is this shown? Is he too confident?

7. Would you re-read this book?

8. Did you have a least favorite character?

9. How would you describe the connection between Maximilian and Mary and how did it change throughout the book, if at all?

10. If *Loved by the Last Knight* were a Netflix series, who would play Maximilian and Mary?

Character Interview

Loved by the Last Knight

Want more? Of course you do. Hop on over to Lily Harlem's website and enjoy an exclusive interview with Maximilian and Mary.

www.lilyharlem.com/maximilian-and-mary-interview.html

Suggested Playlist for

Loved by the Last Knight

"Crusaders" – Harry Gregson-Williams

"Girl on Fire" – Alicia Keys

"Blackbird Song" – Lee DeWyze

"You Should See Me in a Crown" – Billie Eilish

"Hero" – Enrique Iglesias

"Never Back Down" – Kat Meoz

"Kiss Me" – Ed Sheeran

"Dance Me to the End of Love" – The Civil Wars

"Look What We Started" – UNSECRET & Rayelle

"So in Love" – Hailey Tuck

"Don't Forget About Me" – The Cloves

"Dandelions" – Ruth B

"River" – Leon Bridges

"In Case You Didn't Know" – Brieanna James

"Never Say Never" – The Fray

"Let It All Go" – Birdy & Rhodes

"Turning Page" – Sleeping At Last

About the Author

Lily Harlem wears many colorful, feather-adorned hats but being an author is one of her very favorites.

Since leaving an adrenaline-packed eighteen-year career in acute nursing and picking up a pen she hasn't looked back. With industry awards and bestsellers, she has over one hundred novels to her name and many short stories. She's an indecisive butterfly when it comes to genres and pairings though historical romance has become a firm favorite in the last few years – dashing dukes, dominant Vikings and surly Highlanders, what's not to love?

She's British through and through with a Scottish father and English mother. Lily has lived in England, Scotland and presently resides in rural Wales with a desk overlooking rolling hills. Mr Harlem is a constant source of inspiration, and his family are Irish so a great deal of time is spent on the Emerald Isle too.

Her characters' love stories may span the centuries, but they all have a few things in common—passion, romance, adventure, a happily ever after...oh and the bedroom door is always left wide open. If you've fallen for the hero in a Lily Harlem book you'll get to know him intimately and discover all of his skills, and his kinks. Enjoy!

Website – www.lilyharlem.com
Facebook – facebook.com/groups/188731774881774
Amazon – amazon.com/stores/Lily-Harlem/author/B004MHRTQK
BookBub – bookbub.com/profile/lily-harlem
Twitter – @lily_harlem

Made in the USA
Middletown, DE
17 May 2024

54272471R00136